A PIRATE'S GEM FOR RI

SERIES BY NELLIE H. STEELE

Cate Kensie Mysteries

Shadow Slayers Stories

Lily & Cassie by the Sea Mysteries

Pearl Party Mysteries

Middle Age is Murder Cozy Mysteries

Duchess of Blackmoore Mysteries

Maggie Edwards Adventures

Clif & Ri on the Sea Adventures

Shelving Magic

A PIRATE'S GEM FOR RI

A HIGH SEAS PIRATE ADVENTURE

CLIF & RI ON THE SEA
BOOK TWO

NELLIE H. STEELE

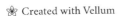

CHAPTER 1

*T*he ship listed hard to the side as a massive wave smashed into it. The helmsman fought hard to keep her steady as the storm raged.

"Please, sir, let's turn back," Johnson said as he clung to the railing. Water dripped from the hat that had miraculously stayed on his head despite the torrents of rain and the wind whipping.

"Onward," Clif answered as he set his sights on the horizon.

"But, sir–"

"We must make it to our island."

A moan escaped Johnson's lips as the ship rolled again. His features shifted from worried to hopeful as he spotted a lithe figure moving across the deck, hunched over as the rain pelted her.

"Captain!" he shouted. "Please, talk some sense into the Commodore."

"Can't do it, Johnson," Henrietta shouted as she bypassed him and climbed the stairs to the helm.

Clif creased his brow as he spotted his sister. "What are you doing here? Who's captaining your ship?"

"I swung across. Abby has it well in hand."

Clif arched an eyebrow at her. "You swung across to my ship during this storm, leaving your *Grandmistress* under the guidance of a very green First Mate and an untested helmsman."

"I trust them. If only because I will murder every last one of them should they wreck my beloved ship. Besides, I had to come."

"What is it? Is something wrong?"

"I had a question."

"A question?" Clif repeated.

Henrietta bobbed her head up and down as rain continued to pound around them. "Might we step away for a moment into the privacy of your cabin to discuss it?"

Clif pressed his lips together into a thin line. What could have prompted his sister to take such a chance? It must be something vital. He bobbed his head up and down.

"Mr. Johnson, you have the deck."

"Wonderful," Johnson murmured as they clamored down the stairs past him. They crossed the slippery deckboards and ducked into the cabin under the helm.

Clif peeled his hat from his head. It dripped across the floor as he ambled to the desk and tossed it on the top. A capuchin monkey leapt from a pillow on the hammock and scurried to him, climbing up to perch on his shoulder.

Henrietta pulled her tricorn from her head and stared at it ruefully. "I really must find a way to make the feathers waterproof."

"Perhaps a hat without the feathers just for rainy days."

"Do not make ridiculous suggestions, Clif. I am a ship's captain. It is now more important than ever that I sport the feather in my cap."

He tossed his hat onto the desk. "I am a commodore, and my hat is featherless."

"It's not my fault you have no style, Clif."

He narrowed his eyes at her as he pulled a flask from his drawer and took a long swig. "What is your question?"

The ship rocked roughly. Henrietta stamped a foot to stay upright. She tossed her hat on the hammock and dug into her long duster jacket.

Clif's heart skipped a beat as he waited to see what object had driven his sister to flee from her ship in a storm onto his. The monkey screeched and grinned at her.

"Quiet, Jack," Clif said to the small animal.

She tugged a small black book out and waved it in the air. Papers escaped the worn edges at all angles.

Clif sucked in a breath, letting his jaw gape open. "You're joking."

Henrietta froze with the book still high in the air. "What?"

"You did not make a dangerous crossing from one ship to another in the midst of a storm, leaving your ship captain-less, to discuss something from my idea book."

"It's not that hard to believe. And my ship is hardly captain-less. She is right next to us, and I trust Abby implicitly."

Clif let his features settle into an unimpressed stare. The monkey tilted his head and grinned at her.

"Jack is amused. Do you not trust Johnson?"

"Yes, I do, but—"

"But nothing. If you had discovered something important, you could have felt entirely comfortable leaving your crew and your ship in the hands of Johnson to discuss it."

"Johnson has proven himself time and time again. And he has considerable experience."

The corners of Henrietta's lips turned upward and she

offered her brother a wry glance. "Seems he has had many experiences of late."

Clif tossed a hand in the air before he reached for his flask again. "Now, *there* is something we should discuss. *That* is becoming a problem."

"Is it? For whom?"

"Don't joke, Ri. I'm being serious."

Henrietta crossed to the desk, setting the book's spine against it. She flicked her dark eyes to her brother's and offered him a consoling half-smile. "I know you are. But Carolina is an adult, Clif."

"You were an adult on many occasions when I protected you."

Henrietta sucked in a breath as she considered her response. He had killed a man for her, not on purpose. It had been an accident. But still…he had ensured no harm came to her, no matter the cost.

The situation with Johnson was far trickier. The bond between a captain and his first mate was strong…but was it strong enough to survive this?

She decided not to delve into the delicate matter. "Let's put that aside for the moment. We are at sea. Nothing will come of it now."

Clif balanced himself against the desk with a deep sigh. "Fine. What in that book has you swinging through a storm to see me?"

Henrietta grinned, tracing a finger along his chiseled chin. "You're a good sport."

A slight smile played across his features. "I had better be. My sister is poised to become a better pirate than I've ever been. The ribbing I take knows no bounds."

"Hardly. I am only a smidgen of the pirate you are, Black Jack."

Clif straightened and sucked in a breath. "Black Jack is dead."

"Oh, but he lives. Haven't you heard? Rumors of the dreaded ghost ship carrying Black Jack? Davy Jones himself spat the man back from the depths of the sea. And now he roams the waters in search of more victims."

"You must have a big request."

She fluttered her eyelashes, plastering an innocent expression on her soft features. "Why would you say that?"

"You're trying to butter me up."

"I'm doing no such thing."

Clif grabbed the monkey from his shoulder and sat him on the desk. The creature scurried off to find a banana from a bowl of fruit. "You are. Reminding me of Black Jack. And how fearsome he was as a pirate."

"Is," Henrietta interjected. "How fearsome he is. That's my point. Black Jack lives on, and many still fear him. I am hardly poised to besmirch your reputation as a pirate."

Clif arched an eyebrow at her as the ship rolled perilously again. "All right, out with it. What have you found that's got you itching to speak to me?"

Henrietta frowned at him. "I won't discuss this with you when you have that condescending tone."

"I haven't any such tone. But you came across to my ship in rough waters for something. And it wasn't to toss about ideas for waterproofing your feathered cap." He plopped into his chair and eyed her.

"Need I remind you that this venture—"

"Was it all my idea? I'm well aware of that, Ri. But this very danger makes this island worth looking at for a hide-away. We need somewhere to stash all our finds. We can't keep carrying everything on our ships."

"Why not use Hideaway Bay? With Carolina—"

"No." Clif leaped from his seat, slicing a hand through the air.

"You're being unreasonable."

"I am not. The last time I hid treasure in Hideaway Bay, it nearly cost me your life."

Henrietta scoffed, tossing the book on his desk and setting her hands on her hips. "That is hardly true."

"Ri, we faked our deaths. It's very true."

She sucked in a breath and blew it out in a slow, controlled manner. "All right, we'll be more careful this time."

"No, no, and no. That's final. We are not endangering Carolina's life to hide our treasure. We'll use Stormy Island, or we'll find another spot."

The ship lurched again, and they struggled to remain on their feet. "This place is appropriately named."

"And most dare not come anywhere near it. So the treasure will be safe. And so will Carolina."

"Are you worried about her being robbed or about her seeing too much of Mr. Johnson?"

"I thought we were setting that aside."

Henrietta crossed her arms and dropped into the hammock. "We were. That was before. Now, I want to talk about it."

"Carolina is a married woman–"

"An unhappily married woman."

Clif pressed his lips into a thin line and huffed, his nostrils flaring.

"She will want to see us. And when she does, she may see Johnson."

"We'll dock in another town and travel by carriage. There, it's solved. No treasure near Carolina, and no Johnson near her either. Now, enough playing about. Out with your demand."

Henrietta clicked her tongue. "It's hardly a demand."

Clif sank into the chair again and tented his fingers, allowing his elbow to rest on the carved wood arms. "All right, out with your request."

With a grin plastered on her lips, Henrietta leapt from the hammock and hurried to the desk. She flipped open the book and paged through it, pausing a few times before continuing.

Clif arched an eyebrow as he lifted his chin to peer over the edge. She flipped through another few pages before he placed a hand down on the book. "Is this it? This may be a worthy treasure to seek?"

Henrietta wrinkled her nose at it as she studied his scrawled handwriting on the yellowed page. "The Lost City of Gold?"

"Your Spanish is getting better," he said with a grin. "Yes."

Her shoulders slumped, and she grimaced at him. "We just searched for a city. That seems...a weak follow-up."

"It's a perfect follow-up adventure to our City of Diamonds conquest. We already have practical experience searching for cities."

"Be serious, Clif. Did Black Jack search for the same treasures constantly?"

"Black Jack robbed ships regularly, so yes."

"Well, we could do that," she said, pausing to think it through, "that may be fun, too. And with our fleet, we could easily win."

Clif bobbed his head up and down.

"Though it's not as exciting as searching for these. I enjoy the puzzles. We'll rob someone along the way."

Clif clucked at her as she shoved his hand away and continued her paging. A few more supposed treasures flipped by before he rose and pointed at the paper. "There. That one. That's quite a good one."

She squinted at the messy writing. "The Cursed Diamond? You jest, brother."

"I do not. You love diamonds."

"And I have a load of them in my cabin from the last bounty. And besides, why would I want a cursed diamond?"

"Well, firstly, because it is a bigger diamond than we have now and is supposedly flawless."

"Except for the cursed bit."

"Yes, but you enjoy puzzles. We could work out how to break the curse." He waved a finger in the air.

"Maybe later. For now, I had something else in mind."

She shoved his finger away from the book and continued her search.

"What about the Pirate's Diary? Is that what you seek? It could prove very profitable."

"Isn't that what I've got here?" She motioned to the book.

He shook his head. "That's my idea book. Not The Pirate's Diary."

"What is that?"

"Haven't the read the whole book?" He skirted the desk and slipped his hands around his sister's shoulders, steering her toward the door. "You should spend some more time perusing this before you decide. If you don't know what The Pirate's Diary is—"

She planted her feet against the floorboards and pushed back against him. "No. You are not going to put me off. I have a bounty in mind and demand to be heard out."

"I thought you said it wasn't a demand?"

"I said the bounty-seeking wasn't a demand. This is." She narrowed her eyes at him, looking down her thin nose at his bearded face.

"All right," he said with a sigh, and an arm waved toward the desk. "Go ahead. Why you didn't mark the page ahead of time is beyond me."

"I did. My marker must have slipped down when I made the treacherous journey to *The Henton.* "

She thumbed through the book until her eyebrows flicked up. "Here it is. See, I've marked it with one of my destroyed feathers."

With a triumphant grin, she flipped the book around for him to see. He brought the candle closer to the paper and read the words he'd scrawled ages ago on the paper.

His heart skipped a beat as realization dawned on him. Any amusement on his face disappeared, and he flicked his eyes to hers. "No, Ri, we can't."

CHAPTER 2

*H*enrietta studied the lines suddenly etched in her brother's features. She's only seen fear dance in his dark eyes once before and never over something like this. He'd been daring as a child and a pirate. Nothing frightened him. Nothing except harm coming to his family.

"Clif? Have you gone soft on me?"

He flicked his gaze away from her and rose to stand, licking his lips as he considered his response. "No."

"Then what is it? I've never known you to shy away from a challenge."

"This isn't a challenge, it's a death sentence."

"You're starting to sound like Johnson. All woe and worry."

"Johnson worries needlessly," Clif answered. "I do not. If I'm telling you it's too dangerous, you ought to believe me."

"I don't disbelieve you, but I'm surprised you consider it too dangerous. I didn't think you knew the meaning of those words."

"This is no time to jest, Ri."

She crossed her arms and narrowed her eyes at her brother's profile. "What makes it too dangerous?"

"Everything," Clif answered with a slice of his hand through the air.

Henrietta set her hands on her hips, ready to argue, when a cry sounded above them.

A hurried knock pounded at the door a moment later. "Captain, we've spotted land!" Johnson called through the door.

"I'm coming. Prepare to weigh the anchor." Clif shifted his eyes to Henrietta. "You should go back to the *Grandmistress*. Your sailors await your orders."

"This conversation is not finished. We'll discuss it once we're safely on land."

"I have no doubt about that," Clif answered as he skirted around his desk. "But first, let's determine if Stormy Island will be our new hideout."

Henrietta followed him onto the deck. The rain had tapered off to a drizzle, and a dark form of land blotted out part of the night sky on the horizon.

"The waters have calmed considerably. I'll lay a plank and walk across to my ship." Henrietta approached the side rail and waved to her first mate on the other deck.

Abigail hurried closer to her. "Captain, what orders?"

"I'm coming across," Henrietta said. "Bring the ship closer."

"Starboard!" Abby called to the helmswoman. Slowly, the ship inched toward them. Mr. Johnson slid a plank between the two railings, and Henrietta carefully picked her way across to the opposite side.

She leapt onto the deckboards of her ship and stalked toward the helm. Abby hurried to match her pace. "Well? How did the discussion go with Commodore Nichols?'

"It didn't," Henrietta said with a wrinkle of her nose.

Abby arched an eyebrow at her captain.

"We will discuss it further once we are on land. We were sidetracked by other things, and then Clif had an…interesting reaction to the gambit. Before we could hash it out, Mr. Johnson informed us of the land."

"Yes," Abby said with a nod. "I have had them trim the sails. I gave orders to circle the island in search of the inlet the Commodore said existed."

Henrietta climbed the stairs. "Excellent, you are quite a good first mate. Spyglass."

Abby slapped it into her hands, and she extended it to full length, peering through it. "It will be difficult to spot anything in the dark."

"Perhaps moonlight will help once these clouds break."

"Perhaps we should venture closer on our own," Henrietta mused aloud.

"I shall gather volunteers to man a skiff, Captain."

Henrietta slammed the spyglass shut and nodded, sending Abby scurrying off to attend to the collection of a small crew to row a boat closer.

She stared at the dark blob with her naked eye for another moment before she left the helm and descended to the main deck.

"What do you think of her at first sight?" Clif called from *The Henton*.

"She's not very exciting, though she looks like a blob at the moment."

"If there is a waterway leading to her heart, we may like her more."

"Abby is preparing a search party. Perhaps you'd like to come along."

Abby hurried toward Henrietta, flinging her hand up in a salute. "Captain, the search party is prepared."

After another wave of her hand at Clif, she spoke again. "Commodore, will you be joining us?"

"I don't mind if I do," he said with a grin. "Mr. Johnson. Keep her steady while I join Captain Blanchard to search for an inlet."

"Aye, Captain. Helmsman, hold her steady."

"Mr. Johnson," Henrietta called across the gap between their ships, "you are responsible for the *Grandmistress*. Abby is with me."

"Thank you, Captain. I'm very pleased to be joining you." She motioned for Henrietta to head toward the skiff they freed for the journey.

Moments later, they rowed away from the two pirate ships bobbing in the water off the island's coast.

Henrietta lifted a lantern above her head as she stood at the front of the small boat. "What manner of animals live on this island?"

"Hard to say," Clif answered. "Rumors are quite wild."

"Are there large cats? Like the ones we ran into on Moaning Isle."

Clif joined her and studied the rolling hills covered in tropical trees. "Perhaps. But perhaps not."

"What say the rumors?"

"That there are man-eating cats on the island."

Henrietta arched an eyebrow. "Good thing you didn't bring Jack along."

"I think that monkey needs a new home. Perhaps one with a more feminine environment."

"He seems perfectly happy in his current environment."

"I don't like him," Clif said, wrinkling his nose.

Henrietta suppressed a chuckle.

"What?"

"Yes, you do. Don't try to deny it."

"I am fully denying it. I don't like the little devil. I only keep him around because I feel sorry for him."

Henrietta flicked her amused gaze back to the island. "Keep telling yourself that, brother. Where is this supposed inlet to the heart of the island?"

"Does not seem to exist," Clif said as he scanned the dark waters around them.

"No. Perhaps you were misinformed."

Clif slid his eyes sideways to glance at her. "Doubtful, though possible."

She crossed her arms as the boat rocked back and forth. "So, is it possible you were misinformed about my pick for the next treasure hunt?"

"No, it is not. That I am sure of."

She let her arms fall to her sides with a click of her tongue. "Clif! You cannot be certain. This is the stuff of legends. They are embellished all the time. Just like this island. "

She waved a hand toward the land mass rising from the water. "Clearly it has no watery inlet allowed for discreet entrance into its heart."

Clif pressed his lips together into a thin line as he considered his response. Before he could answer, something caught his eye.

He leaned forward, squinting at the water.

"What is it?" Henrietta asked.

He raised a finger, his lips parting and curling at the corners. "Look."

"At what?" she asked.

"At the water. Look at the ripples and the current."

"I don't understand."

He squatted down and lifted the lantern high, motioning for her to join him. "Where is the water flowing?"

"Toward the island."

"Yes, but it's not coming back, is it?"

"What do you mean?"

"If it is heading toward the island, it should smash off the shore and ebb back toward us, but this does not."

She arched an eyebrow high. "The inlet." Her gaze rose toward the island before she gave it a puzzled look. "But that's solid rock."

"Is it? Looks can be very deceiving." He twisted to the crew rowing. "Starboard."

Half the crew lifted their oars while the others continued to dunk them in the water to turn the small boat.

Abby rose from her seat, staring at the wall before them. "Commodore, those are rocks ahead."

"I see them," Clif said. "Continue forward at a slow pace. There is an inlet here, and I aim to find it."

"Aye, sir," Abby answered, sinking back onto her bench. "Forward."

The boat floated closer to what looked like a stone wall.

Henrietta gnawed on her lower lip. "I hope you know what you're doing, brother."

"Trust me, Ri. A bit more to starboard."

The small craft pulled to the side a bit more.

"Oars up!" Clif called.

Paddles lifted from the water. The small skiff rocked back and forth before being pulled closer to the island.

Henrietta's knees wobbled, though she forced herself to stand firm and not show her fear. They'd soon smash into the rocks and be plunged into the water.

The dinghy's stern scraped against the stone before shifting to the side and floating under a rock canopy.

Henrietta sucked in a deep breath, allowing her gaze to rise to the stalactite-ridden ceiling above the underground river. "Clif! We found it."

"Indeed, we did. I told you my source was correct."

They continued until they found a place to drag the boat ashore and explore. Henrietta lifted a torch high as she wandered under the tropical trees.

"What do you think?" Clif asked.

"We cannot hide the ships here."

"No, the entry is far too tight. Particularly for the *Grandmistress's* girth."

Henrietta shot him an annoyed sideways glance. "Are you saying my ship is fat?"

"No, merely too wide to fit her thick stern through the small passage."

"As if *The Henton* could fit." She scoffed as she continued to explore a cave entrance.

"I did not claim it could. Though we could use skiffs to bring ashore any treasure, and there are sufficient caves to store it. It should be fairly safe. Reaching this location is difficult, and finding a safe entrance is even more so."

Ri swept the torch around and spun to face him. "Yes, it does seem a worthy spot. I agree."

"So, have we found a hideaway that pleases us both?"

Henrietta bobbed her head up and down with a grin. "We have."

"Then we should celebrate." He pulled the flask from his pocket and took a swig before he held it out to her.

"Must I? The rum is not as appealing as you made it seem."

"I insist. It's part of pirate life."

Henrietta grabbed the metal container and drank from it. "There. Now we have celebrated. And we have settled the matter."

He took another drink before he slowly screwed the cap back on. "And now I suppose you'd like to settle another."

"I would," she answered when a contingent of crew approached them.

"Ah, Mr. Johnson, you have perfect timing. Please, join us." He clapped a hand around the man's shoulders.

"And Abby," Henrietta said. "You should also be here." Henrietta clasped her on the shoulder and shot an arched-eyebrowed glance at her brother.

"Is the island suitable for you both? I can have the crew bring over any bounty left on the ships."

"It is most suitable, and both Captain Blanchard and I have agreed to claim this space as ours."

"Excellent, I shall order the crew—"

"Just a moment, Johnson," Clif said, tightening his grip on the man's shoulder.

Johnson's skin blanched, and he swallowed hard. "Is there some further way I can assist, Commodore?"

"Indeed there is, my good man." Clif released his grasp on his first mate as he stalked across the cavern. "Captain Blanchard and I are having a...spirited discussion about where to set our sights next."

He twisted to face Johnson. "You have much knowledge of the sea, and I'd like your opinion."

Johnson arched an eyebrow. "My opinion, Commodore?"

He slid his eyes sideways to Henrietta. "S-surely, you and Captain Blanchard are the best to decide this."

"I would agree, except we cannot seem to do that. Decide, that is. Captain Blanchard has her heart set on a specific treasure, and I'm afraid I have to disagree."

"Unsurprising," Johnson murmured.

"Wouldn't it be grand, Mr. Johnson, if we were to seek the Pirate's Diary?" Clif grinned at him.

"A worthy goal, Commodore."

"Or perhaps The Cursed Diamond?"

"Oh," Johnson said, his voice wavering, "well, that's quite a gambit, though we could make a try for it."

"Indeed, or even The City of Gold."

"Ah, there's one I could get on board with." Johnson wagged a finger in the air as he bounced on his toes. "Yes. The City of Gold, it is. I shall begin charting a course to find the first bit of information—"

"Just a minute," Henrietta said. "I have agreed to none of those."

Johnson swallowed hard again as she continued. "I have quite another plan."

Clif sucked in a breath and shook his head. "Mr. Johnson, I want you to give me your honest opinion when I tell you what Captain Blanchard seeks. Don't hold back anything. Do you understand?"

"I do." He bobbed his head up and down.

"The esteemed captain of our sister ship would like to seek the Gemstone Islands."

Johnson's hand flew up to his gaping jaw as he gasped. "No. Not there."

He shifted his gaze to Henrietta. "Please, Captain."

"Tell her why."

"We'll die. We'll all die."

CHAPTER 3

*H*enrietta screwed up her face at the dire statement before she crossed her arms and cocked a hip. "Mr. Johnson, aren't you being just a bit dramatic?"

Johnson shook his head, his face still pale. "No."

She arched an eyebrow at him. "Johnson, you are always dramatic. You said we'd die if we went to Moaning Isle, too. Yet here we are alive and well—and richer for it."

"We almost died, Captain. Those beasts nearly killed us and then the volcano."

"But they didn't. We are all capable pirates. We needn't worry about such things. We have proven ourselves able to handle these situations."

Johnson shook his head again. "But the Gemstone Islands are much worse for many reasons, Captain."

Henrietta narrowed her eyes at the man. "Oh? Are there beastlier felines that lurk through its jungles?"

"Ri, you're being ridiculous."

"I am not. What are these supposed dangers that will kill all of us?"

"They are three," Clif answered, waving three digits in the air. "First, another pirate. He holds a piece of the map to find these islands. He has for years. He is quite savvy and ruthless."

"Will he trade for it? We have amassed quite a fortune."

Clif shook his head. "No. It is his most prized possession."

"Why? If it leads to a place that will kill us, why does he cling to it?"

"Because it stops anyone else from daring to search for it," Clif answered.

"Fine. He has a piece of the map and is to be feared. That's one danger. I suppose the other two stem from other pieces of the map? Are they all held by other pirates?"

"No. The other piece is supposedly hidden deep in the jungle. A treacherous journey, but hardly too difficult."

"The other?" Henrietta asked. "There are only two?"

"Yes, two. One is too dangerous to retrieve, and the other is dangerous but hardly unattainable."

"So, what is the second danger, then?"

"Assuming we should retrieve both pieces, which I maintain we cannot, the map is still incomplete and cryptic. We would need to solve that puzzle to even try searching for them."

"You know how I love to solve puzzles," Henrietta answered.

"I'm certain you could do it, too. It's what comes next that concerns me."

"Which is?"

"Treacherous waters, filled with all manner of sea creatures," Johnson said. "Maybe even some that no one has encountered before."

"Some rare form of shark?" Henrietta asked.

Johnson shook his head. "No. Jellyfish venomous enough to kill a man with one sting."

"Stay out of the waters." Henrietta shrugged.

"Whales large enough to overturn a large vessel."

Henrietta arched an eyebrow as she considered the statement. Could such things exist?

"And…" Johnson swallowed hard and slid his gaze to Clif before he returned it to Henrietta.

She arched her eyebrow in a silent prompt for him to continue.

"Sirens."

"Sirens?" Henrietta repeated.

Johnson bobbed his head up and down. "Aye, sirens. Beautiful sea creatures who lure men to their deaths by singing beautiful songs."

"Yes, I know what a siren is, but I cannot believe you are concerned about them."

"They are deadly, Captain."

A chuckle bubbled up and escaped her lips. She pressed them together before another escaped, then turned into a full giggle. "Mr. Johnson, please. You cannot be serious. You expect me to believe in mermaids?"

"No, sirens."

"Same difference," she said, the amusement leaving her features. "And a ridiculous notion. Mermaids or sirens are fictional. Created to spin compelling yarns around the fire. I'm an author. I know this."

"Many a man has been lost to the sea because of the sirens."

"Oh? And how do you know this? Have they returned to tell the tale? I thought no one could find these islands. How do they know these supposed deadly creatures surround them?"

"Someone found the island, Ri. How do you think the story was passed on and a map made?"

"Well, good, then someone found them and lived to tell the tale. We shall be the second party to do so."

Clif heaved a sigh. "You haven't heard the third danger."

"What is it? The Kraken? The Leviathan? Please, enlighten me."

"The terrain of the islands themselves. Said to drive a man mad and send him wandering for days until he starves to death."

"Or is eaten by the local wildlife," Johnson added.

"Yet someone managed to return with that tale, too."

"Yes," Johnson answered. "Yes, someone did. A lone survivor, bloody, terrified. He couldn't speak for weeks. And when he did...the tale he uttered made blood run cold."

"Or he killed his fellow explorers and pocketed the gemstones for himself, then made up a tale to frighten others off from learning of his misdeeds."

"Please, Captain," Johnson said, wringing his hands, "we'll try for another treasure. There are many great bounties out there for the taking. Just not this one."

Henrietta crossed her arms and glanced at her first mate, who shrugged. She set her eyes on her brother and Mr. Johnson. "You two are quite a pair, aren't you?"

"I told you," Clif said. "This is a bounty even I would avoid."

"Believe in mermaids, too, do you?"

Clif shrugged in response. "I believe something is in those waters."

"Fine. The *Grandmistress* will sail for it. You and your crew can hide away somewhere until we return triumphant."

"Ri, you are being impossible."

"I am being a pirate." She stepped past him toward the mouth of the cave. "Now, if you will excuse me, my first mate and I have much to discuss."

As she reached the entrance with Abby in tow, her brother's voice stopped her from leaving.

"Wait."

She hesitated, one foot dangling in the air. The corners of her lips turned up. She returned her features to a neutral expression and twisted to face him. "Yes?"

"You cannot go alone."

"Can't I? I suppose I shall have to. I have no one else willing to go."

Clif heaved a sigh and shook his head. "I will–"

"Please, no, Commodore." Johnson wrung his hands and shook his head.

"I am afraid you will need to gird yourself, Mr. Johnson. We plan to seek the Gemstone Islands."

A groan escaped the first mate's lips.

"Don't worry, Mr. Johnson," Henrietta said as she stalked back to him and tipped his chin up. "We'll make it up to you."

"Not if I'm dead, Captain."

"You'll survive it. And have a wonderful tale to tell…" She shifted her eyes sideways to her brother before she returned them to Johnson. "Well, you know."

The deep sigh from Clif didn't escape her as she spun on a heel to leave. "Shall we seek the jungle map piece first or your pirate friend's?"

"First, he is not my friend. Far from it. If caught when we attempt to recover that piece, I will be shot on sight."

Henrietta arched an eyebrow before she stepped out of the cave. "Interesting. I suppose we should be careful, then."

"Very," Clif answered.

She spun to face him as she walked backward. "I have an idea for that. We can discuss it later. We've got a course to plot. Come along."

"Mr. Johnson, have the crew shift of valuables to this cave."

Johnson nodded. "Aye, Captain."

Clif jogged to catch up with Henrietta and Abby. They marched along through the jungle toward the waiting skiffs.

"I do not believe you will be quite so gleeful once we are trudging through a jungle."

"Why? I quite liked the jungle."

"I certainly hope we do not come across another exploring party."

Henrietta pushed a large leaf aside. "What you mean to say is you hope we do not come across Carolina's party."

"Carolina is not in the jungle now. She's gone home."

"Lucky for you. Unlucky for Mr. Johnson."

Abby chuckled next to Henrietta.

Clif snapped his gaze to her. "I do not find it humorous. She is a married woman."

They reached the boats and climbed inside.

"I find it charming," Abby said.

Clif grabbed an oar and shoved the craft further into the water. "I cannot believe what I am hearing."

"Why, Clif? You, of all people, should understand how the heart works."

"I do not. I cannot understand any of it. The same goes for your attraction to that pig who nearly ruined your life. Nor your marriage to Blanchard."

"Both mistakes."

"And Carolina's...I don't even know what to call it," Clif said as he rowed them through the cavern.

"Attraction, Commodore?" Abby suggested.

Clif puckered his lips. "I cannot see it."

Abby flicked her eyebrows up. "Mr. Johnson is a..."

"Yes, I know, I know," Clif said with a groan. "A very handsome man. If he is so bloody handsome, why aren't you pursuing him?"

Abby scoffed as she shot a glance at Henrietta. "Like the

Captain, I would prefer to make my own way. My...experiences with men have left me with no desire to pursue any of them, no matter how attractive."

They emerged under the starry canopy of the cleaning sky. "Could you make an exception?"

"Oh, really, Clif, stop. Abby is right. It's charming how he looks at Carolina. You should be happy a man thinks so much of her."

Clif grumbled under his breath as they reached the *Grandmistress*. They scaled up the ship's side and swung over the railing onto the deck.

"Have you any idea where this map piece may be in the jungle?"

Clif trailed behind his sister as she led them to her cabin. "Perhaps. However, we really should consult with someone."

Henrietta pulled her door open and stepped inside with an eye roll. "Oh, no, not another Blind Bill."

"No, this one is sighted," Clif answered.

"And I hope not as strange."

"Bill isn't strange. He's quite nice," Clif answered. "However, perhaps you should remain here whilst I take *The Henton* to Tortuga and seek information."

"Why would I stay here?" Henrietta asked.

Clif lifted a shoulder. "Give the crew a rest. A chance to frolic on the island and enjoy themselves."

"And what of *The Henton's* crew? Will they not have the chance to frolic?"

"Certainly. I'll give them the day, and we'll sail at sunset tomorrow."

"Hmm," Henrietta said as she rubbed a finger against her lips. "Let's switch. Give your men a chance to frolic whilst I collect the informant at Tortuga."

"That's ridiculous."

"Why? My crew has less need to relax. They are newer. It

will allow them to gain more sailing experience for the rough seas surrounding the islands we seek."

Clif wrinkled his nose as he tried to think up a response to settle the matter without causing an argument.

Henrietta narrowed her eyes at him. "What aren't you saying?"

"Nothing," he claimed.

Abby arched an eyebrow as she flicked her gaze between them. She tilted her head as her eyes met Henrietta's.

"Oh, put that eyebrow back in its place, Abby. I'm only suggesting that this is not a two-crew trip."

"Of course, Commodore," she answered.

"I disagree. I think you're suggesting something quite different."

Clif rocked on his toes, hoping to convey an air of nonchalance. "I'm not."

"Then, we'll both go. There is no harm in it."

"Actually…" Clif said.

"Yes?" Henrietta asked, cocking her head.

"There is harm."

"What? Please do not tell me you now find Tortuga too dangerous."

"It is when you are involved. You pick fights at every turn in that village. The last time, we were driven off with pitch-forks and torches."

"*That* was different," Henrietta claimed, crossing her arms.

"Hardly. First, you quarreled with that prostitute. Then you picked a fight with the drunkard. Then another drunkard–"

"Attacked me, and I defended myself."

"And then you kicked in a door at the brothel, got on the wrong side of the owner, and ended up covered in mud as we attempted to slink away from the island."

"I'm certain tempers have cooled. Besides, I argued with the brothel owner because he had been completely unfair, and it was a matter of Abby's life."

"And I am most grateful, Captain."

Henrietta smiled at the woman as she lifted her chin.

"It doesn't matter *why* you did it. What matters is what you did. You got them so riled up they chased us off the island. We barely made it off with our lives."

"All the more reason for me to go with you. You'll need the backup."

"I can manage."

"Are you trying to cut me out?"

"No, merely saying that perhaps I can smooth things over, but I would have an easier time of it if you weren't picking more fights."

Henrietta leaned forward, stretching her arms to grab the corners of the desk. "I'll behave."

Clif arched an eyebrow at her. "If only I believed that."

Henrietta snapped straight and crossed her arms. "I cannot believe you. You would turn on your sister."

"I'm hardly turning on you."

"Then let me go."

Clif heaved a sigh. "Fine. You will likely need provisions anyway, and we can secure them there. If there is anyone left willing to sell to us."

"The only request I have is that Abby remain aboard. She should not be subjected to that man again."

"Absolutely not, Captain," Abby answered. "I am capable of returning to Tortuga. I will not hide on this ship, quivering in fear. I shall face my demons and be better for it."

"I knew there was a reason I saved you." Henrietta grinned at her.

"It seems we have a plan. We sail for Tortuga in the morning."

* * *

As the sun rose in the east the following day, the two ships left Stormy Island behind and made for the island town of Tortuga, arriving as the sun set over the harbor.

Henrietta strolled down the plank to the floating dock below.

"Ah, Ri, perhaps you should stay aboard," Clif said as she hurried to catch up to him.

Henrietta chuckled, adjusting the gun on one hip and the sword on the other.

"I'm being serious."

She narrowed her eyes at him. "So am I."

Clif wrinkled his nose before he flicked his eyebrows up. "All right, fine."

"We agreed," she said as she strolled toward the town with him, "that I would come with you."

"To the island. I didn't recall agreeing that you would visit town to meet with my source."

"Why do you always have a source?" Henrietta asked.

"Stop avoiding the issue here. You really could wait–"

Henrietta strolled forward, her eyes set on the town ahead. "Don't say another word, Clif, lest the next fight I pick be with you."

He took another few steps before he slid his eyes sideways. "I would win, though, you know?"

Henrietta's jaw clenched, and her nostrils flared. "You really want me to draw my sword, don't you?"

"I'd rather you didn't. I'm just pointing it out. The last time we sparred aboard *The Henton*, I won."

"That was ages ago. I've now survived boarding Whitmane Webb's ship, fought my way to disable the rudder, then fought my way back."

"Yes, I remember all too well. I thought I'd pulled your burned body from the waters, remember?"

"Yes. And with my new experience, perhaps I could beat you."

"I doubt that," Clif said as the pub came into view. "Why don't you wait out here while I determine where Stargazer may be."

Henrietta grabbed hold of his elbow. "Just a moment. Did you say his name was Stargazer?"

"Well, I don't believe that is his actual name; however, that's how he's called by most who know him."

"And we are pinning our hopes on a man named Stargazer?"

Clif wrangled his arm from her grip. "Yes. Stay here, and I'll see where we may find him."

He stepped away as a figure wobbled its way toward them. As she stepped from the shadows between two buildings, Clif recognized a prostitute from the brothel down the street.

He grabbed Henrietta's arm and dragged her toward the pub. "On second thought, come with me. Before you pick a fight with that woman."

Henrietta rolled her eyes as her brother dragged her toward the tavern's doors. Since she'd much rather enter than be shut out of the search, she went along with him.

They pushed inside. The din of slurred conversations and drunken laughter assaulted their ears for a moment before a shout resounded.

"Hey!"

The crowd quieted as a man rose to his feet and poked a finger at them. "You dare to set foot in this town again after the last time?"

Clif grinned at the man and cocked his head. "A simple misunderstanding. It should be all cleared up now. I'm wondering if anyone can point me toward Stargazer Santiago?"

"I'd like to point you in the direction of something else," the man said, his hand falling to the hilt of his sword.

"Now, gentlemen," Clif said, "really, it was all just a misunderstanding."

"You shot Isaac."

Clif lifted his eyebrows. "I did not."

Henrietta whipped her sword from its sheath. "I did. And if you'd like to discuss it further, you will do so at the tip of my sword."

CHAPTER 4

*C*lif heaved a sigh as his sister thrust her sword forward toward the man. "Ri," he murmured under his breath.

The man stared at her for a moment before his features twisted into an amused grin. He slapped his thighs as he doubled over in laughter.

Henrietta flared her nostrils in irritation.

"Look, fellas, we've got ourselves a female pirate. Or so she thinks."

The crowd burst into laughter along with the man.

Incensed, Henrietta gritted her teeth and inched her sword forward. "I *am* a female pirate. With my ship, thank you. And unless you will stand down, I'll add another notch to my belt on men I have disposed of."

This statement gave the man another chuckle. "And how many notches do you have already, sweetheart? Zero?"

Clif winced at his comment as he directed his sister's sword toward the floor.

"Do you know of Whitemane Webb?" she asked.

He raised his chin. "I did."

"And do you know what happened to him?"

"Certainly. The ghost of Black Jack pursued him in open waters and sank his ship."

Henrietta's jaw unhinged at the words before she clamped it shut. Her features settled into an angry frown, and she tightened her grip on the hilt. "That's not–"

"Possible," Clif said, stepping between them with a chuckle. "Ghosts are not real."

"It is the truth. Black Jack returned from the sea to take his revenge on Whitemane."

Clif slid his eyes closed before he shot a glance over his shoulder at his sister. She shook her head at him, her eyes narrowing.

"Listen, that's not possible. And do you know how I know that?"

"I know you're wrong." The man rocked back on his heels as he adjusted his belt.

"I can't be."

"Oh? And how's that?"

Clif licked his lips, holding back some of his irritation. "Because I am Black Jack."

The man squinted at Clif, cocking his head before he burst into laughter. The crowd gathering around him joined in.

Clif sucked in a breath, his chest rising high as he shot another glance at his sister. She raised her eyebrows and lifted a shoulder.

He shook his head as he returned his gaze to the man and held up his hands. "Please stop laughing. I'm not joking."

The man snorted another laugh. "Listen, boy, you may wish you were Black Jack, but he was a far more fearsome pirate than you'll ever be."

Clif frowned at him and wrinkled his nose. "Impossible. I *am* him."

"Black Jack is dead."

"But he's not. He's right here in front of you. I didn't die when *Neptune's Servant* sank. I lived. I bought another ship, and now I prowl the waters again."

"That's awful," another man said.

"What is?" Clif asked.

"That you're trying to make your name on a dead man's legacy."

"I am not. It's my legacy. I'm Black Jack!"

"You are not," someone answered.

Another man shouted from further back in the crowd. "You don't even look like him."

Clif fluttered his eyelashes at the words.

Another man spoke up. "We all knew Black Jack. And he'd spit on a man like you."

"A liar," the original man said, wiggling his eyebrows.

"This is unbelievable. All right, fine. Black Jack is dead, and it is he who sank Whiteman's ship. That is beside the point. We are looking for Stargazer Santiago. Can anyone point us in his direction?"

"And you are parading around as him, shooting Isaac, and now making demands."

"I'm hardly demanding–"

"You're not nearly as personable as Black Jack. I cannot believe you expected to pull this off."

Clif puckered his lips at the statement before he shook his head. "I just–"

"You just expected to waltz in here and use another man's reputation to complete your business." The man stalked toward Clif. "But you don't have the savvy to pull it off, see? And we aren't going to stand for it."

Clif shifted his tricorn hat on his head as he studied the floor. "This is becoming tiresome."

The man continued forward, poking Clif in the chest.

"You think you can walk in here and just lay claim to a legacy?"

"I haven't done any such thing."

The man called over his shoulder. "Round them up, boys. I know just who'd like to deal with this liar."

He reached for Clif's arm, but Clif skirted away and drew his sword. Henrietta raised hers, stepping closer to Clif, and Abby did the same, closing ranks on his other side.

"Now," Clif said with an arched eyebrow, "I have been more than patient. But this is ridiculous. I am Black Jack. And I am tired of being insulted. If you don't believe me, that's up to you, but I will not be held captive because you are too stupid to see what is right in front of your face."

"You cannot defeat all of us."

"Black Jack could," Clif answered.

"But you ain't Black Jack."

Clif grinned at him. "We're about to find out, aren't we?"

He inched the sword forward, his jaw flexing. "I would recommend you abandon this gambit before you regret it."

The man ripped a knife from his belt and twisted it in the air. "I doubt I will."

"Captain," Abby whispered, "perhaps we should take our leave?"

"And walk away from a fight?" Henrietta asked. "Never!"

She slashed her sword in the air at one of the men who circled toward them.

He chuckled at her as he pulled his weapon. "That's darling, sweetheart, but I prefer my woman in a different position."

"I'll bet you do, you old codger." Henrietta dove forward, shoving the sword toward him.

He danced backward, escaping her thrust. Another man dove toward her with a sword leveled. He stopped short as Clif's weapon clashed against his.

"I think not."

"You can't fight us all."

Clif grinned at him. "Watch me."

He spun in a circle, driving back three men at once before he swept a leg out to upset another. The man toppled onto his backside. Clif whipped around to find his sister engaged in a sword fight with another man.

She seemed to be holding her own. Across the room, Abby smashed a beer stein over a patron's head before she climbed from a chair to a table and leapt to another before spinning to survey the crowd.

Clif left her to fight her battles, and he returned his attention to the three men still pursuing him. He slashed his sword again before he cocked a fist and punched one in the jaw.

The man stumbled sideways but regained his balance quickly. The liquor in his system must be numbing the pain. He snapped his gaze back to Clif, his nose wrinkling with anger. With bared teeth, he stormed forward.

Clif frowned, realizing his opponent would be more challenging than he'd hoped. He spun in a circle and slashed his sword toward the man. It met resistance as his opponent's sword clashed against his.

The man brought his grizzled face closer to Clif's. "You only wish you were Black Jack, you imposter."

Clif held back, rolling his eyes at the statement. It was becoming tedious to constantly be accused of not being who he was, particularly by a set of drunkards who had succumbed to a crowd mentality.

"You people are fools. I have spent many a night here. I *am* Black Jack." He shoved the man away and parried to slash at another attacker.

"Black Jack would have put down every man in this crowd already. You clearly cannot. You are a liar!" the man roared as he flung himself forward with his sword flying through the air to strike at Clif.

"You really are an idiot." Clif smacked his sword against the man's before he kicked him in the stomach, knocking him back.

He slammed into the table behind him. It skidded across the floor with a screech before he toppled underneath it.

"Black Jack wasn't rude, either."

Clif spun to find another man barreling toward him. He ducked, allowing the man to fall over his back and sprawl onto the floor before he left him behind to move on to another opponent.

Across the room, his sister climbed onto the bar involved in a sword fight with another angry crowd member. She glanced behind her at a large barrel of beer.

Her eyebrows knitted. She scanned the room, finding Clif. He offered her a nod, reading her mind. She returned the gesture before she swept a leg under the other man, sending him sprawling on his back and landing hard on the bar.

She danced back a few steps and sliced at the cork. It fell from the cask. Liquid poured from it, splashing onto the floor and snaking across it.

A man charged forward toward the bar where Henrietta stood. He trod on the liquid and lost his footing. With his arms flailing in the air, he slipped and fell onto his backside.

Henrietta leapt over him and landed on a table nearby. She jumped to another, wobbling as the table rocked underneath her.

"Abby!" she shouted.

The woman snapped her gaze to Henrietta, her gaze questioning.

"The casks!" Henrietta pointed her sword in the air.

Abby whipped her head around to glance in the direction

Henrietta indicated. A grin crossed her features. She offered Henrietta a nod before she slashed at another rowdy patron and sailed to another table.

She and Henrietta worked their way to the back of the room while Clif brawled with the men near the front of the tavern. He swiveled as he sparred with multiple attackers, fighting off one before switching his attention to another. He drove them back repeatedly with punches, kicks, and sword flicks.

Henrietta and Abby reached the back of the room.

"Break them all!" Henrietta shouted to her first mate.

Abby nodded as she leapt off the table and landed on the floor. Henrietta whacked corks from the top barrels while still standing on her perch on the table.

Abby hacked at something near the floor, ignoring the corks. "Captain, when you have knocked loose several of the corks, try to free the casks themselves."

"Excellent idea, Abby," Henrietta shouted over the din in the room. Swords clashed together, and shouts resounded.

Henrietta jumped to the floor. A sword grazed her chin before she could break the wood holding the barrels. She slid her eyes sideways to a grizzled man who offered her a toothless grin.

"Look what I caught."

"I don't think so," she growled. She straightened, pulling the knife from her boot and flinging it at him.

He gasped as it struck him in the arm. Blood bloomed on his white shirt, seeping onto the vest he wore and running down his arm.

"You bi–" he started when Henrietta tugged the knife from his blubbery flesh and kicked him away from her.

She returned her attention to freeing the casks from their perches.

"I've got my end, Captain," Abby shouted as she wrapped her fingers around the wood that held the barrels.

Henrietta grabbed hold of the wood on her end and tugged backward. Her arm and back muscles strained as she yanked toward her.

The barrels quivered but didn't budge much. She gritted her teeth, squeezing her eyes closed as she heaved again.

This time, the holder gave way. Henrietta danced backward as the barrels began to topple. Abby sprinted to the opposite side of the pub and dove through a window.

Henrietta tucked herself in the back hall as the barrels splashed through the beer and wine she'd emptied onto the floor. They rolled through the crowd, knocking down patrons in their path and clearing out many in the crowd.

Clif ducked out the front door as pandemonium erupted. Henrietta scanned the bar. She needed to find a way out. If she recalled correctly, there was a door in the back through which she could escape into the back alley.

She'd circle around and meet Abby and Clif to discuss their next steps and regroup.

She hurried down the hall with her sword sheathed, and the knife returned to her boot.

"Hey!" a man shouted behind her.

She shot a glance over her shoulder at the man's soaked clothes. He must have been a victim of one of her ploys.

"Where do you think you're going?"

"Buzz off," she said before continuing down the hall.

"I don't think so." He raced down the hall toward her. She drew her sword a moment too late. He slammed her into the wall, and she lost her grip. The sword clattered to the floor as he wrapped a beefy hand around her arm.

"You're coming with me."

"No!" she shouted, struggling to free herself from his iron grip.

"Yes," he growled. "I have someone who would be very interested in a woman who claims to be sailing with a man calling himself Black Jack. He pays well, too."

"I do not care what you have. Let go of me."

He offered her a harsh laugh. "I don't think so, dearie."

She desperately attempted to reach her sword as he tugged her down the hall toward a closed door leading to a back room.

"Let go of me!" Henrietta shouted again as they reached the door.

He shoved the door open and pushed her inside.

She stumbled forward, landing on her hands and knees. With a glare over her shoulder, she scrambled to her feet.

"What's going on out there, Clarke?" The voice came from the dark shadow in the corner of the room.

"Brawl. Someone came in claiming to be Black Jack."

"You don't say. And what have we here?"

"Someone who came in with him. She claims she killed Whitemane Webb. Liars both of them. But I caught her. And I remembered you said to bring you any evidence of Black Jack."

"Yes, I did," the man answered, still hiding in the darkened corner.

Clarke lifted his chin and rocked on his feet, a grin crossing his fat face. "You can count on me, sir."

"I suppose you'd like the payout I mentioned."

"I wouldn't mind it."

A small pouch flew from the corner and landed on the floor near the man's feet. He snatched it up and tugged it open, smiling at the contents.

"Now, get out."

The man's brow wrinkled. "Is this—"

"I said, get out!"

Clarke's features blanched before he tripped over his feet and raced from the room.

Henrietta crossed her arms and frowned at the corner, unimpressed. With just one man left and one who preferred to hide, she should be able to escape this situation.

She spun on her heel and headed for the door. A knife sailed through the air, coming dangerously close to slicing her cheek before it landed in the wooden door.

"I don't think so."

She whirled around, searching the shadows for the man. "What sort of *man* hides in the shadows like you? A coward?"

"I think you'll find I am anything but." The man's boots tapped across the wooden floor as he stepped forward.

Shadows shifted, and his figure formed as he moved closer to the light. With his head bowed low, his hat covered most of his face.

Henrietta knitted her brow as she searched for a clue to his identity.

It became clear a moment later as he lifted his chin. Flaming red hair escaped beneath his hat, framing his bearded face and deep-set dark eyes.

"Hello, Henrietta."

She swallowed hard as she stared into the face of an old enemy. One that had caused her death once before.

CHAPTER 5

*C*lif slashed his sword through the air twice before it met resistance. His weapon slid toward the floor as it screamed against the other blade.

"Give it up, liar. You can't win. Black Jack could have. Too bad you're not him."

Clif wrinkled his nose at the ridiculous statement as he shoved the man away. The man swung his sword as he stepped backward, slicing through Clif's sleeve and causing a trickle of blood to run down his arm.

Clif grabbed his pistol, but before he could aim, another man leapt onto his back and wrapped an arm around his neck.

The pressure on his windpipe caused him to gasp for air. He stumbled backward and slammed his attacker against the wall.

His former foe stalked forward with his sword raised. "Looks like you lost."

"I...don't...think...so." Clif struggled to push the words out in a hoarse voice.

"What's that, son?"

Clif tugged at the man's arm around his neck, loosening his grip before he slammed the man against the wall. His grip went slack, and he slumped to the floor.

Clif adjusted his clothing and raised his eyebrows. "I said, I don't think so."

A crash sounded behind the man. He glanced over his shoulder, his eyes going wide. The casks from the back of the room barreled toward them, cutting down anyone in their path. The floor, slick with liquid, made escaping all the more difficult.

"Looks like I win," Clif said with a cheeky grin.

He scanned the room before ducking through the front door into the dirt street. Abby had dove through the window to escape, and Henrietta had disappeared into the back hall.

She would likely remember a back entrance she could use to escape.

He'd circle around to meet her, and they'd return to the ships to discuss their next move.

He sheathed his sword and shoved his gun back into its holster as he hurried around the corner. Abby climbed to her feet, dusting herself off.

"Commodore," she said with a crisp salute despite the dirt still smudged on her cheek and chin.

"Excellent work, Abby. Using the barrels was a brilliant move."

"Thank you. I thought of it all because of the captain's use of the wine. Speaking of, where is she?"

"She ducked into the back hall. I'd expect we'll find her in the alley."

"Excellent," Abby said, retrieving her hat from the ground and affixing it to her head.

They continued to the corner of the building. Clif hugged close to it before he peered around the corner. His brows knitted as he found an empty alley. Where was his sister?

Abby took a step forward, but Clif blocked her. "No."

"Where is she?"

"That is exactly my concern." Clif chewed his lower lip. She should have been out by now. What delayed her?

"Commodore, if she is not here, we should find out what happened. Perhaps she needs help."

"That is precisely my worry."

Abby tried to step around him again, but he stopped her.

"Commodore! The Captain may need help."

"Yes, but we cannot help her if we become ensnared ourselves."

Abby stamped a foot into the dirt. "But Commodore–"

"Ri is smart and savvy. She will know how to stay alive and well until we reach her. We cannot walk into the situation unaware."

They waited around the corner for a few more moments before Clif slipped around it and crept to the door. He held up a finger to signal Abby to wait. With a wince, he tugged with a slight amount of pressure. The door shifted toward him before catching on something. He yanked a bit harder, but it refused to open.

"Now, I am convinced something has happened to her."

"But what? And how can we get to her?"

"Whatever it is, it's trouble we were unprepared for. And I don't like that kind of trouble."

* * *

Henrietta's breath caught as she eyed the man before her. He pulled his hat from his head, his flaming red hair gleaming in the candlelight brightening the space.

"You," she spat.

He grinned at her. "Yes, me. Surprise. I'm not certain we've met in person, but I can see you recognize me."

She stared at the man. He looked so much like his father, a pirate Clif had battled several times. A man her brother had killed. "I'd recognize that red hair anywhere. You're Ronan O'Rourke's son."

"Indeed, I am. You are as clever as I've been told."

"What are you doing here?" She asked the question despite already knowing the answer. He sought her brother to kill him in revenge for his father's death.

He arched an eyebrow. "That's a funny little story. You see, I was sailing the seas, minding my own business, when I heard a tale of Black Jack risen from his watery grave."

Henrietta frowned at him as she took shallow breaths. Her eyes darted around the room in search of a way out.

The man stalked a few steps closer to her. "Imagine my surprise when I confirm that wild story with several other sailors, including one who claimed the ghostly version of Black Jack downed Whitemane Webb's ship."

"Nonsense," Henrietta said, dismissing the room with a simple shrug.

"Is it?" He narrowed his eyes at her, one corner of his lips tugging back in an amused grin.

"Of course. Clif is dead."

A sharp laugh escaped the man. "Do you honestly expect me to believe that lie?"

"It's not a lie," she answered, holding his gaze without flinching.

"Says his supposedly dead sister."

"That was all a misunderstanding," she answered, crossing her arms. "Unfortunately, Clif's death was not. You should know. You were there."

"Yes, I was. And I searched the waters for his mangled body. I did not find it."

Henrietta arched an eyebrow. "Those are shark-infested waters. I am unsurprised you did not find it."

Ronan Junior crossed his arms and sighed. "This is a frustrating conversation."

"I find it quite tedious myself."

"Do you? I find it bothersome that you lie with such ease. Why do you find it irritating?"

"Because you cannot be reasoned with."

He slammed his hand against the table, clutching the edge with white knuckles. "I am quite a reasonable man. I—"

"Doubt that," Henrietta spat back, interrupting him. "You are a coward."

He snapped his gaze to her, his features twisting with anger. "How dare you?"

"How dare I? I think not. You threatened my sister. An innocent woman who had nothing to do with your seafaring gambits. But you used her. You couldn't be bothered to fight Clif outright, likely because you knew you would not win. Instead, you used an innocent life to make your play."

"Ah, but according to you, I did win. I managed to surprise him and sink his vessel with him aboard."

"But you do not believe you did. Perhaps Clif does live somewhere. Perhaps he managed to escape. I do not know, but what I know of you turns my stomach. You are a vile man who can only win by stooping so low—"

He lunged at her, wrapping a thick hand around her neck and squeezing. "I would take care not to say something you will regret."

She gritted her teeth as her windpipe closed. "I... regret...nothing."

He tossed her backward, releasing his grip on her. She stumbled before she fell, gasping and choking for air.

"Your brother is the vile man. Can you not see him for what he is?"

Henrietta picked herself up off the floor and glared at

him. "A fine man. An excellent pirate. A legend whose name still passes over the lips of many."

Ronan scoffed at her. "A fine man? A murderer."

"Of whom?"

"My father."

"Your father was a pirate. He knew the score. He picked a fight with Clif he could not win. He was outmaneuvered on the battlefield. Such is the way of it."

Ronan pressed his lips together as he tugged at his beard. He stalked a few steps closer to Henrietta. She refused to back down, lifting her chin as she squared her shoulders.

"Yes, it is, I suppose. But this time, it appears Black Jack has been outsmarted. Here I stand with his sister. I wonder what he would do to save you?"

"Nothing, he's dead."

"For your sake, you'd better hope not."

"What are you saying?"

The redheaded pirate stalked away from her. "If he is not alive, you will join him in the afterlife very soon."

* * *

Clif rounded the corner into the alley. "We must find a way to see inside that tavern."

"We cannot go back inside now, Commodore," Abby said as she trotted beside him.

"No, obviously not. We must find someone else to do that and gather the necessary information."

"Perhaps one of the other crew members."

Clif pressed his lips together as he considered it. Sending in one of his men may raise eyebrows if they ask the wrong questions. He would have preferred Johnson to handle the matter, being a trusted associate…except when it came to matters of the heart. However, Mr. Johnson's presence may prove too obvious.

"I have an idea. Come along, and we'll discuss it with Mr. Johnson."

"Shouldn't one of us stay here in case the Captain should come out of the pub?"

"If she hasn't come out yet, I doubt she will. And if she does, she should know to return to the ship." Clif rubbed his chin as he stared at the tavern wall next to him. "But perhaps someone should keep an eye on things. You must stay hidden, though."

"Yes, Commodore. I will. And I will report anything I see or hear that may be of interest."

"Good. I will return as soon as I can." Clif nodded at her before he hurried down the alley and peered into the street.

A few men still sat on the steps leading to the tavern. One wrung out his vest before he slung it around him.

Clif chewed his lower lip. He couldn't stroll past them. Instead, he'd need another route. And he knew of just the one. With a final glance, he tiptoed to the building next door and skirted around it, keeping to the shadows as much as possible. Once he reached the far corner, he ducked down another alley.

The pungent stench of the pig pen hit his nostrils halfway down the dirt path. He'd have to cross the blasted thing to return to his ship. He hoped not to find it a soggy mess like the last time they'd used it to escape an angry mob.

He hastened the remainder of the way to the fence and hopped over it, landing neatly on the opposite side. A pig snorted beside him, and he shot it a sideways glance. "I'm not pleased either."

He picked his way across the sty, avoiding most of the muck before he jumped the fence and circled to the docks.

He safely boarded his ship as men hauled provisions on board.

Johnson coordinated the stowing of the new supplies. "Mr. Johnson, a word."

The dark-haired man uttered a few instructions to men hauling aboard food before he followed Clif into his cabin.

"Have you located Mr. Santiago?"

"No, we have hit a snag."

"Is he unavailable?"

"I wouldn't know. We were not able to get any answers. A fight broke out in the pub."

Johnson arched an eyebrow. "Oh? Was it Captain Blanchard who started it?"

"Yes and no," Clif said with a sigh. "Someone did not believe she was a pirate, but what they said next led to the issue."

"And what was that, Commodore?"

"Apparently, the ghost of Black Jack has been roaming the waters. He is responsible for many deaths, including Whitemane Webb's."

"Interesting."

"Yes, also false. When I mentioned this, I was accused of many things including being a liar. And then I was accosted for impersonating Black Jack. It's when they attempted to take me to some unknown person to 'deal with me' that the brawl ensued."

"It seems you're no worse for the wear at least."

"No, I am not. However, Captain Blanchard did not fare as well. She did not emerge from the fight, and I don't know where she is. I need someone to go into the pub and locate her."

"I will do it," Johnson said.

"No. You may be recognized. We need someone who will not be."

"Perhaps Crowe or Doyle," Johnson suggested.

"What about Quinn?"

Johnson's knuckles pinched tighter as he gripped his hat in front of him. "We don't have a Quinn, Commodore."

"Captain Blanchard does."

Johnson's brows knitted. "Do you mean…the woman?"

"Yes, Johnson, I mean the woman. Who better to slink amongst the men than a woman? She would be discounted at every turn. And if we dress her like a woman, she likely could pass through the tavern and into the back room where Captain Blanchard disappeared with ease."

"I don't know how I feel about entrusting an important task to a woman."

"It's good that Captain Blanchard isn't here to hear you say that."

"I know. And while I believe the Captain to be extremely capable, somehow…"

"I had the same reservations, but we must do something quickly. I cannot imagine what would be keeping her."

"I will speak with Quinn." Johnson spun on his heel and stepped toward the door when it burst open.

A breathless, red-faced Abby rushed inside. "Commodore! There is no need to send an agent to the pub. I have information about the Captain."

From her wide eyes and paler-than-normal complexion, Clif imagined the news was not good. "What is it, Abby?"

She swallowed hard, her forehead pinching. "She has been caught by someone named Ronan O'Rourke, Junior. And he means to hang her."

CHAPTER 6

*R*onan offered Henrietta a devious grin as he grabbed her arm and dragged her toward the door.

"Get your filthy hands off me," she shouted as she dug her feet into the floorboards.

Her actions failed to stop him from shoving her forward. He wrapped his arms around her and lifted her off the ground to make the task easier. "I think not, dear lady. When your brother killed my father, it set into motion many things. Many things that Black Jack will come to regret. This is the first."

"What are you planning to do?"

"You'll find out soon enough," he answered before he flung the door open and carried her into the hall.

"I demand to know your plans."

"Too bad," he said as he burst through the rear door leading to the alley behind the pub.

He wrangled her forward around the corner and down the side street. They emerged at the tavern's front. Another man hurried toward him. "Captain?"

"Find my rope. We have a criminal to hang."

Henrietta's heart skipped a beat, and she yanked at her arm, struggling to free herself from his grasp.

The man bobbed his head and hurried away to complete his task.

"Get off me."

"I don't think so. You're going to pay the price for your deception. And I hope your supposedly dead brother is here to witness his lovely sister taking her final, strained breaths."

"You're a pig," Henrietta shouted as he continued to drag her toward a platform near the town's center.

"Aye, and I'll admit it. But at least I'm not a thief like your brother."

"Clif was not a thief."

"Was…that's clever. You continue to insist he is dead." He plowed up the stairs with her in tow, her feet banging off each tread as she tried to free herself.

"He is. You'll see. You will hang me, but no one will come to rescue me. Because my brother is gone."

The crewman Ronan had spoken with earlier raced forward with two lengths of rope. Ronan used the first to secure Henrietta's hands behind her back. The rope burned her wrists as she tried to wiggle out of them, but he'd tied her bonds too tightly.

He tossed the second piece of rope over the beam looming above them and tied a knot to secure it to the post before he fashioned a loop.

He tugged off her hat and tossed it away before he slipped the noose around her neck and tightened it. The scratchy fibers scraped at her neck as she glared at him.

"Give me my hat."

"You won't need it."

"I'm a ship's captain and wish to die with my hat."

"You're a bloody pain in the arse is what you are. And you're hardly a ship's captain."

"I am. Of the *Grandmistress*. The least you could do is allow me to die with my feathered cap on my head."

"O'Malley?" the man shouted over his shoulder, his eyes not leaving Henrietta.

"Captain?"

"Bring the lady her hat." He grinned at her, his yellowing teeth peeking through his grizzled red beard.

The other man snatched the cap from the ground and shuttled it to Ronan, who placed it on her head. "There we are. Happy now?"

"Hardly," Henrietta said. "Your gambit here is ridiculous."

"I do not agree."

A crowd gathered at the foot of the platform, murmuring about the current situation unfolding. Ronan twisted to address them, pacing back and forth as he spoke. "Men, we have here a situation unlike most others. This woman is the sister of Black Jack. She is supposedly dead. Yet, here she stands among us. Alive and well. But not for long.

"You see, she assisted her beloved brother, Black Jack, before his untimely demise. She helped him rob me and others. And she hid the bounty, refusing to pay it back. And for that crime, she will pay with her life."

Henrietta slid her wrists up and down, hoping to free herself and slip away somehow, but the ropes held. Her stomach turned over as more men gathered to watch the spectacle. She searched the group for any hint of her brother, but she found none.

He was right to stay away, she reminded herself. Coming here likely meant certain death for him. He had once been accepted in this town and even well-liked. But with Ronan O'Rourke poisoning the people against him, he didn't stand a chance.

Today, she would take her last breaths, but Clif would live on. He would avenge her. She was only sorry she wouldn't be around to see that vengeance.

"That's the woman who caused the trouble in the tavern earlier," one man shouted. "She came in with a man claiming to be Black Jack."

Ronan ceased his pacing and shot a wide-eyed glance at Henrietta.

She shrugged. "A simple deception. The pub's patrons were able to sniff out the lie immediately. Ask any one of them. They'll agree he didn't even look like my brother."

Ronan faced the crowd again. "Which of you saw this man?"

Hands raised throughout the crowd.

"And was he Black Jack?"

"He couldn't have been!" a skinny man shouted. "Black Jack is dead."

"Did he or did he not look like the man once known as Black Jack?"

A few men shouted an affirmative while others shook their heads.

Ronan returned his attention to Henrietta, wrapping his fat, dirty fingers around her neck. "Are you lying to me again? Is your brother here?"

"You heard them," she choked out. "He was a fake."

Ronan narrowed his eyes at her. "Well, I suppose there is one way to flush him out if he does walk among us. And that is to dangle his precious sister at the end of her rope."

"Wa–" she began, but he had already pulled the lever that opened the panel on the floor.

Time slowed as Henrietta felt the air whoosh around her. Her feet kicked in the air, trying to find purchase, but not able to stop her fall.

Her heart stopped as she realized she'd likely just taken her final breath.

* * *

The words stabbed Clif in the chest as they escaped from Abby's lips. "What?"

"Ronan O'Rourke, Junior has the Captain. He means to hang her in the square. He's taking her there now."

Clif collapsed into the desk chair behind him, his eyes wide and his stomach churning. His old enemy had resurfaced and once again threatened his family. "We must stop him."

"Aye, Commodore. But how? A crowd was gathering when I left. They will not take kindly to us interrupting their business."

Clif leapt from his seat and yanked open a drawer, retrieving another small pistol and two knives. "We must create a diversion while someone spirits Ri away from the platform."

"What sort of diversion, Captain?" Johnson asked.

Clif blinked a few times as he mind vetted options.

Johnson slid his head forward, trying to catch Clif's eye. "Captain?"

He snapped his gaze to his first mate and arched an eyebrow. "We're going to burn the pub down."

"Burn the pub down?" Johnson cried, his face blanching.

"We must rescue the Captain," Abby argued. "I will do it, Commodore. Leave it to me and the crew of the *Grandmistress*. We will help you get our beloved Captain back."

"I do not object to rescuing the Captain, but I'm not certain we can pull this off."

"We don't have to reduce it to ashes," Clif said as he shoved his extra weapons into his belt or boot. "We only have to divert enough of the crowd to be able to slip in, grab Ri, and sail away."

"Commodore, the ships aren't yet prepared to sail. We still have several provisions to bring aboard if we plan to search for the Gemstone Islands."

"We will have to find them elsewhere." Clif skirted around the desk and stormed toward the door.

"But, Commodore–"

Clif whirled to face them. "Prepare the men for the rescue mission. Do it now, Johnson. We haven't time to waste."

"I will prepare the crew of the *Grandmistress*," Abby said with a nod. "Mr. Johnson will handle *The Henton's* men. We'll split in half. Send four volunteers, two from each crew, to the pub. Send another six, three from each crew with the Commodore."

"The others should stay back to ready the ship. We will likely need to depart with haste," Johnson said with a nod. "I shall go with the Commodore whilst you stay back to ensure both ships are ready to sail when we return."

"Like fun," Abby answered, her hands on her hips. "I, too, shall go with the Commodore. It is my Captain who is about to be murdered. She saved my life. It's time I repaid that favor."

"Someone in authority should remain here," Johnson said.

"Then give someone the appropriate authority," Abby answered. "We are both needed elsewhere."

"Let Simmons prepare the ships, Johnson. I need you with me," Clif said.

"Aye, Commodore. I will do that. I only mean to ensure there are no slip-ups."

"And to ensure that, I'd prefer you involved in the land operations." Clif nodded before he spun on a heel and stepped onto the deck.

Abby and Johnson followed him. Johnson quickly assembled a set of men for the risky operation to retrieve Henrietta, leaving the second mate in charge of readying the ship.

They met the women from the *Grandmistress* on the floating dock.

"You four set the pub aflame, make sure it catches well, then return immediately to this ship. If you do not, you risk being left behind," Clif said. "The others, including Mr. Johnson and Ms. Abby, are with me. O'Rourke means to make a spectacle. We cannot let that happen."

With nods all around, they strode to the town. Four sailors split off with matches and makeshift torches in hand to create the diversion.

The others stormed forward toward the large crowd gathered around the platform. Henrietta stood with her hands bound behind her and a noose around her neck.

Her feathered cap sat atop her head after Ronan retrieved it and placed it there.

Clif maneuvered his way closer, trying to remain discreet and hidden in the throng of men. One member of the crowd thrust his hand forward. "That's the woman who caused the trouble in the pub earlier."

A conversation broke out about the man claiming to be Black Jack. Ronan wrapped his fingers around Henrietta's neck, his eyes wide as he spoke to her. She choked out a response, inaudible to Clif at the distance he stood away from her.

Whatever she said prompted Ronan to narrow his eyes at her. His hand reached for the lever to open the panel on the floor and hang her.

Clif's heart leapt into his throat. "He's going to hang her."

"We won't make it in time, Commodore," Johnson said.

"Johnson, Abby, O'Connor, prepare to break for the Captain. You'll need to help her get free. As for the others, you remain with me."

"Commodore, the rope will snap her neck. She won't survive," Abby answered, her eyes wide with fear.

"No, it won't." Clif withdrew a knife from his boot.

"Commodore…" Johnson began.

Clif's eyes remained fixed on the slackrope attached to his sister's neck. "I have the aim to make it. Go, now."

Johnson, Abby and Clif's third mate, fought through the crowd toward the platform.

Ronan finished his statement to Henrietta. His lips twisted into a sneer, and his bicep flexed as he began to put pressure on the handle.

Clif tried to steady his nerves. His aim needed to be impeccable. If he hoped to save Henrietta from a broken neck or strangulation, he needed the knife to slice the rope attached to her neck cleanly away.

The next few seconds of his life would determine if he saved his sister or if she died. There was no margin for error. Even a one-second misjudgment could mean the end for Henrietta.

Ronan flipped the lever from one position to the other. The platform swung open underneath Henrietta, and she began to fall.

Clif whipped the knife at the rope and held his breath as he waited to determine if he'd just cost his sister her life.

CHAPTER 7

*T*he wooden platform beneath Henrietta dropped, and she began to fall toward the ground below. She gasped in a breath as her heart seized in her chest. Seconds from now, her neck would break if she was lucky.

If not, she would choke and gasp for breath until she finally died of strangulation. She kicked her feet in a desperate attempt to stop herself from falling, but she could find nothing to brace herself against.

She waited for the rope to tighten around her throat. But that didn't happen. The ground rushed at her quickly. And before she knew it, she landed in a heap on it, knocking the air from her lungs.

For a moment, she lay unmoving, wondering if she'd died. Blue sky peeked at her through the open panel on the platform. She realized she was lying on the ground. Her lungs hurt. The pain reminded her she was still alive and forced her to suck in a breath.

The influx of air cleared her mind. She had fallen. Her neck had not snapped, nor had she been strangled. The rope must have broken. *Lucky.*

She struggled to get to her feet, but with her hands tied behind her back, she didn't make much progress.

Hands grabbed at her arms and tugged her upward. She struggled against them, assuming Ronan was dragging her back to her death.

"Quickly, Captain, we must get away," Abby said.

Henrietta blinked to clear her clouded vision and snapped her gaze toward the woman. She swung her head to the opposite side, spotting Johnson hauling her to her feet.

"Abby! Johnson!"

"Aye, Captain. And we have no time for idle chatter. We must break away before you are caught again."

Henrietta bobbed her head up and down. The rope rose over her face as Abby pulled it away, and her hands broke free as Johnson cut the bindings around them.

Abby wrapped a hand around her arm and tugged her away from the crowd. Henrietta stumbled a few steps before she broke away from Abby's grip.

"Captain!" Abby shouted. "This way! Quickly."

"My hat!" Henrietta dove for the tricorn with the feather sticking from it.

"Leave the hat!" Johnson shouted.

She snatched it from the ground and dusted it off before placing it on her head. "I cannot be a pirate captain without my feathered cap!"

"Or your life," Ronan growled from behind her.

Henrietta whipped around to face him.

He swung at her, knocking her to the ground before she could draw it. Abby and Johnson drew their guns, and so did Ronan.

He pointed it at Henrietta. "Shoot me, and the last thing I do is snuff out her life."

A sneer crossed his hardened features. "Now, I suggest

you two return to your ships unless you'd like to forfeit your lives with your captain."

Abby stuffed her gun into its holster and stepped forward. "I will. I would be proud to stand shoulder-to-shoulder with my Captain. I will not run away."

"As will I," Johnson answered.

"Fools." He shifted his gaze to Henrietta. "Get up."

She scrambled to her feet, hands raised in the air.

"A valiant attempt to rescue you, but alas, a doomed one. Though I would like to know who has the aim to have sliced that rope from a distance."

"That would be me," a new voice answered behind them.

Ronan twisted to face Clif, who held a knife in one hand and a pistol in the other. Redness rose into Ronan's cheeks, and his features twisted with hatred. "Men! We have Black Jack! We have—"

"Fire!" a shout resounded. "Come quickly! There is a fire at the pub!"

Clif's lips twisted into an amused smile. "I think you'll find them otherwise engaged."

Ronan reached for Henrietta and pulled her closer, settling the gun under her chin. "I think you'll find yourself at a disadvantage, Jack."

"Let her go. Your fight is with me, not her."

Ronan waddled his way backward, his eyes darting from Abby and Johnson to Clif. "She'll come with me. Or I'll kill her. No quick moves now. Unless you want her dead."

"I think not," Henrietta growled. With a quick movement, she stamped on his insole with the heel of her boot before she slammed her head backward into his. His grip loosened. She plowed an elbow into his gut before she slid lower and escaped from his arm.

As she ducked backward, she knocked the hat from her head again. Clif fired his weapon at the man as Henrietta scurried away. Blood bloomed on his shoulder, knocking him back a few more steps. With his hurt arm, he tried to pull his weapon, but another shot from Abby stopped him despite it going wide. The man side-stepped to avoid another bullet, stamping on Henrietta's hat and snapping the feather. It hung limply from its broken rachis.

Clif grabbed hold of a stumbling Henrietta and steadied her. "Let's take our leave, shall we?"

"Wait, my hat!" she cried.

"The feather is broken, leave it." Clif bent and caught her around the legs, throwing her over his shoulder before he ducked from under the platform and hurried through the street, filled with frantic men trying to stop the fire blazing at the pub.

"Put me down!" Henrietta shouted as she flailed her arms and legs.

"I'll put you down the moment you are safe."

"I am not a child, Clif. Put me down!"

They reached the floating dock, and he set her down, keeping a firm hold of her arm. "I hope we are far enough from that hat to stop you from racing back for it."

"It was a good hat. Though Ronan ruined the feather." Henrietta shook her head as she lamented the death of another hat.

"Those hats will be the death of you. Come along, we are preparing to sail." Clif caught her arm and dragged her forward another few steps.

"Just a moment! We are not prepared to sail, and we have yet to find Sunwatcher."

"Stargazer," Clif corrected, "and we have changed our plans. It is not safe here. I will not slink about the island in search of Stargazer when O'Rourke Junior is lurking around every corner."

"And now that he knows you are alive, it is even more

dangerous," Johnson added. "He has his sights set on both of you."

Clif nodded. "Yes, he does. And we would do well to skedaddle."

Henrietta frowned as she dragged herself forward. "Well, this certainly ruins my day."

"Sorry, Ri, but we'll find a way."

Henrietta stopped in her tracks as they approached the ships. "Find a way? Do you mean you are not put off the entire thing?"

Clif wrinkled his nose as he scowled. "No. Now, I want to find them more than ever. Let O'Rourke find out I have put another feather in my cap."

Henrietta scowled at him. "Must you use that turn of phrase after yet another beloved cap of mine has been ruined?"

"Sorry, Ri. If we find the Gemstone Islands, I will buy you enough feathered hats to sink a ship."

"Please, Commodore," Johnson said, "they are so very unlucky."

"They are not," Henrietta insisted. "And we will have plenty of time to discuss our options in pursuing this whilst we take our detour." She strode forward toward her ship.

Clif hurried to catch up to her. "What detour?"

"Why, to check on Carolina, of course. You heard Ronan. He threatened her again. We must check to ensure she is fine."

"I second the plan," Johnson said.

Clif slid his eyes sideways in a glare. "Of course you would."

"Oh, come on, Clif. We should go check on her."

Clif arched an eyebrow at his sister. "You want to check on Carolina?"

Henrietta clicked her tongue at him, sticking her hands on her hips. "What does that mean?"

"It means you usually avoid anything to do with Carolina. You prefer her out of the picture entirely."

Henrietta shook her head as she crossed her arms. "Complete lies."

"Is it? She is fine, Clif. Leave her go, Clif. She is a grown woman, Clif. Or perhaps you recall…she stole my house. She stole my life. Mousy little Carolina—"

"That's enough," Henrietta said with a flick of her hand in the air. "Carolina and I have had our differences; however, we resolved many of them during our escapade in the jungle."

Clif sucked in a breath.

"You must admit it would be prudent, at the very least, to warn her about Ronan. He is a threat. And she is unprotected. She has no idea who he is or what he looks like. He could charm his way into her home easily."

Clif slid his eyes closed before he nodded. "Fine. One quick stop. And everyone but you and I shall remain aboard their respective vessels."

He shot a pointed glance at Johnson.

"That is ridiculous. Thanks to Ronan, we need to attend to securing the provisions we could not bring aboard. Mr. Johnson and Abby shall see to that whilst we visit Carolina."

"Mr. Johnson and Abby will see to *only* that. Is that understood?"

"Understood, Commodore." Johnson nodded at him before he slid his eyes sideways to Henrietta with a slight smile.

"Don't look at her. She is not your commander; I am."

"Yes, Commodore," Johnson said with another nod before he scurried aboard *The Henton*.

Clif heaved another sigh as he stepped aboard the plank. "I hope I do not regret this."

"I have no doubt you will," Henrietta said as she continued down the dock toward the *Grandmistress.*

"Ri!" he shouted after her before he let out a curse under his breath.

Henrietta chuckled as she continued along with Abby at her side.

"Will Mr. Johnson visit her?"

"I have no doubt he will. Much to the Commodore's chagrin."

"Do you not mind, Captain? Or do you merely wish to unsettle the Commodore? Is it a sibling prank?"

Henrietta shrugged as she climbed aboard her ship. "Both. The Commodore needs to understand that women can make their own choices. Though, it is enjoyable for him. He spent almost seventeen years doing the same to me. A little payback isn't unwarranted."

Abby giggled as Henrietta shot her a devilish grin. "Now, set the course for Hideaway Bay. I want to arrive as quickly as possible."

"Done, Captain," Abby said with a salute before she hurried away to prepare the ship to sail.

They sailed away from the port town shortly after, leaving Ronan O'Rourke and a burning tavern behind. Smoke still curled into the sky as the island became a speck on the horizon.

They aimed north for the seaside town of Hideaway Bay on the East Coast, arriving the following day.

"Ahoy, there," Henrietta called over the railing to her brother on the deck of *The Henton* as the town came into view.

"You are far too happy about this pitstop, Ri."

She grinned at him. "Carolina will be pleased to see you."

"I fear I am not the only one she will be pleased to see. Ready your skiffs. We'll use your crew to go ashore after we hide the ships in the back of the Bay."

"With Mr. Johnson in tow, of course."

Clif offered her an unimpressed stare as his crew prepared to weigh anchor. Henrietta fluttered her eyelashes, shooting him a haughty glance as their crews readied to go ashore.

When the sun crested the horizon, they dragged their boats onto the sandy beach in a hidden bay near Whispering Manor, Henrietta's former home.

"Mr. Johnson, straight to town and back. We sail as soon as we are able."

"Of course, Commodore." With Abby in tow, the man set off toward the town.

Henrietta and Clif walked the beach toward her former home. "Do not be so hard on him. He's a man in love."

"Please stop saying that."

"You must accept it, Clif. It will not change simply because you do not wish it to be true."

Clif wrinkled his nose at the statement as the Victorian house came into view. Candlelight glowed from within in the early morning hours.

"Oh, good, Carolina is awake," Clif noted. "Let's hope we can make quick work of this."

"Likely reading or doing some other mundane task." They circled the house and climbed onto the porch. Clif gave a soft knock at the door and waited.

It opened seconds later, and the petite blonde peeked out the door. Her features cracked into a smile, and she flung the door open before throwing her arms around Clif's neck. "Clif!"

"Hello, Carolina," he said as he wrapped his arms around her.

Henrietta crossed her arms and offered him a knowing glance before dramatically tapping her sister on the shoulder. "And me."

"Henrietta," the woman said as she settled back on her heels and smiled, giving her sister a much less ostentatious hug. "It's lovely to see you both. Are you docked in town?"

"No, in the bay, and we don't plan to stay." Clif shot an uncomfortable glance at Henrietta, who failed to hide her amused grin. Her sister's question was less about where they were docked and more about if a specific first mate had traveled with them.

"Please, come in." Carolina stepped back and motioned them into the house.

They stepped inside as the sun began to paint the floors a rich red color.

"Is James about?" Henrietta asked as she glanced up the stairs.

"Asleep."

"Still?" Henrietta said. "Rather a layabout, isn't he?"

Clif cleared his throat. "Ri, it is not our business and has nothing to do with the reason we are here."

He guided both women into the sitting room.

"And why are you here? Not that I'm complaining," Carolina said. "I do enjoy your visits. Can I offer you tea?"

"Uh, no," Clif began.

"I'd love some," Henrietta said with a smile.

"Ri, we really–"

"I'll make it. I was just about to put the kettle on for myself before I journaled."

"Lovely," Henrietta said as Carolina hurried from the room.

Clif sucked in a breath as he twirled his hat in his hands. "Ri, we are not to be making ourselves at home. We are here to warn her."

"Yes, I understand that. But warn her and then do what?"

"Leave. Wasn't it you who was insistent that we find the Gemstone Islands? We will not find them in Hideaway Bay. I can assure you of that."

"Obviously, however, you mean to say you plan to simply tell Carolina, a gruff, red-bearded pirate with an axe to grind may pay her a call, attempt to kill her, and race off into the rising sun to pirate another day?"

"When you put it like that…"

"Exactly." She pressed her fingers to his temple. "Use your brain, Clif. We cannot simply leave Carolina to her own devices."

"And what do you plan to do? Invite her to join the fleet? Perhaps she, too, can captain a ship, and then we'll have three."

"It's not a bad idea, though I do not think she has it in her to do so. Clif, sometimes you don't think things through."

"I am so pleased you find this amusing. I will leave a contingent with her to ensure there is no trouble."

Henrietta crossed her arms as she considered the move, weighing it against her idea, when a shuffle of feet sounded behind her. She spun, expecting to find Carolina returning with the tea.

Instead, she found a rifle aimed at her. She slowly lifted her hands as her heart skipped a beat.

CHAPTER 8

"What are you doing here?" James growled from behind the rifle.

"James!" Carolina shouted as she returned. The teacups clattered on the saucers as she plopped the tray on the coffee table and rushed toward him. "Put that gun down."

"I will not. These persons are not welcome in this house, and you know that."

"This is *my* home," Carolina cried as she tugged at his arm, trying desperately to get him to lower the gun. "My siblings are welcome in it."

"Yet it is not, *dear*," he spat. "It is mine."

Henrietta arched an eyebrow at the conversation before glancing sideways at Clif. "This was my home to start with. And I do not recall willing it to you when I 'died.'"

"I do not recall asking for your opinion about simple law," James said through clenched teeth. "Do not insert yourself between a husband and his wife."

"I am only saying–"

"I do not need counsel from a woman who behaves like you."

Clif lowered his hands and stepped forward. "We are here for a very important reason, and I will thank you not to speak to either of my sisters that way."

"I shall speak to my wife in my own home in whatever manner. As far as the other." He eyed Henrietta with disdain. "I should prefer not to speak with her at all."

"You really are an insufferable jackass," Henrietta said.

Clif shot her a stony glance. "As I said, we are here for an important reason. The visit could not be avoided."

"What is of this much importance that you would show up on our doorstep before sunrise?"

Clif licked his lips before he explained. "Carolina's life has been threatened."

"No doubt by one of your illustrious counterparts."

"Unfortunately, yes. By a very dangerous one. The same man who led to Henrietta and my decision to disappear in our previous forms."

James heaved a disgusted sigh. "You should not have come. You should distance yourself from her entirely."

"It is too late," Henrietta answered. "O'Rourke is well aware of her. And when we saw him, he specifically mentioned her. We wanted to ensure she is safe and remains that way."

"I will do that."

"You are no match for this man," Henrietta argued.

"And what do you propose? That she disappear? She has a life, a home, and a husband to attend to. She cannot simply vanish."

Henrietta stepped forward. "Do you care so little about her that you prefer she remain exposed to this danger?"

James closed the distance between them, poking a finger at her. "You brought this trouble to our doorstep. You handle it."

"Oh, I intend to." Henrietta sneered at him before she

flicked her gaze to Carolina. "Pack your things. You are about to travel the seven seas, sister."

James stepped back, placing himself between Clif Henrietta and his wife. "No."

"What do you mean, no?" Henrietta questioned. "She is in danger here. Surely, you do not wish to risk her life."

"It is you who continues to put her life in danger. You should leave. I shall deal with this as I see fit."

Henrietta shifted her gaze to her sister. "Carolina? Are you comfortable with this?"

The woman swallowed hard, glancing demurely at her husband before she studied the floorboards under her feet. "Yes. Whatever James feels is best."

Henrietta raised her eyebrows before she shot a glance at her brother. He cleared his throat, unhappy with the turn of events but unwilling to push further. "Well, I suppose we shall take our leave then. If you should need anything–"

"We will not," James said as he stepped back, allowing them to pass to the front door.

"Then we will be on our way." Clif stopped next to Carolina, tipping her chin up to him. "Take care, sister."

She forced a fleeting smile onto her lips as tears showed in her eyes. "You as well, brother. Please be safe."

"We will be."

Henrietta sauntered behind her brother, stopping at Carolina. "Carolina, if you–"

"Please leave," James huffed at her.

She shot him a glare, her jaw tensing and her nostrils flaring before she flicked her gaze back to Carolina. "Take care, Carolina."

"I will," she said curtly before Henrietta strode to the door.

They let themselves out into the brisk morning air. "Is that it then?" Henrietta asked as they strode toward the town.

"What else would you like me to do?"

"You are the one who did not wish to leave her with that man in South America. Now, you walk away willingly when we could make the case to take her with us."

"She does not belong on the sea, Ri."

"She does not, or you do not prefer it because she may spend too much time with your first mate?"

"She is a married woman, and her husband has agreed to care for her. Carolina, herself, has chosen to remain with him. There is nothing I can do."

"You did plenty when I was involved with a man I should not have been."

"That was different."

"Was it? I do not find it so."

Clif shook his head as the buildings of Hideaway Bay filled in around them. "We sail tonight."

"For where?"

"I have some idea of where we may find the map piece hidden in the jungle. We will head south and try to find that first."

Henrietta gritted her teeth as she shook her head.

"Commodore!" Mr. Johnson called before he and Abby closed the gap between them. "Finished already?"

"Yes, we are. We sail tonight."

Johnson raised his eyebrows at the statement. "That quickly?"

"Carolina, in her infinite wisdom, has chosen to trust her husband to deal with this threat. There is nothing more we can do," Henrietta said with a sigh.

"We cannot sail tonight, Captain. Mr. Johnson and I have arranged for all the provisions to be delivered early tomorrow morning. We must stay until then."

Clif slid his eyes closed and shook his head. "We should–
"

"That will be fine, Abby," Henrietta said. "We sail tomorrow morning."

"Shall I give the men permission to come ashore?"

Clif huffed out a sigh. "Yes. That's fine. We will be on the water for quite a while after this. Allow them their freedom tonight."

Henrietta stared down the street as the others turned to return to the ship. "Ri, you coming?"

"I wanted to see the milliner."

"Milliner?"

"I'm running low on hats."

Clif squeezed his eyes closed again. "Honestly, with those hats. They will be the death of us. Mark my words."

She shifted her belt. "Consider them marked. I will see you later on the ship."

She strode off in the direction of the businesses in town to secure a fresh set of feathered caps. After she concluded her business, she returned to the beach, passing by her former home. Something nagged at her about the way Carolina behaved.

Her mother was meek. But not that meek. Miriam may have deferred to her father, John, but she did not look at him with the same eyes Carolina had for James. It bothered her.

Before she could consider it further, she rounded into the hidden cove. Abby stood with another man near one of the skiffs.

"What are you doing?" Henrietta asked as she approached.

"Waiting for you, Captain. You need not row a boat yourself. Have you secured your hats?"

"Yes. They should arrive with the other provisions you secured."

"Excellent. Let us return to the *Grandmistress* then."

They rowed back to the ship. While the others spent time

ashore, Henrietta spent it in her cabin. She would normally have plotted a course or studied the region they planned to scour, but instead, she spent it pacing the floor.

By the time light peeked over the horizon, she had decided. She strode across the deck and climbed down to a skiff still bobbing in the water from the previous night.

"Captain!" Abby called as she settled onto the seat. "Where are you going?"

"To visit my sister. I will return shortly."

Henrietta wrangled the oars into place and began her row to shore. She splashed into the cold water and dragged the boat onto the sandy beach before she strode to the house.

Only a few candles lit the inside at this hour. She didn't bother to knock, instead letting herself in through the open front door. The house remained quiet at this hour. She glanced in the library but did not find Carolina.

With another flick of her gaze up the stairs, she passed by them into the kitchen. Her sister's blonde hair glistened in the morning sun peeking through the windows.

"Carolina."

The woman was startled but did not turn to face her. "Henrietta?"

"Yes. I came to say goodbye. Privately."

"Thank you," she said, turning ever so slightly from her work. "I appreciate that. And your warning. I am sorry for James's reaction, but he worries."

"Does he?" Henrietta asked, crossing her arms as she leaned into the door jamb. "Does he worry enough to let you make the choice you are most comfortable with?"

"I am comfortable with this," Carolina answered.

"While I realize a pirate ship is perhaps not the home you'd prefer, it will not be as bad as you may think."

"I do not think it bad. In truth, I would likely find it exhilarating." She huffed out a giggle. "I always wanted to ride on Clif's ship."

"Yet, you turned him down."

"I have a husband now."

Henrietta narrowed her eyes at her sister's back. "Yes, but you should do what you are most comfortable with. If that is coming with me and Clif, we can–"

"It's not. Please, Henrietta. I appreciate you checking, but you should leave." Carolina twisted to peer over her shoulder before returning to her work at the counter.

Henrietta considered her next move. Should she leave? Something nagged at her, and she decided against it. She crossed to her sister, placing a hand on her shoulder and turning the woman toward her.

"Carolina, I think–"

Her jaw unhinged as she caught sight of her sister's face. One blackened eye was swollen shut. Purple bruises marred her cheeks, and dried blood crusted on her split lower lip.

"My God, Carolina, what happened?"

"I tried," her sister squeaked out.

"That's bull. Did James do this?"

"Please, Henrietta, you must understand he has a bit of a temper."

Henrietta pulled her sword from its sheath as disdain wrinkled her lips. "Oh, I understand perfectly."

Carolina grabbed her arm and tugged. "Please, Henrietta. He won't do it again once you've left."

"You're damned right he won't." Henrietta shrugged off her sister's grasp as she stormed into the hall and toward the front of the house.

She rounded the curved railing on the stairs as Carolina hurried after her. "Please, Henrietta, you'll only make things worse for me."

"James!" Henrietta roared as she set foot on the first stair.

"Henrietta, please! Go before he harms you, too," Carolina shrieked as tears streamed down her cheeks.

A door flung open at the top of the stairs, and James staggered out in pants and an unbuttoned shirt. He glared at Henrietta. "*You* again."

"Me again. Though, take comfort in knowing this is the last time you will see me."

"Oh, good. We cannot be rid of you soon enough." He stumbled forward and plunked his way down the stairs toward her.

"Funny, I have the same sentiment about you."

She raised her sword, but a firm hand stopped her from swinging forward. "Ri, let's not do anything we'll regret."

She twisted to find Clif behind her. Abby and Johnson stood on the porch.

"I'm sorry, Captain. He insisted to know your whereabouts," Abby said, wringing her hands.

"It's fine, Abby. I'm glad he is here."

"Ri, let us take our leave. We are not welcome here."

Henrietta yanked her arm from his grasp. "Mr. Johnson, keep Mr. Edmonton under watch with a pistol aimed at him."

Johnson shifted his wide-eyed gaze to Clif, who held up a hand.

Henrietta spun to find Carolina, but the woman was gone.

"Do it, Johnson." Henrietta switched her gaze to Clif. "You come with me."

She sheathed her sword as Johnson stepped with his weapon drawn.

"Ri, you should not have come. We are not welcome here."

Henrietta held up a hand as she made her way toward the kitchen. "Do not speak until you have witnessed what I did this morning. Carolina! Come out right now."

"Henrietta, please," the woman sobbed from inside the space.

Henrietta entered, finding her sister crouched in a corner, her face hidden as she sobbed.

Clif shot Henriette an unimpressed stare. "This is no doubt upsetting to her. Perhaps we should—"

Henrietta strode to her sister and ripped a hand away from her face. "This is what is upsetting to her, Clif."

Clif's eyes went wide as he stared at his sister's face. "What the hell has he done to you?"

Henrietta bobbed her head up and down. "Yes. This is the man we nearly left her with. This is what he did to her. And I'd wager it is not the first time. Is it, Carolina?"

Her sister shook her head, her face red and pinched from crying.

Henrietta set her hands on her hips. "I will not leave her here."

"Please, Henrietta," Carolina cried as she latched on to her sister's arm. "It will only be much worse when I return."

"You will not return. You will stay with us," Henrietta said. "If you choose to return to this house, you will do so without him here."

"He will come back," she squeaked.

"No, he will not." Clif backed from the room. "Have no fear of that."

"Clif!" Carolina shrieked as he spun on his heel and stormed from the kitchen. "Stop him. He will be in trouble."

Henrietta followed her brother from the room.

He thundered past Abby and Johnson, squeezing James's cheeks between his thumb and forefinger and driving him to the stairs below him. "You put your hands on my sister?"

"No, Clif, do not do anything that will cause trouble for you," Carolina wailed as she hurried behind Henrietta.

"My God," Johnson breathed as he caught sight of her.

"Mr. Johnson, take Carolina to the skiff and see that she safely boards the *Grandmistress*," Henrietta ordered.

Johnson hurried forward to scoop Carolina into his arms, hugging her close as he skirted around them to head out the open door.

"My things..." she called, shooting a glance to Henrietta.

"I will collect them. Abby, go with them."

"Yes, Captain," Abby said with a bob of her head as she scurried after the departing couple.

Clif squeezed the man's cheeks tighter in his grasp. "Now, with Carolina safely away, let us deal with you in the appropriate manner."

"Another murder, you foul pirate?"

"Let's call it justice, shall we? You will never lay another finger on my sister again. Do you know what I did to the last man who threatened one of my sisters?"

James wrinkled his nose at him. "I can imagine you dealt with it in the manner to which you are accustomed using violence and your version of justice."

"I believe it is you who is accustomed to violence," Henrietta said as she slid a knife from her boot. "Tell me, James, what sort of man hits a woman?"

He sneered at her. "The sort who wishes to keep his wife in line and make a God-fearing woman out of her."

"Don't you mean James-fearing? I don't believe God is involved in any of this," Henrietta spat back.

"No, you wouldn't. You are a filthy excuse for a woman. Dressed in trousers and parading around like a man. You have no class, no values, and no morality at all."

"I have more of those in my little finger than in your entire body." She tightened her grip on the hilt of her weapon.

James grunted as he shifted around under Clif's weight. "Do you know why I did it?"

"Because you are an insufferable jackass who finds it amusing to hit a woman?" Henrietta questioned.

He shook his head as far as Clif's iron grip would allow. "No. Because your sister deserves it; she needs a firm hand to stop her from giving in to the types of behavior you exhibit. She needs to be reminded of her place in life. Which is groveling at my feet."

"You bastard," Johnson's voice shouted.

Clif and Henrietta twisted to find him limned in light in the doorway. He flew across the room at the man before he landed blow after blow against him.

Blood flew in the air, spattering the railing and wood stair treads.

"I'll kill you myself, you vile bastard!" Johnson screamed.

"Johnson!" Clif shouted, letting go of James to pull his first mate away from his victim.

Henrietta held out her knife, keeping James at bay as he picked himself off the floor, wiping at the blood trickling from his lip and a cut above his eye.

"She's an angel of a woman. How could you harm her?" Johnson cried.

"I told you. She deserved it."

Clif slid his eyes closed and stepped forward to react, but Johnson quickly pulled a knife from his belt and raised it. "I challenge you to a duel for her hand."

James spit out blood and wiped at his mouth. "A duel with a pirate?"

"I am an honorable man. And I am challenging you, sir. Do you accept?"

James's nostrils flared. "Accepted. And when I win, you will return her to me before you bury your man at sea."

"I don't think so," Henrietta said with a scoff. "Clif, do something."

Clif held his hands up in the air. "The challenge has been set. Let them settle this as men."

Johnson nodded at him. "Commodore, if I can ask you to be my second."

"Of course, Mr. Johnson."

Henrietta fluttered her eyelashes. "Surely, you jest. Let's get him and be done with this!"

"Don't worry," James said with a sneer. "It will all be over soon. And then we can get on with our lives. Oh, except for Mr. Johnson."

"Your second, Dr. Edmonton?" Clif inquired.

"I need none."

"Where?" Johnson growled.

"The beach. Allow me to fetch my pistol." The man stepped past them, heading into the library.

"Clif, are you insane? Stop this, now!"

"Johnson is an excellent shot, and it would end the matter."

"I don't care if he is the world's best shot."

Clif dragged her several steps away, lowering his voice. "Ri, this is the way of it. The man has issued a challenge, and I would be wrong to step in."

"Who gives a fig? I'd rather see James dead than Johnson."

"Are we ready?" James asked, toting a pistol as he re-entered the room.

Henrietta slid her eyes closed before wrenched her hand from her brother's grasp. "I will not be a party to this."

She stormed from the house with them following behind her. They rounded toward the beach. With a shake of her head, she followed, desperate to see the outcome despite disagreeing. A winded Abby ran toward her as the others marched toward the lapping water.

"What is happening, Captain?"

"Mr. Johnson has challenged Dr. Edmonton to a duel for Carolina's hand. And the nitwits plan to go through with it."

"Oh, no. Johnson could be killed. Have we any idea how good a shot Dr. Edmonton is?"

"None. I tried to stop it, but no man would hear reason. Even Clif supports this ridiculous method of problem-solving."

The two men stood facing each other in the distance as Henrietta curled and uncurled her hands. Johnson thrust his hand out toward James. The man stared down at it before he snubbed him, spinning to face the opposite direction with his pistol against his chest.

"Ten paces, then turn and fire," Clif said. "May the best man win."

Clif began the count, and each man took steps away from the other. The sun glistened off the waters as the scene played out in slow motion.

When Clif reached six, James spun and aimed his weapon as Johnson continued to march toward his spot.

A cloud passed over the sun, blotting it out momentarily and plunging the area into dimmer light. Then, a single shot rang out, and blood bloomed as it hit its mark.

CHAPTER 9

"**J**ohnson!" Clif shouted as he spotted James turn far too early.

The shot rang out before he could react. His heart stopped, but he continued to reach for his weapon, withdrawing it from its holster and aiming it at James's form.

His brows knitted when he found the man already dropping forward to his knees. Blood bloomed, turning his white shirt crimson. James's lower lip trembled as he reached a hand toward his chest, his features showing signs of shock as blood-colored his fingers.

He sucked in a shaky breath before he fell forward, collapsing onto his face as his body shuddered with his last breath.

Clif flicked his gaze to Johnson. The man stood with empty hands and a gaping jaw. His gaze raised from the dead man to Clif. "Captain?"

Clif shook his head, understanding the implied question. He hadn't shot James, and neither had Johnson.

He let his gaze roam across the beach toward the house. Henrietta stood with her weapon aimed, smoke still curing from the barrel, and one eye closed. She lowered it and opened both eyes wide. "Best to check that he's dead, though I believe my aim is as good as yours. Perhaps better."

"Ri…you…he…"

"He cheated. Or tried to. Once a louse, always a louse. Now he's a dead louse." She shrugged as she holstered the pistol.

Clif stared at her for a moment with a shocked expression before he let his gaze fall on James's dead form. The water lapped at the man's outstretched hand, covered in sand.

"Well, chop, chop, brother. We haven't all day. We must sail."

"We'd better help, Captain. I believe they are stunned." Abby took a few steps forward.

"Quite right. Typical men. All bluster and blowhard until the deed needs to be done." Henrietta stalked forward with her. "Come on, brother, we shouldn't leave the body here. The seagulls will make a mess of it."

"That shot…how did you…at that distance," Clif stammered.

"Well, I couldn't let him kill Johnson. And he planned to. I did what needed to be done."

"Yes, but…"

"I suppose it runs in the family." Henrietta grabbed the man's hand and tugged. "Now, come on. Best to get underway before the town wakes."

"Captain," Johnson said as he approached them, "thank you."

"You are quite welcome. Now, please, may we finish this nasty business and move on."

Clif reached to lift the body as Henrietta dusted the sand from her hands. "Oh, we should return for some of Carolina's things. She will undoubtedly need several items since she will remain aboard one of our vessels until she can safely return here."

"I will help you, Captain," Abby said.

They trudged back to the house while the men dealt with the disposing of the body. Henrietta pushed into the foyer and started up the stairs with Abby trailing behind her.

"This is quite a lovely home, Captain. Did you enjoy your time here?"

"No. I hated it mostly. I'm much happier where I am."

Abby smiled at her. "I understand."

They pushed into the main bedroom. Henrietta tugged open a drawer, gathered several dresses, and handed them off to Abby before she strode to the small desk. She shifted a few papers around on the top, then pulled the drawer open.

"What is it you seek, Captain?"

"These are James's things. Where are Carolina's journals? She enjoys writing and reading. We should take them with us to comfort her."

"That's very kind, Captain. Perhaps she writes in another space."

"Undoubtedly. The swine she had been married to most likely kept this space for himself."

They left the room, and Henrietta crossed to a linen closet, pulling a sheet from within before descending to the first floor. "Do you think Mr. Johnson and Miss Carolina will marry?"

"If Clif doesn't kill him first, I should think so. At least, I should hope so," Henrietta answered as she entered the library. "Ah, here we are."

She grabbed the leather-bound books from the writing desk, along with a supply of ink and quills, before gathering a few books from the stack near the armchair.

"Do you believe the Commodore will bar them from marrying?"

"I believe he will hem and haw, but he should come around to the idea. It is rather obvious how they feel."

"Yes, very," Abby said as they left the house behind and made their way to the skiffs.

"I brought a sheet to cover him. I'm sick of looking at his face," she said, tossing the item over James's body before she settled onto a seat.

Abby and Johnson began rowing them toward the ships.

"I will come aboard with you. We should tell Carolina together."

"All right," Henrietta said. "We shall inform her together, then we will sail. I trust you have a location where we will begin our search?"

"Yes," he answered as they arrived at the *Grandmistress.* "I shall pass the information to your crew in case we are separated."

"I should hope not," Henrietta said as she climbed aboard. "It would be a terrible shame if I were to find the Gemstone Islands without you."

"You find yourself quite amusing, don't you?"

Henrietta grinned at him, stalking across the deck to her cabin. "I do."

"Try to break the news gently to Carolina," Clif said before they entered.

Henrietta let her hand linger on the door handle. "Me? She'd take it better from you. You break the news."

"I think this would best come from a woman."

"And I think it would best come from the brother she adores."

They stared at each other for a moment, neither willing to give in.

Clif finally heaved a sigh. "Fine. I will do it."

"Good, I'm glad we agree." Henrietta smiled at him before she pushed into the cabin. She stepped inside when

Carolina raced across the space and flung her arms around her neck.

She sobbed as she clung to Henrietta.

Stunned, Henrietta wrapped an arm around her sister's shaking shoulders. "There, there. It will be all right."

Clif placed a hand on his sisters' shoulders as he drew them closer. "Carolina..."

She unburied her face from Henrietta's chest and flicked her gaze between them before she sniffled and wiped at her tear-streaked face. She settled her focus on Henrietta. "Thank you."

Henrietta offered Clif a sideways glance. "Uh, you're welcome."

"I saw everything." Carolina hiccupped as she wrung her hands. "He nearly killed Mr. Johnson. If it hadn't been for you..."

"Oh," Henrietta said as realization dawned. She flicked her eyes to the window of her cabin. Her sister had seen everything from her vantage point. At least she didn't blame her for her husband's death. "Yes, well..."

"He could be a cruel man...though he did help me through a difficult time."

Henrietta rubbed a thumb against the bruise on her sister's cheek. "That's no reason for you to have stayed with him when he hurt you."

"It wasn't always this bad."

Henrietta lifted her chin. "Now, it will never be this bad again."

Clif wrapped an arm around his younger sister and kissed her hair. "You are safe now, Carolina."

"Am I?" She twisted one hand around the other again. "What will become of me? I cannot do what you do, Henrietta. I am not strong like you."

Clif squeezed her shoulder. "You will sail on our ships

until the danger is passed with O'Rourke. After that, you can do as you wish. Continue along with us or return to Whispering Manor. The choice is yours."

"You are not like me; that is obvious. You cannot be a pirate ship's captain. But there is no need for you to fill that role. I do it quite nicely already." Henrietta offered her sister a cheeky grin before her gaze fell on her sister's black eye. "As for your strength, I'd beg to differ. You lived through far more than I could have."

"You would have never tolerated this from your husband."

"No, I would have. But I am different from you. It does not make either of us better or worse. Just different. I imagine you will quite enjoy our adventures on the sea. Though there is no need for you to participate in them as I do."

"And your crew…they will not mind?"

Henrietta stalked across the cabin and collapsed into the seat behind her desk. She kicked her boots up on the wooden surface. "They will not be given the choice."

Carolina raised her eyes to Clif. He smiled down at her. "We're happy to have you with us, baby sister."

"Please tell Mr. Johnson, thank you."

Clif wrinkled his nose as a chuckle escaped Henrietta. "Perhaps you could tell him yourself, sister."

"That won't be necessary. We really should be underway," Clif said. "I will pass along the message."

"I would very much like to speak with him. Perhaps when I am a bit tidier than I am now."

Henrietta swung her feet off the desk and rose to cross the room and open the door. "Abby, the dresses, please."

"No need to dress right away. I am taking Mr. Johnson and returning to *The Henton*. We sail immediately." Without waiting for a response, Clif hurried from the room.

"I have caused such a disruption," Carolina lamented as the door slammed shut behind her brother.

"Not really. We have no set schedule. Clif is simply being...difficult."

Abby laid the dresses out on the desk. "I think he hoped to avoid an emotion-filled conversation between Carolina and Mr. Johnson."

"That, too," Henrietta said with a laugh.

Carolina wrinkled her forehead.

"Oh, come off it, Carolina. There is no need to play innocent with us. We have each seen the look you give each other."

"But...I can't..."

"Can't what?" Henrietta asked. "You are a free woman now. And he is a free man."

"It's not proper."

Henrietta chuckled as she stalked back to her seat behind the desk. "I think you'll find most of what we do isn't proper, sister. But it's fun."

"And don't you worry a bit about these bruises," Abby said to Carolina, taking her hand and guiding her to Henrietta's bed. "I tended many a split lip or a blackened eye during my time at the brothel. I know just how to fade these quickly. I'll have you looking right as rain before you can say, Mr. Johnson."

Carolina froze as she perched on the edge of the bed, her delicate fingers tugging away from Abby's hand. "Brothel?"

"Aye," Abby said with a grin as she tugged a blanket over Carolina's lap. "I worked at the brothel on Tortuga before your sister rescued me and offered me a new life."

Carolina eyed the woman, her delicate features a mask of shock.

"Her drunkard father sold her. Men can do terrible things, Carolina. As you well know."

"I'm very sorry…Abby, is it?"

"That's right." Abby smiled at her as she poured water into a basin. She added a few ingredients to it before she dunked a rag into it and wrung it out. "Now, let's get these feeling a bit better."

Carolina winced as the woman pressed the rag over her bruised eye.

"Sorry, dearie, but it will help ease the throbbing you feel quite a bit."

Carolina's features pinched, and her shoulders shook with sobs. Abby shot Henrietta a glance.

She rose from her chair and shifted to sink onto the edge of the bed next to her sister. "It's over now, Carolina. These bruises will fade, and so will the memory of how you got them."

"I'm sorry," her sister cried. "I did not sleep well last night. I am exhausted."

"No doubt. You were likely too sore. Close your eyes now and try to sleep. We should have smooth sailing for the first bit. Let the ship's rhythm lull you into a slumber."

Carolina collapsed back into the pillows, clutching the blanket tighter as she pulled it up to her chin. Within minutes, she had dozed off.

"I can stay with her, Captain."

"She will be fine," Henrietta said. "She needs rest. And we have a long journey ahead of us. Come, we'll discuss our trip with the helmswoman."

"Yes, Captain," Abby said with a nod.

They tiptoed from the cabin, leaving Carolina behind to sleep. Bright sunshine met them as they strode onto the deck, along with shouts."

"Miss Weatherby," Henrietta called to her third mate as they crossed toward the main mast, "what is the commotion?"

"A stowaway, Captain. Found in the storeroom."

"Stowaway?" Henrietta questioned her hands on her hips. "Bring him forward."

"Aye, Captain. Hendrix is fetching him now for you to deal with."

"And deal with it, I shall." Another member of her crew wrangled a wiry figure from below deck, shoving him forward. He stumbled a few steps before he fell onto his knees at Henrietta's feet.

With his hat pulled low, he glanced up at her, shielding his dark face with his hands. "Please. I can help you. I can help you find the Gemstone Islands."

Henrietta's eyes grew wide at the words, and butterflies fluttered in her stomach. Could this trespasser help them achieve their goal?

CHAPTER 10

*H*enrietta crossed her arms and stared down her nose at the person before her. "You can help? How do you figure that?"

"I know where to begin the search. I know the location of the first map piece."

Henrietta narrowed her eyes at him. "Impossible. Only one person knows that location, and it's–"

"Stargazer Santiago."

"Yes. And unless you're–"

The man leapt to his feet and thrust out a hand. "Stargazer. I heard you were seeking me. I sneaked aboard the ship."

Henrietta drew her sword, pressing the tip against the man's throat. "Liar."

He raised his hands and swallowed hard. "I'm not lying."

"You are. You couldn't have known we sought you."

"I did. You made inquiries. Inquiries that tipped me off. When O'Rourke tried to hang you, I sneaked aboard, hoping to sail with you undetected."

"I don't believe you."

"Perhaps once I successfully lead you to the map piece, you will."

"Or lead us into a trap."

"I'm not leading you into a trap," he insisted.

"Aren't you? Do you know why I don't believe this story?" He shook his head.

She used her sword to knock his hat from it. It fell to the deck below, sliding across as the ship rocked. Long, dark hair spilled from underneath, falling past his shoulders.

"Because you are not a he but a she."

She arched an eyebrow. "I did not expect to face such an issue from a female pirate captain."

"I have no issue with your gender, but I was led to believe Stargazer was a man."

"A common misconception. I often disguise myself as such to live a freer life."

Henrietta considered it. Perhaps she was telling the truth. She had done the same in search of a freer life. Or was this person merely seeking shelter away from some issue and using the *Grandmistress* to get it? If that was the case, should she deny a fellow woman her chance at a better life?

"Fine," Henrietta said. "Suppose I believe you. Where should we go to find the map piece?"

"I need a map to study. Then I can tell your navigator where to go."

"Miss Weatherby, secure this individual until we can discuss this further."

Her third mate nodded and hurried to find a rope to bind Stargazer's wrists behind her back. Henrietta stalked toward the railing and eyed the ship diagonal from her. Leading their small fleet, *The Henton* sailed toward Southern waters.

She waved her hands to signal them, not having any luck raising anyone. With a huff, she let her hand down, slapping her thigh.

"No answer?" Abby asked.

"None. We really need a better way of signaling."

"I can send a crew to row to them. They are not going exceptionally fast yet. We can catch them."

Henrietta narrowed her eyes at the ship. "No. Fire at them. That ought to get their attention."

"Fire at them?" Abby cried.

"Yes. One volley. Forward cannon."

"Captain!"

Henrietta offered her first mate an incredulous glance. "I didn't say to hit them. Merely to fire toward them."

Abby arched an eyebrow. "All right." She spun on her heel. "Miss Asher. Fire one volley from the forward cannon. Do not...and I repeat, do *not* hit *The Henton*."

"Do not hit it. But I'm meant to fire at it."

"Fire near to it. To get their attention."

"Aye, Miss," the woman said as she hurried across the deck to give the order.

Henrietta thrust her open palm at her first mate. "Spyglass."

Abby tugged it from her belt and handed it over. Henrietta extended it and set her sights on her brother's ship.

A cannon roared beneath her, and a cannonball shot out of the front of the ship. It splashed into the water ahead of Clif's ship moments later. Shouts resounded from *The Henton*. Sailors aboard raced around on the deck, trimming sails to slow their progress.

The *Grandmistress* pulled alongside them, slowing their pace, too.

"Is it Carolina? Has something happened?" Clif asked, his knuckles white as he gripped the railing.

"No, she is asleep. We really must discuss a better way to communicate between ships."

"Ri, why did you just fire at me?"

"Oh, right. We have had a development on our end."

He arched an eyebrow.

"A stowaway who claims to be Stargazer Santiago."

Clif's eyes went wide. "What? Where is he? And why would he be aboard the *Grandmistress*?"

Henrietta wrinkled her nose and crossed her arms. "What kind of question is that? Why wouldn't he be aboard *my* ship? It *is* the larger of the two vessels. The crown jewel of the fleet."

"But *I* am the one who knows of him. You would think he would see *me*."

"Yet he hasn't. Perhaps because he is a she."

Clif furrowed his brow. "What? He is not. He is most certainly a he."

"Yet this individual is a she. It's plain to see that once you get past the large hat."

"Then this person is a fraud. A fake. Simple as that."

"Perhaps we should listen to this fraud and see if she has anything to offer. Stargazer says–"

"Stop calling her Stargazer. Stargazer is a man, not a woman."

"Well, the person calling herself Stargazer claims she can lead us to the first map piece. I would like to hear what she has to say."

"Perhaps it's a trap."

"Perhaps it is. And perhaps it isn't. I think we should at least hear the information and then make our decision."

"Fine. Mr. Johnson, fetch me a grappling hook."

"What for?" Henrietta asked.

"I'm boarding to discuss this."

She arched an eyebrow at him and crossed her arms. "Are you? You haven't asked permission."

Clif offered her an unimpressed stare. "I am the Commodore of this fleet. I can–"

"I'm still the captain of this ship."

"Fine. Permission to board the *Grandmistress?*"

She turned up the corners of her lips. "Permission granted."

Clif rolled his eyes as he clamored to her ship and landed on the decking. "You are taking this Captain role a bit too seriously."

"I am not. I would not allow anyone to swing over and board my ship."

"I *am* the Commodore of this fleet."

"Still," she said with a shrug.

"Now, where is this fraud who claims she is Stargazer?"

"With the navigator." Henrietta pointed toward the ship's wheel to three women bent over a map stretched across a barrel.

Clif arched an eyebrow, staring at them with a sour expression. "I cannot believe some woman is masquerading as Stargazer. How ridiculous."

"Is it? Is it ridiculous because it is a woman doing it or for another reason?" Henrietta asked as they wandered toward the stairs leading up.

"For the reason that she is claiming to be Stargazer. It has nothing to do with her being a woman. You know I'm not that sort. However, it is far more ridiculous because Stargazer is a man. So, she's even got the gender bit wrong. Which makes it infinitely more ridiculous."

"Have you seen Stargazer before?"

"No," Clif admitted. "Never. But he has quite a reputation, and no one mentioned he was a she."

Henrietta considered the information as they climbed the last stairs and joined the others.

"Ladies," she said, "please make room for Commodore Nichols."

Abby stepped back from the map as Clif narrowed his

eyes at the woman studying it. "I presume you are the woman claiming to be Stargazer?"

"I am Stargazer," she said without removing her eyes from the paper.

"Except you are not. I happen to know for a fact–"

"That I am a man? Yes, a rumor that often circulates, and I have failed to correct. It works to my advantage for others, particularly your lot, to assume me to be a man."

"What's that supposed to mean?" Clif asked.

She flicked her dark eyes to him. "I know all about you, Black Jack. Tell me…is every legend about you spot on? Are there any stretches of the truth?"

Clif pressed his lips together in an unimpressed frown. "This is far from a stretch of the truth."

"Aren't you, in fact, dead? Isn't this the legend? That you are a ghost?" Stargazer clamped a hand around his wrist. "You seem very much alive to me."

"The rumors surrounding me are of no consequence in this discussion. What matters is that you are not Stargazer. And as such, you have nothing to add to our plans. However, you are a stowaway on one of my vessels, and for that–"

"I wouldn't go further with that statement unless you are prepared to eat your words. I know the location of the first map piece. And you will never find it if you follow the asinine plan you have now."

Henrietta and Abby exchanged a quizzical glance before offering each other an amused smile. This woman, whether she was Stargazer or not, refused to back down, which won her a point in Henrietta's book. Though she trusted her brother, she was sufficiently intrigued by the woman's tale.

Clif stood with his jaw unhinged before he raised a finger in the air. "Now, see here–"

"Just a moment. I would like to hear what she has to say."

Clif glared at his sister, his nostrils flaring.

"What?" Henrietta said with a shrug. "It can't hurt. Please, tell us where we have gone wrong."

"Simple," Stargazer said. "You are going to the wrong location."

"Perhaps so," Clif shot back, "but we can reach it from wherever we land. It may take an extra day's journey, but my men…" He paused, his gaze darting around at his present company. "And women are hearty. They can make the journey."

Stargazer snorted a laugh. "No. You cannot reach the destination from your landing point."

"That's ridiculous, why not?"

"Because," she said with a shrug, "you are assuming the map piece is in the jungle here." She pointed to the land mass of Central America. "However, it is not."

"Oh?" Clif crossed his arms, rocking back on his heels. "And where is it?"

She let her finger slide away from the continental mass to a speck of an island. "Here."

"Really?" Henrietta asked.

Stargazer nodded. "It's not in the jungles where the pyramids are. A common misconception. It is, instead, in the jungle on Verdant Isle."

Henrietta slid her eyes to him, trying to gauge what was going on in his mind. Clif remained expressionless. "And why would you openly give us this information?"

"You sought me when you came to Tortuga. You must have expected me to share something with you."

"Yes, for a price. We have promised you nothing, yet you have told us the location of the map piece. Well, supposed location."

"It is the location. And I have told you it as a show of good faith. Retrieving the map, however, is another matter entirely."

"What do you mean?" Henrietta questioned.

"I mean, Verdant Isle is a dangerous location. You need someone familiar with it to lead you. I am that someone. Without me, you will not survive it."

A chuckle escaped Clif's lips. "You underestimate us."

"You underestimate the Isle."

"And you know it?" Clif asked.

"I grew up on the neighboring island. My father and I used to go across to it on many occasions. I am intimately familiar with the island. I can lead you to the map piece."

"If you are intimately familiar," Clif said, "why do you not already have the map piece in your possession?"

"Because I never sought it. As I said, it is quite dangerous."

"And what do you ask for in return?" Henrietta asked the woman.

"A life away from the odd jobs I cobble together in Tortuga. I want to be your first mate."

Abby's lips parted, and her brow wrinkled.

Henrietta crossed her arms and shook her head. "That job is taken. But you can become a crew member and work in a suitable position."

Stargazer matched her stance. "Or I could not help you."

Clif shot the woman a skeptical glance.

"That is an option, of course," Henrietta said without skipping a beat, "but it's not good. You should take the deal on the table. My sailors of any rank are well compensated and enjoy their work."

"Why would I take less than I deserve?"

"The mate's position is taken. I am quite happy with her and am not looking to replace her. The position is not there. However, I can offer you a position on the crew, and once we have had a chance to assess your strengths and weaknesses, we will funnel you into the correct position."

Stargazer gave her an unimpressed stare with a slight frown on her features. "You need me more than I need you."

"Doubt it," Henrietta said. "At this point, if we don't agree, I can simply toss you into the water and sail away. Maybe I'll find the Gemstone Islands, and maybe I won't. Either way, I'll continue along my merry way. You, however, will suffer a terrible death in one form or another."

Stargazer's features crinkled as Henrietta detailed her predicament.

"Second, you sneaked aboard *my* ship. While I may have sought you out, I did not find you, yet you took it upon yourself to find me. Which tells me you need me more than I need you."

The woman wrinkled her nose as she eyed the map on the barrel's top before she flicked her eyes back to Henrietta. "Fine. I'll accept the position with the potential to move up into a suitable position."

"And you will help us acquire the first map piece?"

"Yes. I will make sure you find it and continue to sail with you until we reach the Gemstone Islands."

Henrietta thrust her hand out toward the woman. "Deal."

They shook on it as Clif furrowed his brow. His sister had become quite the negotiator. "It sounds like we have a new course."

"Yes, we do," Henrietta said. "Miss Williamson set a new course for Verdant Isle."

"Aye, aye, Captain," the woman answered.

"I shall return to *The Henton* and pass the message along." Clif followed his sister down to the main deck. "I'd say we should reach the island by early tomorrow morning."

"Excellent. Then we begin our search for map piece number one." Henrietta lifted her chin with a grin.

"Yes. Let's hope it's not a setback."

"Do you believe her?" she asked as they approached the railing.

"We will find out. See you there."

Henrietta nodded at him before he returned to his ship. Her crew worked to change their course and gather more speed. Henrietta sucked in a deep breath as she watched the entirely female crew scurried around.

Satisfied, she stalked across the deck and slipped into her cabin. Carolina still slept soundly in her bed. Henrietta grabbed Clif's journal and collapsed into her hammock.

She flipped through the book until her eyes grew heavy. The toll of the sleepless night and tense morning overtook her, and she nodded off.

Shouting awoke her. Carolina still slumbered across the cabin. A loud rumbling overhead drove Henrietta from the hammock. Clif's journal slapped to the floor below.

Still groggy, she retrieved it and tossed it into the swaying bed before she stumbled across the room and opened the door.

Rain soaked the deck, falling from the sky in torrents. Henrietta squinted through it as a soaked form hurried toward her.

Abby called out, clinging to the railing near the cabin. "Captain!"

"Abby! How long until we're out of this?"

"I don't know, Captain. We cannot seem to navigate properly. The compass is not working."

"Have you spoken with Mr. Johnson or the Commodore?"

Abby's features pinched as Henrietta spoke the words. "No, Captain."

The expression on her first mate's face made the worry nestling in the pit of her stomach grow. "What is it? What's wrong?"

"We've lost sight of *The Henton*. We cannot find her or our way out of this storm."

CHAPTER 11

enrietta swallowed hard. *Lost?*

"What do you mean you lost them? They cannot be far. We're likely turned around because of the weather. Have you checked in all directions?"

Abby bobbed her head up and down, water dripping off the tips of the hair that framed her face. "Yes, Captain. We have. No sign of them. Nothing."

Henrietta crossed her cabin and retrieved her jacket, tugging it on as she returned to the door. She ducked into the heavy rain falling, becoming drenched immediately. "When were they last seen?"

"Off the starboard side just behind us no less than a quarter of an hour ago."

"A quarter-hour? We have lost them completely in a quarter hour?" Henrietta stalked toward the stern.

Abby hurried behind her as they climbed the stairs. "The storm came out of nowhere, Captain. We struggled to trim the sails and avoid it, but…she hit us. And now we seem to be alone."

Lightning tore through the sky above them. "Spyglass."

Abby slapped the item into Henrietta's hands. She extended it fully and swept it across the dark horizon. No sign of the other ship existed.

"I have never seen it so black during the day, Captain."

Henrietta squinted as she glanced up at the sky. "This is quite bad. We must find a way through it. Let the sails out further."

"Captain! If we let the sails out…"

"We will sail faster. We need to sail faster. We cannot dally in these waters. They are tossing us about like a rag doll."

"But, Captain, the gusts of wind could topple the mast. And without the mast…"

"I understand, Abby, but we are no better with it if one of those massive waves turns us over."

Abby stared out over the rocky sea. The waves crested higher and higher.

Henrietta braced herself as one smashed into the ship's side and washed over the deck. The *Grandmistress* stood firm against it despite the broadside hit.

She blew out a shaky breath. They could weather this storm. But where was Clif?

He was an excellent captain. He, too, would come through it if he hadn't already. This would test her mettle. It was her first difficult scenario as captain of her ship.

She'd sailed through challenging weather with Clif. And she'd done an excellent job. She reminded herself of that as she leaned against the railing, her eyes scanning the horizon for the best way through the storm.

She wondered how far off course they were and how much further they would be once they sailed free of this.

It didn't matter. What mattered was sailing through it unscathed. They could make up the time, and they could reorient themselves later.

The second objective was to find Clif. Where had he gone? Becoming separated in weather like this could mean they'd never reconnect.

She pressed her lips together, trying to quash the panic building in her. At the worst, they would find each other at Verdant Isle. They were both going to the same place.

She closed her eyes for a moment and imagined the sun shining as they sailed to the jungle-covered island. He'd probably arrive first. Then he'd tease her about it for years to come.

"I beat you, Ri. You're getting slow as a Captain."

She'd roll her eyes and chuckle, but she'd work all the harder to ensure it never happened again.

"Captain!" Abby's voice called, snapping her back to reality. She opened her eyes and spotted a massive wave rolling toward the ship. "Hard to..."

Her voice wobbled, and she swallowed hard. "HARD TO STARBOARD."

The woman at the helm stared at her with wide eyes.

"Move!" she boomed and shoved the woman aside. She spun the wheel as quickly as she could. The ship would never turn in time, but she could mitigate the impact by turning into the wave. It wouldn't broadside them.

"Come on," she murmured as the ship continued forward.

The wave smashed into them hard. The ship rolled to the side on the rocky sea. Abby clung to the railing. Her helmswoman tumbled toward the ship's opposite side before catching herself on the stairs.

Ocean filled the port view and sky the starboard as the ship fought to stay upright. The main mast bent toward the water.

Henrietta's muscles burned as she fought to keep the wheel hard over and keep her feet on the slippery deckboards.

Her heart skipped a beat as they reached the point of no return. *We will capsize.*

Just before the ship plunged into the water, she began to right herself, tipping slowly upward before she slammed back into another wave. This time, they cut through it at an angle, able to withstand its force without a precarious roll.

Henrietta's stomach settled as they sliced through the crashing waves diagonally despite the ship's bouncing.

"Captain!" Abby shouted as she clung to the rain-soaked railing and climbed up.

"Keep the sails out," Henrietta answered. "I see a break up there."

"Aye, Captain."

They spent another fifteen perilous moments fighting the sea and the skies to make progress. As they neared calmer seas, a wind gust stretched the sails to their limits.

"Trim the sails!" Henrietta shouted.

Abby had already begun the process, with the main sail threatening to tear in two. With the help of several other crew members, she managed to rein it in before it ripped.

Their progress slowed, but they continued to move forward toward quieter waters. Henrietta whipped her head behind her to study the raging storm they left behind.

They'd made it through unscathed, but she'd slow their progress to assess any damage and then chart a new course to their destination.

A drenched Abby slogged up the stairs toward Henrietta. "Order, captain?"

"Assess the ship and the crew. We'll chart a new course after we've ensured we can sail without issue."

"Yes, Captain," Abby said with a weak salute.

"And Abby, allow the crew some time to recover."

The corners of her first mate's lips ticked up, and she

nodded. "Of course, Captain. Though rest is not required, I'm certain they would like to find *The Henton*."

"As would I," Henrietta said. She made another scan of the horizon. No signs of the other ship.

Her heart sank. She had hoped to sail into calmer waters and find Clif waiting for her. The ocean was vast. Perhaps they'd turned before the storm and sailed in a different direction.

"Captain," her helmswoman said as she took over the wheel, "shall I assess how far off course we are?"

"Yes. Then, we'll discuss recharting. We may not see *The Henton* until we reach our destination."

"Shall I rechart us back to the original course and search for them?"

Henrietta considered it. "No, we may waste too much time that way."

"I'll do some figuring and present options to you."

"Good," she nodded before she descended the stairs and pushed into her cabin.

Carolina clutched at the blanket, her face white.

"Are you sick?" Henrietta asked, peeling off her drenched overcoat.

"No, surprisingly. Was it a storm?"

Henrietta dug around in her trunk for a fresh set of clothes. "Yes, but we've come through it."

"And Clif?"

"I don't know," Henrietta said, trying to stop her voice from trembling.

"What do you mean?"

She let the trunk's lid fall shut with a bang. "We were separated whilst navigating the weather. I am uncertain of his whereabouts."

Carolina flung the covers back and leapt from the bed. "We must find him."

"I agree. However, we must also be smart about it. We cannot sail about randomly in search of him. Instead, we should stick to our plan. We will both be going to Verdant Isle."

She turned to find Carolina staring at her, her eyes shining with tears. "He will be fine, Carolina. He has sailed the seas much longer than I have. I have no doubt he can take care of himself."

Carolina frowned, the split on her lip more pronounced by the action. "How can you be so brave?"

"Clif is an excellent captain. He will–"

"No, not about that. Yes, I agree Clif can likely take care of himself, though I still worry, but…"

"But?" Henrietta asked as she stepped behind a screen in the corner and peeled her damp clothes from her before she pulled on a fresh set.

"We are alone."

Henrietta stepped around the privacy screen and sorted her clothes to hang them. "What do you mean?"

"We are alone on the sea. How can you be so brave? How can you not be hiding until Clif finds us?"

"Hiding until Clif finds us? Carolina, I am the captain of this ship. It is my duty to ensure we reach our destination safely."

Carolina sank into the hammock and shook her head. "I would be shaking if I was you. I would fear every gust of wind, every passing ship."

"We are well-equipped to defend ourselves, and the girls know how to handle the ship."

Carolina glanced up at her sister. "I don't know how you do it."

"I learned. I learned quite a bit from Clif before taking on my ship. And I continue to learn. Every situation teaches me something."

Carolina shook her head. "I could not do it."

"Yes, you could. You went into the jungle, did you not?"

"With James. And guides. And men to protect us."

"You still did it. Many women would not. You are braver than you think." She finished hanging her clothes to dry and stalked to her desk.

Carolina rocked back and forth on the hammock, quiet.

"You are still reeling from what happened with James."

"I'm not," she said, snapping her gaze up. "It's...surprising, but I'm not unhappy and don't blame you."

"I should hope not." Henrietta rolled out a map and studied it.

"I'm being honest."

Henrietta flicked her gaze to her sister. "I did not mean you are reeling from James's death. That is likely a relief for you. I meant you are reeling from what James has done to you since you married him. The abuse you endured has made you more timid than you were in your youth. Give it time—your courage will come back."

Carolina slicked a lock of her hair behind her ear before approaching the desk. "What are you doing?"

"Examining our options. We need a plan. And we need one quickly."

* * *

Clif squinted through the rain as he stood at the helm. "And you say you saw them only moments ago?"

"Aye, Commodore," a soaked Johnson said with a bob of his head. "They were off our port side only moments ago. A wave hit us both. When I looked again, they were gone."

Clif extended his spyglass and scanned the dark horizon. "They couldn't simply have disappeared, Johnson."

"There are no remains in the water."

Clif shot him a glance that stopped any further discussion on that front.

"I'm certain we became separated in the storm. Likely, each of us was blown off course. What are your orders, Commodore? Do we search for the *Grandmistress*? Or shall we sail clear of the weather and regroup."

Clif sucked in a breath, his jaw flexing as he considered it. Every fiber in his being wanted to search the waters for his sister's ship. She could be lost, have sustained damage, or worse.

He flicked his gaze to his first mate, nervously awaiting his orders. If they stayed in the storm, they could become lost, sustain damage, or worse.

He had an entire crew of men depending on him to make the right choice. He would be useless to Henrietta if they did not survive this storm.

He pictured her as he limped his battered ship to hers. She crossed her arms and raised her chin, offering him a haughty glance that only she could pull off. She'd arch her eyebrow, and the feather in her cap would bob around as she said, "There you are. And what happened to your little ship?"

He slammed the spyglass closed. "Get us out of this storm, then we will regroup. If we haven't found the *Grandmistress* by then, we will devise a plan to track her."

Johnson nodded before he issued the orders. If they turned to the starboard side now, they could skirt the worst of the storm.

He descended the stairs as the rain continued to beat against the deck. He strode to the front of the ship, extending his spyglass again to search the stormy skies. Lightning ripped through the dark clouds, and the seas swelled.

Was Henrietta in the thick of that storm? His decision wavered. If she was, she might not have made it through unscathed. The sea looked treacherous.

He second-guessed himself, turning to call to Mr. Johnson as the ship began to swing around. No, he couldn't go into the heart of that storm to search for his sisters. He had to take care of his ship and crew.

Henrietta was a good sailor. She'd navigated *The Henton* through many storms, some worse than this one. Of course, he'd been at her side, then. Guiding her and ensuring she didn't do anything that would cost them dearly.

But still, had to keep his crew safe and then help Henrietta. They had to maintain their course to avoid the worst of the weather. No matter how bad of a feeling lodged itself in his gut.

CHAPTER 12

*T*he ship rocked on the still-rough waters as they slowed after skirting the storm and reaching clearer skies.

"Commodore," Johnson said as he approached Clif, "your orders?"

Clif pressed his lips into a thin line. "We must assess how far we are off course."

"Aye. I will report to you once we've determined our location."

Clif waved the statement away. "I will come with you. We should move quickly and try to find the *Grandmistress.*"

"Of course, Commodore. Would you like me to have the ship brought about to search the waters here?"

"No, let's assess our location and determine the most likely place they could be based on where we last saw them, the storm's track, and how they would have navigated it."

They climbed the stairs to the helm and consulted their compass and map.

Clif jabbed his finger at a location in the water. "That puts us somewhere in here."

He glanced over the waters. "And the *Grandmistress* was off our port side, correct?"

"Aye, Commodore," Johnson said with a nod.

"Then she likely took the brunt of the weather." His stomach turned over as he considered it. "She would have continued sailing west to escape the weather with as little damage as possible."

"We turned east to avoid the storm," Johnson said. "So they are likely somewhere..."

"What is it, Johnson?" Clif asked.

Johnson stared at the map for a moment before he shook his head. "They would be close to these small islands. If they were blown off course..."

"They could be smashed into them. They have hazardous rocks," Clif said. "If they survived the storm."

"She is a large vessel able to withstand quite a bit, Commodore," Johnson said, though his pale face suggested he, too, worried about the odds that they hadn't capsized from the rolling waves.

"Yes, she is. And Ri would have sailed west right into those waves. And right into those islands."

* * *

"Captain!" Abby's voice shouted from outside. "Quickly!"

Henrietta snapped her gaze to the door before she sprinted around the desk, raced to it, and flung it open. "What is it?"

"Land. Dangerously close off our port side."

"Turn starboard."

"The storm, Captain. It's moving this way."

Henrietta stepped out of her cabin and scanned the horizon. Dark clouds marched toward them. She swung her gaze to the opposite side. Sharp rocks jutted out of the crashing waves.

She cursed under her breath, and she quickly vetted options. They'd run back into the storm if they turned toward the east. But if they did not, the storm would push them into the islands before they could skirt them.

"Captain?" Abby questioned, shifting her weight from foot to foot.

Henrietta swung her gaze back to the islands. She could not sail into the storm again. "Turn toward the islands."

"Captain, we will be smashed against the rocks!"

"Turn toward them. We cannot sail around before the storm pushes us toward them, nor can we sail back into the storm. Turn toward the island. We will shelter between them as the storm passes over us, then sail into clear water."

"I'm not certain…"

"Sail between the islands," Henrietta insisted.

Abby pressed her lips together as she bobbed her head and gave the order.

The helmswoman spun the ship's wheel, turning them toward the treacherous rocks.

"When we reach the center of those islands, drop both anchors and lower the sails. As the storm passes, we will sit between the three islands in that pocket."

Abby gave an unconvinced nod as the ship turned toward the islands. "Captain, one wrong move…"

"I'm certain we can handle it. Miss Williams is an excellent navigator." Henrietta crossed her arms as she monitored their progress forward. With her chin lifted, she projected confidence, though she did not feel confident. It was a risky move, but the gamble was all they had. Any other options would put them in far greater danger.

"There is debris in the water," Abby said as they sailed closer to the islands. "Appears to be the remains of another ship."

"Yes, likely one not savvy enough to sail into the little pocket like we will."

The large ship sailed closer to the small area in the center of the three islands. Sharp rocks jutted from the water on either side of them. Abby ordered the sails to be lowered as they cleared the jagged coast and sailed past the island.

The crew quickly brought down the sheets, slowing the ship's progress. They slipped into the pocket created by the islands. Calm waters lapped at the ship's sides.

"Drop anchors."

Abby nodded at her captain's orders and passed it along to her crew. The anchors slid from the ship on either side, grounding them.

"Now, we wait."

All eyes turned toward the approaching storm front. Black clouds marched toward them. Lightning ripped through the sky, and thunder rumbled overhead.

The winds picked up, gusting against the water and the ship. Henrietta narrowed her eyes as she stared into it, her hair blowing wildly.

They were about to live through the storm they'd struggled to escape earlier. Would they survive it twice?

* * *

Johnson rushed to keep up with Clif. "Captain, perhaps–"

"Make for those islands, Johnson. Trail the storm and head east. We must determine if the *Grandmistress* is there. She may need immediate assistance."

"Aye, Captain." Johnson hollered out orders as Clif slipped into his cabin.

He stalked to his desk and rummaged in the drawer for his flask. With a shaky hand, he gulped down a large swallow of rum.

He slowly screwed the lid back on as he imagined the scenarios he might find when they reached the islands.

Bits of a ship smashed against the rocks floated in the water. A few survivors clung to them, bobbing in the water. Would his sisters be among them?

Perhaps. She would be smart enough to stay alive. She was a fighter.

He tried to imagine another scenario, but with the storm pushing them, there likely weren't any other outcomes.

The ship turned underneath him as they changed their course with a new destination in their sights.

They trailed behind the dark clouds that marched toward the islands. Lightning tore from the sky to the sea. Clif eyed it, wondering where his sister was. Was she still fighting her way through the storm? Had she reached the islands and navigated around them?

He refused to believe there could be any other outcomes. His knuckles turned white as he gripped the railing, willing the ship to reach the islands faster.

Their progress seemed painstakingly slow. The storm ahead of them, which had moved at a good clip before, seemed to have stalled.

They approached the edge of the dark clouds. Rain began to patter against the deck boards.

"Captain, it seems the storm has slowed or stalled," Johnson reported. "Your orders?"

Clif stared at the black clouds hovering over them as he drummed his fingers on the wood. The rocky sea swayed the ship from side to side. They couldn't sail through the storm.

"Turn back."

The words stuck in his throat as he said them.

"Turn about!" Johnson shouted.

Clif's heart ached as the ship swung to the south; they tucked their tail and ran from the storm. Henrietta was somewhere ahead of him. Perhaps she needed his help, but he couldn't get there.

He hoped the decision didn't cost him or his sisters. Both were aboard the *Grandmistress*. Both were in danger. And both he'd just turned his back on. He hoped it was not a mistake he'd regret for the rest of his life.

"Captain, we can try to sail south and round the storm," Johnson suggested.

It would stretch the process longer than a straight shot to the islands; however, at least they would make some progress. Perhaps by the time they rounded the storm, the storm would have moved enough for them to reach the islands.

"Yes, fine."

Johnson bobbed his head up and down and shouted the orders. Rather than turning in the opposite direction, they continued south, sailing along the edge of the dark clouds and looking for an opening to move east.

They sailed further south than Clif would have preferred. The block of black clouds seemed endless. Was there an end to this storm?

"Captain!" Johnson shouted from the main deck.

Clif tore his eyes from the rocky sea and the black horizon and gazed at his first mate. The man's face was devoid of color, and his lips formed a deep grimace. "What is it?"

Johnson focused on the water and pointed a shaky finger toward it.

Clif leaned over the railing and studied the waves. His stomach dropped as he spotted the object Johnson called his attention to.

A chunk of wood floated on the foamy sea. He swallowed hard, unable to tear his eyes away from the debris. It looked like a piece of a broken ship.

Was it the *Grandmistress?*

He pressed a hand to his lips, struggling to keep his breathing measured and calm. He pushed away from the railing and strode to the steps, down them, and to his first mate.

"Follow the debris."

"Aye, Commodore," Johnson said but did not move.

Clif flicked an annoyed glance at the man. "Now, Johnson."

"Yes, of course." He licked his lips as he stared at the floating wood before he spun away, shouting orders in a shaky voice.

Clif squeezed his eyes closed. He hadn't meant to be that short with the man. But his nerves, already frayed from being unable to reach his sisters, were at their breaking point.

These were likely the remains of the *Grandmistress*. In a storm like this, survivors would be few and far between. Ri may survive, but Carolina was far more delicate. Ri would do her best, but could she save her baby sister?

"More debris in the water, Commodore," Johnson said with a pinched face.

Clif leaned over the railing, spotting the additional bits of wood. "I see it. Have we seen any survivors?"

"No, Commodore, but also no bodies. Perhaps...perhaps they've only sustained some damage and are still afloat."

"From your lips, Johnson," Clif said as he pulled away from the railing and wandered forward.

He reached the bow and studied the horizon, not finding anything. No ships, no bodies, nothing.

Each second that passed as they continued south felt like an eternity. The dark clouds finally broke up next to them.

"Commodore, we can swing West," Johnson said.

"Do it. Search for remains of the ship."

Johnson nodded and hurried away to give the orders. Clif scanned the horizon, hoping to spot anything that could lead him to his sister's ship.

A shout sounded from the crow's nest. He glanced up, finding the man's arm outstretched. He followed the line of his finger. Smoke rose on the horizon to their east.

"Mr. Johnson, make for that smoke," Clif bellowed across the deck.

"Hard to starboard!" Johnson shouted to the helmsman.

The man spun the wheel to change their trajectory. Clif gnawed his lip as they slowly turned toward the black smoke rising on the horizon.

He hoped they'd reach them in time to save most of the crew. They slowly approached the smoke. A ship, wholly crippled, sinking, and on fire, came into view. Clif's heart thudded as he awaited being close enough to identify the ship positively.

"Spyglass," he said as Johnson joined him at the bow.

The man slapped one into his waiting hand. He extended it and eyed the horizon. He swept it around, eyeing the crew scrambling to survive the sinking ship.

He focused on one crew member who tried to pull another from the hull. His forehead wrinkled as he stared at them. *Men.* His heart leapt. *They were men.*

"Mr. Johnson," he said, breathing a sigh of relief.

"What is it, Commodore? Are there survivors?"

"There are, but that is not the *Grandmistress.*"

"It isn't?"

Clif handed his first mate the spyglass. The man stared through it, the corners of his lips turning up. "You are correct."

Clif offered him a half-grin. There was hope for his sister's ship yet. At least the *Grandmistress* wasn't on fire and sinking in front of his eyes.

He pondered the crew's situation on the unknown vessel. Had lightning struck them in the storm? Why was the ship sinking?

His brows knit as he tried to piece the clues together. Realization struck him, and he sucked in a breath, ready to give a surprising order to his first mate, when a cannonball roared toward them and splashed into the water off their port side.

"What was that?" Johnson asked as he picked himself up off the deck.

"There's another ship. We missed it in the smoke. That ship wasn't in the storm. It was attacked," Clif said as he rose and pointed in the enemy ship's direction. "Prepare to fire on it."

"Aye, Commodore." Before Johnson could give the orders, the enemy ship fired again before running up a Jolly Roger.

"Pirates," Clif said. "Wonder who it is?"

"And it looks like they are taking no prisoners," Johnson said as two more cannonballs sailed toward them.

Clif flexed his jaw. Whoever this pirate was, he meant business. And he didn't plan on letting them slink away. They had nowhere to run and nowhere to hide. They'd have to stay and fight. And hope they survived the attack by the much larger ship.

CHAPTER 13

Chaos broke out as sailors raced to man their stations as the giant ship bore down on their location.

"Prepare to fire all cannons," Clif said. "Hit them hard. Drive them back."

"Yes, Commodore," Johnson said with a nod before he shouted the order.

"We will turn, fire, turn again, and try to outrun them. We are smaller and more agile. We may be able to slip away while they recover from any damage our barrage creates."

"On your order, Commodore."

Clif allowed them to fire again, but one cannonball came dangerously close to striking them. "Hard to starboard."

"Hard to starboard!" Johnson shouted.

The helmsman whipped the wheel around to shift the ship. They moved slowly in the waters, turning their broadside toward the other ship. Clif counted the seconds, hoping to get a round of fire off before the other ship reloaded.

If the other crew were worth their weight in salt, they'd have those cannons blazing in ninety seconds.

He reached seventy-five. They hadn't fully rounded to face them, but it was enough to try for a shot. "Fire," he said.

"Fire, fire, fire!" Johnson shouted.

Cannons roared to life under Clif's feet as they initiated their attack. The first one missed, and the second went wide, too.

Another struck the bow, chipping it but doing no real damage.

"Damn it," Clif growled. He hoped the attack stunned them enough to allow them to escape. "Keep it hard over and make a run for it. We don't have time to engage with him."

"Aye, Commodore. Keep it hard over; let out full sails."

"Are we running, Mr. Johnson?"

"Yes, we are."

"We've never run from a fight," the man argued.

Clif shook his head. "We have other pressing matters, including finding the *Grandmistress*. We do not have time to duke it out with another pirate. We'll leave him safely behind."

They sailed away from the other vessel. Clif kept his eye on the enemy ship as they made their move.

"Commodore, they are giving chase," Johnson informed him. Clif wrinkled his nose. "I see that. It appears they do not wish to give up so easily. Give it a few minutes; let's see if *The Henton* can pull away from her."

"Aye, Commodore." Johnson busied himself, making sure the ship moved as efficiently as possible. He rejoined Clif moments later and studied the horizon.

"She's still on us, Mr. Johnson. Whoever this pirate is, he isn't willing to let us go that easily."

"We're at a decent speed. Can he maintain his?"

"That remains to be seen. However, we have a slight problem."

Johnson arched an eyebrow as he glanced at Clif. "We're

going to run into that damned storm again or those islands. We need to shift course."

"Shifting course will slow us."

"It will slow him, too."

"But he could use the winds to catch and fire upon us."

Clif chewed his lower lip. "We must stay and fight."

"Are you certain, Commodore?"

"Yes. Even now, he closes the gap. His ship is agile and quick. Our best chance is in a battle."

"But, Commodore, we are much smaller and far less equipped than that ship."

"Then we must be smarter than he is. Use every trick we have, take every advantage."

"Aye. We're going to need as much luck as we can get. She's armed to the teeth and looking to shred us to pieces as she did with that last ship."

"Prepare the crew. We fight until the end." Johnson hurried away to prepare the ship for the battle. Clif eyed the pursuing vessel. They'd fight. He hoped it wasn't to their end.

But he couldn't help but wonder if he would end up on the bottom of the ocean.

* * *

The storm bore down on the *Grandmistress* as she sheltered in the pocket of water created by the three surrounding islands. The dark clouds soaked the islands with rain but never inched closer to them.

"The storm, Captain," Abby said. "It seems stuck."

"Yes," Henrietta said with a nod. "It's stalled over those two islands."

They waited for another thirty minutes until the rain in the distance seemed to lighten. The clouds overhead split, with some moving northeast and the rest moving southeast.

The storm never passed over them, driven apart by the islands they'd ducked between. Thunder rumbled in the distance as the sky began to clear.

Henrietta waited longer to ensure they'd definitely escape the weather before she ordered them to attempt to sail between the southern island and the western one.

As the clouds swept past them and continued their march across the sea, Henrietta studied the map. "With the storm now passed, let's get back on our course to Verdant Island. We will hope to catch *The Henton* as we sail. We'll set a hard pace."

"Aye, Captain," Abby said with a nod before she shouted orders for the crew to prepare to set sail. They'd round the southern island and head east to their original course.

The sails billowed as the women raised them. The ship lurched forward toward the westernmost island as the anchors were raised. The helmswoman guided the ship southeasterly until they slid past the islands.

With the eastern horizon in their sights, they allowed the sails out full to increase their speed.

"Captain, we will be back on track within the hour, I estimate," Abby said.

"Excellent. Notify me of any developments, particularly if *The Henton* is spotted."

"Aye, Captain," Abby said with a salute.

With clear skies and the ship underway, Henrietta ducked back into her cabin.

Carolina leapt from the bed. "Have you found Clif?"

"Not yet. We just narrowly avoided being smashed on the rocks, but the storm has passed, so we are underway. I hope to catch his ship soon."

Carolina nodded as Henrietta collapsed into her chair and kicked her feet up.

"Sit down, Carolina, we have quite a ways to go."

"We will find him, though, right?"

Henrietta held back, rolling her eyes. Her sister's devotion to their brother could be maddening at times. "Yes, we will find him. Likely sailing along without a care in the world. Clif is an excellent pirate. He probably avoided the storm, sailed around it, and is waiting at Verdant Island with his feet up."

Henrietta squeezed her eyes closed and sighed. "I will never hear the end of it."

Carolina eased into the hammock, her hands clasped tightly. "Are you two always this competitive?"

"No, because I usually win," Henrietta said. "Though I have to work at it quite a bit. For Clif, it seems effortless."

"He has much more experience on the sea than you do. Perhaps that's why."

Henrietta slumped in her seat. "I suppose so."

"I think you are doing an admirable job as captain. All the girls seem to like you, the terrible weather. I wouldn't have known where to start."

"I sailed through many a storm with Clif. You learn."

"You have learned quite well, I suppose. I'm certain he'd be proud of you."

Henrietta let the corner of her lips curl into a half-smile. "And my ship is bigger than his, so I win."

"It is quite large, yes," Carolina said. "Did Clif buy it for you?"

Henrietta scoffed and shook her head. "Certainly not. I made the deal myself. I think I did quite well. If it was all the same to Clif, he was happy to sail about pretending we were both captains of *The Henton*."

Carolina drummed her fingers against her thigh. "What are you and he searching for this time?"

"Something called the Gemstone Islands. Your beau is

quite against finding them. This will be quite the feat. Even Clif is nervous."

Carolina's cheeks reddened. "If you are referring to Mr. Johnson, he is not my beau."

This time, Henrietta could not hold back the eye roll. "Oh, come off of it, Carolina. The man challenged your husband to a duel for your hand."

Carolina cocked her head, arching one light-colored eyebrow. "I don't understand how that happened?"

"Don't you?" Henrietta asked, settling her cheek into her palm and propping an elbow on the chair's arm.

Carolina shrugged. "No, I do not. I could understand Clif challenging him, or even James challenging Clif, but Mr. Johnson's involvement in a duel over me seems quite surprising."

Henrietta fluttered her eyelashes. "You must be joking. Surely, you see the way he looks at you."

The color rushed into Carolina's face again.

"And we all see the way you look at him."

She snapped her eyes to her sister's face. "I do no such thing."

"Oh, stop. No one here is a prude. Everyone can see you fancy him, and he certainly fancies you. Enough that when your former husband spoke ill of you, Clif and I had to wrestle him off the man. I thought he would kill him with his bare hands."

Carolina shook her head as though understanding still would not come. "Is it because he is a pirate?"

"What does that mean?"

"James never once acted this way. Not even whilst pursuing me. Once, when we were courting, another gentleman made a rude remark toward me."

"And he did not defend you?" Henrietta asked.

Carolina bit her lower lip as she stared at the floor. "No. He laughed."

Henrietta pressed her lips together into a frown. "Why ever did you marry the idiot?"

"I...he proposed and...I..."

Henrietta held up a hand. "Stop. There is no need to go any further. You felt you should accept. He was a good match given his position as a professor, and he seemed quite alluring because you adored studying and books, and you felt it your duty to settle."

"More or less," Carolina said with a nod.

"I suppose I should take some of the blame for your horrid choice. Had I not done the same, you likely would not either."

"You made a good match, Henrietta."

"My husband was a drunk and a liar. He left me destitute. Clif is the only reason I kept Whispering Manor. Clif is the only reason I live as I do now."

"And you prefer it?"

Henrietta bobbed her head up and down. "And so will you once you become accustomed to the freedom it offers you."

"Freedom?"

"I assume James kept quite a tight leash on you, yes? You must stay at home unless you inform him of a task you must complete in town, you must have tea ready when he arrives home, you must prepare a breakfast before he leaves, that sort of thing?"

"Well, yes, we had a routine. And yes, I always ran my plans past him before I would venture into town for anything I needed."

"No one will police you like that here. If you wish to go off on your own, you may. Go to town, go to a pub, see Mr. Johnson." She offered her sister a devilish grin.

Carolina's face turned a new shade of red.

"Oh, correction, outside of getting yourself into trouble, no one on this ship will care. Clif, on the other hand, may try to play protector."

"Clif worries. He's trying to help."

Henrietta heaved a sigh. "Yes, I know. But sometimes Clif's help can be stifling."

"But he means well."

"Yes, I know. But his well-meaning efforts had us sailing about the sea for months with no real aim or action because he didn't want to expose me to anything dangerous."

Carolina cocked her head. "Well, that's quite nice. Like a holiday."

Henrietta pressed her lips together into a frown. "I wasn't looking for a holiday. I wanted a pirate's life. Either way, eventually, we embarked on a journey to find the City of Diamonds and now the Gemstone Islands. So, I cannot complain too much."

"I think you may be more adventurous than Clif," Carolina answered with a grin.

"I just may be. And one day, I will prove I'm a better pirate." Henrietta matched her sister's expression and winked.

A knock sounded at the door, and Henrietta shouted for them to enter.

"Captain, you'd better come quickly. We have a development that you should see."

* * *

"Fire!" Clif shouted again.

Mr. Johnson pushed the crew to fight with everything they had. They had already sustained some damage. Repairable if they were able to survive the fight.

"Mr. Johnson!" Clif shouted. "They are preparing to board us. We cannot fall. Keep firing at them even as they cross. We must disable the ship."

"Yes, Commodore," Johnson said with a nod.

Clif drew his pistol and sword, ready to battle for his ship. So far, he'd managed to stay afloat and not sustain enough damage to cripple them, but being boarded was not a good thing.

Grappling hooks swung toward their ship, most of them latching onto the railings, with a few falling short.

Clif cut the lines on the ones closest to him. Another volley of fire exploded under his feet. Smoke made it challenging to see, but his heart sank as he realized they'd failed to destroy the main mast of the other vessel.

If they could disable it in some way, they could limp away and lick their wounds elsewhere. Plus, he still had to search for his missing sister's ship.

More cannons were fired from the enemy vessel. Wood splintered in front of him as one of the cannonballs smashed through his railing.

Clif swallowed hard, realizing this may be a situation he could not escape.

CHAPTER 14

*H*enrietta swung her feet off the desk and hurried to the door. The expression on her first mate's face concerned her. Something was wrong.

Notions blazed through her mind faster than she could walk. Had they hit something? Had they run into another storm?

Carolina must have sensed her trepidation because she rose from the hammock, wringing her hands before her as she followed behind Henrietta.

"What is it, Abby?"

Abby licked her lips as they stepped onto the deck. Bright sunshine beat down on them. Henrietta crinkled her brow. It wasn't weather.

Abby led her forward, a spyglass in one hand. She pointed to two specks on the horizon. Smoke rose in the distance.

"I first spotted that one," she said, pointing to black smoke puffing upward from an unknown object.

Henrietta grabbed the spyglass and extended it. She studied the magnified object, finding a sinking ship with fire spewing from it. "Hmm."

"Yes. Someone must have attacked and disabled it." Abby thrust a finger slightly north to more smoke. "Then, I spotted that. It must be the aggressor."

"Battling with another ship?" Henrietta questioned. She swung the spyglass in their direction.

Her heart dropped as she made out the familiar form of *The Henton*. "Clif."

"Aye, Captain. And it doesn't look like they are faring well. The other ship is much larger. *The Henton* has sustained some damage."

"Full sails. Sail southeast, around that disabled ship. We will close in behind them."

"Aye, Captain," Abby said with a nod before issuing the order to the crew. "I assume we will attack?"

"You're damned right we will. Ready all cannons on the port side."

"You want to move the cannons from starboard to port?"

"Yes. A full barrage. No one attacks my brother and gets away with it. I mean to send them straight to the locker."

The corner of Abby's lips curled. "Yes, Captain. We are ready. We shall sneak behind them using the cover of the smoke from the disabled vessel, then blow them right out of the water."

"Excellent." Henrietta crossed her arms and waited as the ship maneuvered to change course and sail south of the disabled ship.

Carolina clutched at the railing, her face a mask of worry. "Henrietta, shouldn't we go straight away to Clif to help?"

"We are helping. Under the cover of that smoke, they will not see us coming. We will slip behind them and fire away."

"But this is taking us longer than if we made a direct route to Clif."

"A direct route will not allow us the element of surprise."

"To hell with surprise! Clif's ship cannot withstand much more!"

Henrietta arched an eyebrow at her sister. "Firstly, I am the captain of this ship, not you. We sail under my orders. Secondly, Clif is not so weak that he cannot keep his ship afloat for the extra time this will take. You must give him some credit, Carolina."

"I do, but...he is under heavy fire, and the other ship is much larger."

"Yes, it is. But he has defeated larger vessels on many occasions. He is experienced. I trust that he will hold out until we can finish off his enemy. It does us no good if we race to his side only to become embroiled in an unwinnable battle."

"Unwinnable? Two against one..."

"Isn't an advantage unless we can crush them." Henrietta flicked her gaze to the two ships still battling on the horizon. "And crush them, we shall."

* * *

Clif hacked at another rope attached to a grappling hook. A few sailors from the other ship had boarded. His men battled against them while he tried to stop anyone else from coming across.

The battle wasn't going the way he'd hoped. They were losing. And he didn't like to lose.

They needed something to turn the tides. His mind scoured for a solution. For something that could give them the upper hand.

He found nothing viable to quickly change the course of the battle. They'd need to focus their resources on minimizing the damage to *The Henton*. They couldn't afford to have their mast disabled or their rudder.

He'd have to focus on staying afloat, literally. If a good shot from one of their cannons could blow a hole into the other ship, they may turn the tide.

A slice across his arm drew his attention away from his planning. A man, his gold tooth gleaming in the sun as he grinned, lifted his sword to strike again.

Clif blocked his blow with his weapon. He'd already used his pistol earlier and wasn't able to reload. He'd have to battle with this man with his sword alone.

With a growl, he threw the man backward a few steps and thrust his sword forward. The other pirate danced away before he slashed at Clif again. His swing missed, and Clif took the opportunity to land a blow with his fist, then slice through the air with his sword.

The man escaped the second attack, spinning away. Clif charged after him, and their swords clanged together. The metal screeched as one blade slid along the other. The men backed away from each other several steps, crouching as they circled before making their next move.

"So, the infamous Black Jack lives," the man said.

"Too bad you won't."

"Same old Jack. Always too self-assured. You can't escape this time. Blackheart will be the pirate who finally defeats you. We'll send you and your men to the bottom of the ocean."

"Not if I can help it." Clif thrust his sword forward but failed to inflict any damage.

"Thing is, you can't. It seems like we caught you unaware. You must be going soft in your old age."

"I'm hardly soft," he answered as he danced away from the slicing blade of the opposing pirate. "And I'm hardly beaten."

"Give up, Jack. You can't win. You're outgunned and outmanned."

"Tell Blackheart I'll never give up. Oh wait, you won't be able to because you'll be dead."

"I'll give him the message as we both toast to your severed head." The man swung forward.

"I think not," Clif answered, blocking the blow and burying his fist in the man's gut.

His opponent blew out a breath as he doubled over. Clif kicked him toward the railing. He stumbled backward before crashing into it and flipping backward over the side.

With a deep breath, Clif scanned his ship for another foe to dispatch. Perhaps the tides would turn.

Instead, he found five more men boarding. It was too late to drive them back, they'd have to make a stand on *The Henton*.

"Mr. Johnson," he shouted as he raced toward the men with his sword raised. "We must drive them back before they disable us."

"Aye, Commodore. We caught two making their way toward the rudder and stopped them. But we're losing the battle. We need a break."

"I know that. Perhaps we'll get lucky and damage the ship with the next volley."

"From your lips," Johnson said, setting his sword against another man's.

Johnson and Clif managed to drive their opponents into the water and off *The Henton*. He stared at the horizon before Johnson spun back to find a new opponent. His jaw dropped open as his forehead wrinkled.

"What is it, Johnson?" Clif asked.

The man raised a shaky hand. "They have a backup, sir. We're sunk."

* * *

The *Grandmistress* rounded the disabled ship and swung north toward the ensuing battle. Cannons still fired intermittently between the two ships, though at their current range, they did little to disable the other outside of creating a larger hole here or there.

"Captain?" Abby asked as they studied the battle from afar.

Henrietta crossed her arms and narrowed her eyes at the enemy vessel. "Prepare to fire. Load the central cannons with chainshot. And do *not* miss it. I want their main mast splintered to pieces."

"Aye, Captain." Abby passed along the orders as they closed the gap toward the ship.

Carolina clutched at the railing with white knuckles.

"Captain," Abby whispered, "should not your sister go into the cabin?"

Henrietta slid her eyes sideways to the younger woman before she shook her head. "No. Let her enjoy the show. We will disable them and sail away without even dirtying our hands."

"You do not think they'll try to retaliate?"

Henrietta smirked. "No. They'll never see this attack coming. It will flabbergast whoever is captaining that ship. And I intend to enjoy it."

"Aye, Captain. Shall we begin firing?"

"No. We wait. We should get a little closer so we ensure the chainshot will cripple them."

The distance between the ships grew smaller.

Abby shifted her weight from side to side. "Captain, if we wait much longer, they will surely spot us."

"Yes, I imagine they will. Tell the girls to be ready. Fire on my orders, not before then."

"Aye, Captain. Prepare to fire!" Abby shouted. The orders traveled to the women manning the cannons below.

Henrietta's heart hammered in her chest, but she forced herself to remain calm outside. Clif had taught her well. She should not rush to fire before they could inflict maximum damage. An itchy trigger finger often meant a wasted shot. By the time they reloaded, they could be drawn into a full-blown battle or sustain damage. And she didn't plan to do either.

The tension stretched between them. Carolina's lower lip quivered. Abby bit into hers until it blanched. But Henrietta held firm, unwilling to give the order until the perfect moment.

A shout sounded on the enemy ship. One finger jabbed in their direction. They'd been spotted. Perfect.

The captain, his large tricorn hat covering the tangled black hair hanging past his shoulders, whipped around to study the approaching threat. Henrietta hoped he'd have time to pick up his spyglass and find out the ship was captained by a woman.

Either way, though, the moment had come. With a satisfied smile, she spoke a single word. "Fire."

* * *

Clif stared at the large ship forming out of the smoke blowing across the ocean. Was this how the other ship had been overrun?

He narrowed his eyes as the vessel closed in on their location. They couldn't battle both at once.

Johnson was correct. If this was the enemy ship's backup, they wouldn't survive.

"We should abandon ship, Captain."

Before he could issue the order, he cocked his head and squinted at the second ship.

"Commodore. Should I tell the men? We can still save some of them."

Clif held up his hand. "No. Do not abandon ship."

"But, Commodore–"

"No, Johnson." The corners of his lips turned up, and he sheathed his sword before he set his hands on the railing. "No, we will not be abandoning ship."

"Commodore?" Johnson asked, his brow wrinkled.

"That is not the enemy ship's backup." He jabbed a finger toward the other vessel. "That is our savior."

* * *

"FIRE ALL!" Abby screamed to the crew. Carolina squeezed her eyes closed and clapped her hands over her ears.

Underneath her feet, the cannons roared to life. More smoke filled the air as cannonballs shot out of her ship and barreled toward the enemy ship. One stuck her square in the side, blowing a hole through her.

The chain shot flew out next. Henrietta held her breath as it wobbled its way toward the other vessel. Shouts resounded from the men aboard as they rushed to respond to the second attack.

Before they could retaliate, the chainshot found its mark. It smashed through the main mast, splintering it.

More shrieks resounded as the main mast cracked before pitching over.

"Well done, ladies. Well done."

"Should we leave them to the damage, Captain?" Abby said.

"Fire another round at them. I'm satisfied with the broken mast, but I'd be ecstatic if we sent them to the bottom of the locker."

"Aye, Captain," Abby said with a salute before passing along the order to fire on the ship again.

Henrietta removed her feathered cap and waved it as the cannons thundered again. The other ship's captain hurried to the railing and stared at the damage.

"I hope you've learned your lesson," she shouted to him. "Never fire on my brother's ship."

"Orders, Captain? Shall we fire again? They are still afloat."

She flicked her gaze to *The Henton*. Clif's ship had already begun to pull away.

"Leave it. Follow *The Henton*."

"Aye, Captain. Ladies, we are underway after *The Henton*." The ship swung around, leaving the other disabled vessel floating in the water and trailing behind their sister ship.

"Catch them," Henrietta said as she stood on the deck, staring at the other ship.

"More speed," Abby shouted.

Carolina flicked her gaze to her older sister. "That was something, Henrietta."

Henrietta smirked at her. "Do you feel quite safe sailing with me now? Now that you know I can defend us properly?"

Carolina offered her a sheepish smile. "I suppose you do more than quite well as a ship's captain, don't you."

"I think Clif will agree that I do very well." Their ship slid alongside Clif's, and Henrietta offered her brother a coy smile. "Wouldn't you, Clif?"

With his hat in his hand, he bowed to her. "I am indebted to you, sister."

"I saved you, your crew, and your ship."

"You certainly aided me, though I could have handled the situation."

"Oh? You looked as though you were about to lose that battle."

Clif scoffed. "Me? Lose a battle? Hardly. Though, it presented a challenge I preferred not to deal with."

"Well, I am pleased to have taken it off your hands. She was quite a large ship. Good thing I bought a bigger one."

"That was an impressive barrage. Did you move all of your cannons to the one side?"

"I did. I took no chances. And it seems the girls' aim with the chain shot is second to none."

"Well, now that you have rid us of that issue, we should continue to Verdant. Though, I do have one question."

"As do I. Yours first."

"Where did you go in that storm?" Clif questioned.

"We fought through it, then sheltered among the islands to the west."

Clif crinkled his brow. "The ones with the jagged rocks?"

"Those are the ones, yes." Henrietta set her hands on her hips. "We slipped between them and sheltered amongst the three of them."

"Well, I am impressed," Clif said. "Good work, Ri. Now, what's your question?"

"Who was that pirate? I'd like to know the name of the fool who fired on our fleet."

"Our fleet. I thought I was the commodore of this outfit." He crossed his arms and grinned at his sister.

Henrietta offered him a glowering stare though the corners of her lips turned up. "Well, I've always felt it was shared."

"Did you know?"

Henrietta lifted her chin, refusing to back down.

"Well, in answer to your question, that was Blackheart's ship."

"Blackheart," Henrietta repeated. "Interesting. Well, I wish

I would have sent Mr. Blackheart down to the bottom of the sea, but I suppose next time."

"Something to look forward to."

Henrietta bobbed her head up and down at the statement. "Speaking of looking forward, we should reach Verdant Isle soon. And I am very much looking forward to that."

"As am I. We will soon determine if this person is legitimate."

"I've no doubt Stargazer is who she says she is. She has too much to lose if she isn't."

"We shall see," Clif said with a grin. "Until then. Let's try not to become separated again."

They continued along their route, spotting the island as the sun began to set. They weighed anchor off the coast, planning to go ashore when the sun rose.

Henrietta slept fitfully, taking the hammock and allowing her sister to keep the bed. She rose before the sun and paced the deck as light broke on the horizon and painted the jungle a rich red color.

Blood. The word rattled through her mind as she stared out over the greenery. Would this island prove as dangerous as Stargazer warned? Would this island shed their blood?

CHAPTER 15

"**S**he's as beautiful as she is deadly," a voice said from behind her.

Henrietta spun to find Stargazer meandering toward her. "I was just ruminating about how the morning sun is painting it blood red."

Stargazer joined her at the railing, flicking her eyebrows up. "She's known for drawing blood. Everyone who walks her grounds pays a price."

The woman slid her gaze sideways. "And those who wish to take from her will pay a hefty bounty for that right."

"Oh?" Henrietta asked. "But you have been here before."

"Aye, I have."

"And what price did you pay?"

The woman lifted her chin and stretched her neck, pointing to two dark spots.

"What are those?" Henrietta asked.

"Snakebite. Pit viper," Stargazer said. "Deadly. My father pried him off me with his bare hands before he strangled him. I suffered a fever for two days, but my father is an excellent healer."

"I hope he passed those skills on to you."

"I told you I would see you to the map piece safely, and I will. But it should be known that I cannot work miracles. I expect you to follow what I say."

"You'll have no problems from me or my crew."

"And your brother's?"

"I'll keep Clif and his men in line. You focus on getting us to that map piece."

Stargazer nodded. "We should go to the island soon. It will take us at least two days to navigate to and from the cave. And that's if we do not have any problems."

"I'll ready the girls." Henrietta backed from the railing and headed across the main deck.

Abby met her halfway. "Captain, are we ready to go ashore?"

"Yes, round up those who will go with us. Have you spoken with *The Henton* this morning?"

"Aye, I've already spoken with Mr. Johnson. They are readying a shore party."

"Good. Get the skiffs in the water. We leave shortly."

Abby nodded and, after a salute, strode away. Henrietta ducked into her cabin to collect her weapons and hat.

Carolina yawned and stretched before she climbed from the bed. "Off already?"

"Yes." Henrietta strapped her belt around her and shoved her pistol into its holster. "I assume you will be all right here? Several of the girls are staying behind."

"Yes, I should be, though, I thought I might go with you."

Henrietta snapped her gaze to her sister, her forehead crinkled.

"I've quite a bit of experience with the jungle," she answered. "And various maladies that can befall one when going through it."

Henrietta studied her sister. Slighter in stature than she

was and still so innocent-looking. But she had made it through the jungles on the mainland, and she had survived a violent husband. Who was she to stop the woman from pursuing what she'd like?

"All right," Henrietta said with a nod. "I'm not opposed to you coming, though you may wish to change."

Carolina glanced down at her nightgown. "Yes, of course. I wouldn't dream of wearing this into the jungle."

Henrietta rounded her desk and crossed to a trunk. She dug through it, retrieving a pair of pants and a blouse. "I've got some trousers that may—"

Her words stopped as she spotted her sister shimmying into a dress.

"Are you planning to wear a dress?"

"What else would I wear?" Carolina asked as she paused in the middle of fastening it.

"Trousers. I have an extra pair, though they may be too large on you."

Carolina scoffed and resumed her work with the fastenings. "I wouldn't dream of it."

"Are you serious? You wouldn't dream of wearing trousers? But they are so practical."

"How so?" she asked as she finished with the dress and worked to secure her hair in an upswept style.

"Well, suppose we must run away from some large beast. Trousers are much easier to run in than a dress. Or suppose we must climb."

"I'm certain I will manage." Carolina shoved a pin into her hair to secure it. "And if I do not, I will know better the next time. Though I made it through the jungle once in a dress, and I'm certain I can manage it again."

Henrietta stared at her for a moment until she finished with her hair.

"There we are. Ready."

"You are an odd sort, Carolina. I cannot believe we are sisters."

The woman tugged her chin back toward her chest and furrowed her brow. "Just because I have no desire to run about in men's clothing doesn't mean I'm odd. I'd rather say that it would apply more to you, who challenges society in every role for women. Though I understand it and do not frown upon it."

"Gee, thanks," Henrietta said with an arched eyebrow.

"And we're not so different after all."

"How do you figure that?"

"We both enjoy learning things. We are both bright. And we both enjoy fashion, just in different ways. After all, do you not insist on those feathered caps constantly?"

Henrietta ran her hands over her hat. "I like them."

"And I like dresses. So, here we are. Now, shall we go?"

With a nod, Henrietta led them out onto the deck. Abby approached and squeezed Carolina's chin between her thumb and forefinger. "You're healing quite nicely. Barely a trace of those bruises."

"Yes, and I can open my eyes almost fully today. Thank you, Abby. I appreciate your helping me."

"Of course," Abby said with a nod before she turned to Henrietta and motioned for her to proceed to a boat. Carolina followed them. "Oh, is she going?"

"Yes. Carolina is knowledgeable about the jungle and would like to help. She's quite small, and we can fit her into the skiff without asking anyone to stay back."

"Quite right," Abby said with a nod as they boarded the boat and lowered to the water.

Clif waved from his skiff as they rowed toward the beach.

"Lovely morning to find a map piece, isn't it?" Henrietta called as two of her crew leapt into the water and dragged the boat further ashore.

She climbed out, her boots splashing in the warm, clear water before she trudged onto the sand. Clif swept Carolina out of the skiff and carried her to dry land.

He set her down on the sandy shore as the crews worked to secure the boats before they set off into the jungle. Carolina perched on a rock sticking out of the sand while Clif joined Henrietta, who studied the jungle with Stargazer.

"You brought Carolina?" he murmured as he approached, shooting a glance over his shoulder at his lighter-haired sister.

"She insisted. I did not see a reason to stop her. If she'd like to explore with us, let her."

"I see one reason," Clif said with a wrinkled nose, his eyes still set on his sister.

Henrietta glanced behind her. The corners of her lips turned up as she spotted Mr. Johnson speaking with Carolina. "You're fighting a losing battle, Clif. Let it run its course."

"It's the course that I'm worried about. And what if it doesn't?"

Henrietta returned her gaze to the jungle in front of her. "What do you mean?"

A soft giggle from Carolina floated on the morning air, followed by a groan from Clif. "That's what I mean. I mean, what if this doesn't dissipate?"

"Then I suppose we will have a new brother-in-law."

"New broth–" Clif pressed his lips together tightly before the rest of the statement escaped.

"Why don't we concentrate on navigating this jungle and retrieving the map piece? We will need our wits about us, so if you could pull your focus away from Carolina's flirting…"

Clif snapped his gaze to his sister. "Do you think they're flirting? Is that what they're doing?"

Henrietta sighed, letting her features settle into an unimpressed frown. "Clif, focus. There are snakes and wild cats in there."

"And sudden weather changes as well as quicksand," Stargazer added. "This jungle is a veritable fortress, protecting what is hers. If you take from her, she will take from you."

Henrietta crossed her arms and flicked her eyebrows up. "There, you see? There is no room for your obsession over Mr. Johnson and Carolina."

"It's not an obsession; it's—"

Henrietta clapped a hand over Clif's mouth. "An obsession. Let them be. They are grown adults."

Clif grimaced at her as she pulled her hand away, wagging a finger at her. "Fine. You'll handle the fallout of this."

She rolled her eyes. "Fine. Now, let's concentrate on this jungle. Stargazer, tell us how we proceed."

"We'll need to proceed with caution." She squatted lower to the beach with a stick in her hand and outlined the island in the sand. With an X marked on it, she poked the stick down. "We are here."

She drew another X at the heart of the island. "The map piece is here inside a cave."

"Then we should travel straight toward it," Clif said. "That's half a day's journey at most."

Stargazer shook her head. "There is a stream."

She dragged the stick along a meandering path."

"We'll cross it," Clif said with a shrug.

"And a wild cat's den here. And dangerous pit vipers here."

Henrietta narrowed her eyes at the depiction. "So…"

"So, we must go around the island to here, then go inland. It is the safest way."

"That will take over a day," Clif said. "We should take the

shortest path to minimize our exposure. The men can handle anything this island throws at them."

"That is not wise."

"It is unwise to take two days to complete a journey that should take one. That exposes us far longer than it should," Clif argued.

Stargazer rose, firming her jaw. "Why did you bring me if you planned not to listen?"

"I hear you, but I respectfully disagree with the choice."

Stargazer crossed her arms and raised her eyebrows before she flicked her gaze to Henrietta. "You are my captain. I follow your orders."

Clif shifted his gaze to his sister. "Well, Captain? What are your thoughts on the matter?"

Henrietta stared at the crude map before she gazed at the jungle. "Is there a faster way that would still adequately avoid the dangers of the island?"

"There is one way," Stargazer said, "but it is a much more arduous path. But it would save half a day in travel at least."

Henrietta flicked her gaze up. "Perhaps we should try that path. I'm certain the crew is up to the challenge, and it shortens our exposure without taking unnecessary chances with the local wildlife."

"We would be more subject to the sudden changes in weather on the island's west side."

"Fine," Clif said with a bob of his head. "Weather is something we can muddle through."

Stargazer offered him an amused grin. "We'll see about that."

Clif gathered the crew closer before they set off. "Men... and women, we are about to trek through a dangerous jungle. It will take several hours to reach our destination. Along the way, we must keep our eyes open for deadly wildlife, treacherous terrain and battle the weather. If anyone is not willing to do this, turn back now. We will not think less of you for it."

His eyes fell onto Carolina. She stood with her hands clasped in front of her, politely listening to his warning. "No one?"

Henrietta smacked him in the chest. "No one is turning back, Commodore. Let us proceed. Today, we find the first piece of the puzzle that will bring us fame and glory."

A cheer went up through the group. Henrietta offered her brother a cheeky grin before she twisted to follow Stargazer, who waited at the jungle's edge.

"Fame and glory, is it?" Clif asked as they stepped under the thick canopy of the jungle.

Henrietta offered him a shrug. "I wouldn't say no."

Clif arched an eyebrow at her.

"Though I may have already achieved some fame and fortune. I did, after all, disable Blackheart the Pirate's ship after he nearly bested the legendary Black Jack."

"Having a fleet does come in rather handy," he answered as he pushed away a large leaf.

"And having an exceptional sister who has done quite well at the pirating job."

"That you have. Though I have serious concerns about how you're doing with the sister job."

"What's that supposed to mean?" Henrietta asked as she trudged along a few steps behind Stargazer.

Clif glanced over his shoulder and shook his head before he thumbed toward Carolina. Mr. Johnson held a leaf out of the way as a pink-cheeked Carolina grinned at him.

Henrietta eyed them for a moment before moving on. "You have a problem, Clif."

"Yes, one called Johnson as a brother-in-law."

"Oh, let them go. They are young and in love."

"Father is dead. It is up to me to assume responsibility for Carolina now that she is without a husband."

"Oh? And does that mean keeping her under lock and key?"

"No, but..."

"But what?" Henrietta stopped, setting her hands on her hips and staring at him.

"Well..."

"Are you saying Mr. Johnson is in some way substandard as a man?"

"No."

"Is he dishonest? A liar? A cheat?"

"Certainly not."

"Then what is the problem if Carolina chooses him."

Clif frowned as he studied the ground under his feet.

"That's what I thought." Henrietta spun on a heel and continued through the jungle.

Clif hurried to catch up to her. "But he's a pirate."

"So am I, and so are you. Does it make us unworthy in some way? Or incapable of love?"

"Well, no, but..."

Henrietta pressed a hand against her brother's shoulder. "Clif, let the matter handle itself. If she chooses Mr. Johnson, let her. If she does not, fine. He is an excellent choice, and he cares deeply for her. He is far better than her first husband."

Clif glanced back at his first mate, carefully helping his baby sister over a tree root. With a shake of his head, he agreed with his older sibling and allowed it to run.

"Now, if you're finished bellyaching about Carolina's taste in men, perhaps you can regale me with tales of Blackheart. Have I beaten an excellent pirate? Or is he only so-so?"

"No, he's quite good. He disabled the cargo ship before preying upon *The Henton*."

"Yes, how did he manage to put you in that nasty position?"

"We did not see him. We ventured closer to the cargo ship, thinking..."

Henrietta side-eyed him. "Thinking what?"

"Thinking it was the *Grandmistress* in distress."

Henrietta scoffed. "What? Are you joking?"

"No. We were separated in the storm. I feared the worst." He climbed over a large root poking from the ground.

"Have you no faith that what you taught me had been retained?"

"Even the best captain can be caught by surprise and thrust into a situation they cannot recover from."

Henrietta shot him a devilish grin. "Like being fired upon by another pirate after venturing too close to a disabled ship?"

"Yes, exactly like that. Anyway, you did quite well disabling him. I suppose I can worry less now since you've clearly retained all the knowledge I've passed along."

"Yes, I did learn, didn't I? I'm quite proud of my crew. That was our first entanglement, and they did quite well."

"Yes, they did. Soon, they may be up to the level of my men."

"Very funny. Those girls are every bit as–"

Her words cut off as she bumped into Stargazer, who stood frozen in the path.

"What is it?" Henrietta asked.

The woman answered with one word. "Trouble."

CHAPTER 16

*H*enrietta's brow wrinkled, and her pulse quickened. "Trouble? From what?"

Stargazer arched an eyebrow, though she kept the rest of her body still. Her fists curled at her sides as she murmured her answer. "There is a large cat almost straight ahead."

Henrietta scanned the ground in front of them, narrowing her eyes to peer as far as she could. She glanced to Clif, who shrugged and shook his head. "I don't see anything."

"The large tree twenty paces from us. Second branch from the bottom."

She shifted her gaze higher. Her blood ran cold as she eyed the spotted creature perched on the branch and studied them. "Are there more?" she whispered.

"No, they are usually solitary hunters."

"Can we move past it without trouble?"

"I doubt it. It will prey on one of our group members. Perhaps the first, perhaps the last, perhaps the weakest."

Clif pulled his pistol from its holster and cocked it. "I

should be able to shoot it at this range, and we will rid ourselves of the problem."

Stargazer pushed his arm down as he lined up his aim. "No."

"What do you propose we do? Give it a sacrifice?"

"They are solitary hunters, but that does not mean other cats are not nearby. The shot calls more attention to us than I would prefer. We do not wish any others to know our whereabouts."

"What do you propose?" Henrietta asked.

"That we backtrack and circle around its territory."

Clif shoved his weapon into the holster. "What if we wander into another cat's territory?"

"Then we do the same. Though this side of the island is less populated with the animals, we may stand a good chance of having a clearer path."

"Fine. Then, let's do that," Henrietta said. "Better safe than sorry."

Stargazer nodded, and they backed from their spot several feet before turning and trekking closer to the shoreline before they corrected their direction.

"This will add time to our trip," Clif said as he wiped the sweat from his brow.

"Yes, it will, though I'm certain this is still shorter than the longer route originally mentioned," Henrietta said as they trudged along. Her shirt clung to her skin, slick with sweat.

"We should have gone the most direct route. This exposure is less than desirable."

Henrietta followed the direction of his gaze. "The crew's exposure to the jungle or Carolina's exposure to Mr. Johnson?"

He shifted his gaze to her with an eye roll. "I'm concerned about her exposure to the elements. She is not used to this like our people are."

Henrietta shrugged it off. "She made it through the jungle with her idiot husband once already, she's not that delicate."

"She seems red."

"That's the flirting, not the heat." Henrietta grabbed his arm and tugged him forward. "Come along, we have more important things to deal with than Carolina's giddy philandering."

"Please don't refer to it as that. It's difficult enough watching your sister throw herself at a man without that."

Henrietta snorted a laugh. "She is hardly throwing herself. She's quite timid about engaging in anything with him, to be honest. And he is not a wolf—just let them have their moment and keep your eyes peeled for snakes and cats."

"We should have brought the monkey." Clif snapped his fingers together. "That's it."

"That's what? I fail to see how Jack would help this situation."

"Of course, he would. I will give him to Carolina. That will distract her from these shenanigans."

"A monkey is not going to distract her from a man. And you cannot give Jack to Carolina; he is your monkey. He loves you."

Clif pressed his lips into a frown. "Yes, I know. He screeched at me when I put him in his cage earlier. I felt the island too dangerous for him."

Henrietta's lips tugged back into a smile.

"What?"

"Nothing."

"Why are you smiling at me like that?"

"Because as much as you say you hate that little monkey, you don't. You could never give him to Carolina, and you are fond of him."

"I do not. He's a dreadful little creature, and I don't like him at all."

Henrietta chuckled. "That's not true. You left him on the ship because the island was too dangerous. You care for him."

"I do not. I don't wish any harm to befall him. And, in truth, it is too dangerous. He may have cost us our lives. And it would be quite a mess if something caught him."

"Methinks the man protests too much."

"I'm going to give him to you. And then you can keep him and listen to his screeching and chittering. It'll drive you mad. And the way he leaps onto your arm and scrambles up to your shoulder to sit. He has claws, you know? They're sharp. And sharp little teeth. You'll see."

"I won't. Because his darling protector, Clif, will not give him up."

Clif shook his head at her. "You are very trying sometimes, Ri."

"But you love me all the same," she said with a cheeky smile.

"I love you more on days when you've saved my hide from an opposing pirate."

"Happy to oblige," she said with a salute as they continued through the jungle.

The morning sun beat down on them, and the oppressive, moist heat made breathing difficult. Drenched in sweat, they pressed forward toward their destination.

As the sun rose higher overhead, its rays waned.

"Thank goodness. I hope that cloud stays forever," Henrietta said as she wiped her brow.

Stargazer glanced over her shoulder. "I doubt you'll be that grateful in a few moments."

"Why?" Henrietta asked.

Her answer came in seconds as a downpour drenched them. Thunder boomed overhead, and lightning ripped across the sky.

"Should we stop?" Henrietta called over the loud rain.

Clif shook his head. "No, we keep going."

"In this weather? The crew will be soaked."

"The crew is already soaked, and we would do well to find the cave as quickly as possible. We keep moving."

"I warned you about this route," Stargazer said as they trudged through the mud.

"So, you did," Henrietta grumbled as water poured off her hat. She could only imagine the state of her feather. "And my hat has become the first victim."

"I told you to stop wearing those hats. They are going to be the death of one of us." Clif flicked water from his chin before he continued forward.

"It's not much farther," Stargazer called over the pounding rain. "Just over the ridge."

"Thank heavens. Then, we'll grab this map piece and move on to the next. That one should be infinitely easier."

This time, it was Clif's turn to laugh. "The next one will be far more difficult. I already told you it is in the possession of a pirate who does not care for me. There will be no negotiating for it. We will have to steal it."

"That may be preferable to this. My feather stands a better chance."

They climbed the hill and scanned the landscape below them. The rain began to slow before the clouds gave way to bright sunshine as they descended. The heat rose sharply, becoming more sticky and oppressive than before the rainstorm.

They finally reached the yawning entrance of the cave and ducked inside to escape the beating sun. The air was noticeably cooler inside, and the group settled on the floor to rest before exploring.

Henrietta took a long sip from her flask before wiping her mouth with the back of her hand. "Where is this map piece?"

Stargazer shifted her weight forward as she capped her drinking container. "The heart of the cave. We should take a smaller party and leave some behind to guard the entrance."

"Fine. Clif and I will go with you."

"I can stay behind, Captain, to organize the watch party," Abby said with a nod.

"Good, thank you."

"Johnson, you will go with us," Clif said, "to round out our party."

"I will go with you, too," Carolina said.

"Oh, but–"

"Fine," Henrietta said as she climbed to her feet. "Let's begin, then, shall we?"

"Just a moment, I think you should stay back with the watch party, Carolina. We have no idea what we may encounter in the depths of this cave."

She grinned at him. "Yes, it's so exciting. I enjoyed exploring the caves, pyramids, and the like when I traveled with James."

Henrietta offered her brother an amused glance.

"But these may be dangerous, and–"

"Best we are all together, then," Carolina said as she lifted her skirt and stepped closer to Henrietta.

Clif blew out a controlled sigh, ready to give her a nod, when Johnson chimed in. "Not to worry, Commodore, I will always keep Miss Carolina close to me."

Henrietta pressed her lips together to stop a giggle from escaping them as Clif slid his eyes shut. "I'm certain you will."

"Well, it seems Mr. Johnson has the matter in hand; let us proceed. Stargazer, lead the way." Henrietta swept a hand toward the interior of the cave.

They inched their way into the darkness further before lighting the torches they'd carried with them. The flames' light bounced off the natural brown stone as they continued deeper into the earth.

Drawings decorating the walls depict stick figures fighting with four-legged creatures or wrangling with snakes.

Carolina studied them as they passed. "Fascinating. It seems this island was once inhabited."

"No," Stargazer called over her shoulder. "Never inhabited."

"Then who did these drawings?" Carolina questioned.

"People from my village. Long ago, before even my father's father was born, the story was told through the generations. A warning about this place."

"What is the story?" she asked.

"A group of villagers decided to sail to this island to establish a colony. With the lush rainforest, they thought food would be plentiful. The villagers warned them not to go, but they didn't listen. They wanted more than our village could offer."

"A chance to build something for themselves," Carolina said as she studied more of the drawings.

"But they would not get that chance. They came here and set up a camp. On the first night, one man went missing.

"They searched the island for him. But they couldn't find him. On the second night, another man went missing.

"This time, they tracked him. Finding him in a big cat's den. He was already gone, but they killed the cat in revenge."

Carolina's eyebrow arched as she flicked her gaze to Stargazer. "Did that solve the issue?"

"The next night, two men disappeared. The cats here, usually solitary hunters, banded together to fight back.

"They attacked the camp night after night until only a handful of the men were left. They pushed them inland to the viper pits. Many more of the group perished there. The last remaining survivors huddled in this cave and painted these pictures."

"Did anyone survive at all?"

"One man. People from my village came. They found the lone man, who told them the tale of woe. They came to the island, and the island fought back."

"That's terrifying," Carolina said. "Though, surely with modern advances…"

"This island prefers its natural beauty to remain undisturbed. Taking the map piece is a risk. We should offer her something to appease her."

"Such as?" Henrietta asked.

"Such as a life. But perhaps she will let us escape, but we must tread lightly."

Clif pushed forward. "Let's just press on and finish our business here."

Stargazer eyed him with her dark eyes before she nodded and led them to a branch in the cavern network. She slipped into the right passage. They spilled out of it at a large pool of water. "We must swim."

"Is there not another way?" Clif asked.

"No. We must swim to find it." She pulled a length of rope from her belt. "We should tie ourselves together so no one is lost."

The group worked to secure the rope around each of them, putting Clif at the end of the line with Carolina in the middle after Henrietta.

Stargazer led the way, wading into the cool water up to her chest before she started to swim. She paddled toward the stone wall at the far end of the cavern.

"We must dive. It is far. Take in a deep breath, and do not dally."

They all sucked in as deep a breath as their lungs could hold, and Stargazer sank below the water's surface and moved forward. Bubbles blew from Henrietta's nose as she opened her eyes and moved forward, keeping close to the lead swimmer.

She glanced behind her at Carolina, who kept close to her heels. Her lungs began to burn as she lifted her gaze upward, finding nothing but stone above them. Not even an air pocket to relieve the tightness building across her chest.

She fought to keep moving forward and hold her breath when every instinct in her body begged her to suck in a breath. But she'd only end up with water in her lungs. She continued to swim, wondering how much longer they'd stay underwater.

When she felt she could take no more, the line tugged upward. They were breaking for the surface. She straightened and kicked hard to tug the others behind her upward. When cool air hit her soaked face, she gasped for breath.

Clif used some alcohol in his flask to relight their wet torches, hoping they stayed lit.

Other heads popped up from the water, each doing the same. She counted the entire party, finding everyone still alive. They bobbed for a few more moments while everyone caught their breath before Stargazer tilted her head toward the shore.

"Let's go. We have a bit more to trek."

They swam to the bank and climbed out, loosening the rope and leaving it on a nearby rock to use on their way back before they moved into another large cavern.

"We must cross this, then the bridge of despair, and we will find the map."

"Why are we not taking the most direct route across?" Clif asked from the back of the group.

"There is quicksand. We should keep to the outskirts."

With their backs pressed to the stone wall, they inched

around the cave's perimeter, finally reaching the opening on the opposite side.

"Now, for the bridge of despair," Stargazer said as they passed through the narrow corridor and spilled onto a ledge that poked over a deep chasm.

"Bridge?" Henrietta questioned. "There is no bridge here."

"There is. But many lose their lives on it because they are not careful. Hence the name," Stargazer said.

Henrietta stared down into the blackness. "There is no bridge, and we can't jump it. This is useless."

Carolina pushed her way to the front and squatted closer to the edge. "It is an illusion."

"Illusion?" Henrietta asked.

Carolina grinned at her as she rose to stand and nodded. She took a blind step forward. Henrietta's heart leapt into her throat, and she grabbed her sister's hand, tugging her back.

"I'm fine, Henrietta," Carolina said, tapping her foot against what appeared to be nothing. "See?"

With her hand still firmly clamped around her sister's wrist, Henrietta squatted lower and reached out to trace the stone near Carolina's foot. "There is a bridge. Nearly impossible to see."

"Yes," Carolina said. "It is quite difficult. We must proceed carefully to the opposite side."

"How clever you are," Johnson said.

Henrietta rose and tugged her sister backward. "I will go first. It may be best if Clif and I go and the others stay behind. There is no reason to risk everyone's lives."

Carolina pouted as Clif pushed to the front of the group. "But I wanted to see it."

"You'll see the map piece when we retrieve it. Stay here," he said.

Johnson wrapped his arm around her shoulders, causing

Clif to frown. "Nothing to worry about, Commodore; I will protect her with my life."

"Thank you, Johnson," Henrietta said with a nod. "Most appreciated. We will return posthaste."

Henrietta licked her lips as her heart thudded against her ribs. She took one small step forward before sliding her foot further and dragging the other behind it. The chasm yawned on either side of her. Her throat dried as she continued the painstaking crossing, using her arms to balance her.

"Perhaps you should have stayed behind," Clif said as they hit the middle of the bridge.

"Why?" she questioned, her forehead pinching as she fought to maintain her balance on the tricky passageway.

"Johnson could have come with me. Then, both my sisters would have been safe. Now, both are in danger."

"Neither is in danger," she said as she reached the other side and breathed a sigh of relief. "We have safely made it across, and Carolina is quite safe with Mr. Johnson."

Clif glanced in the direction Henrietta pointed and nearly lost his balance as he spotted Stargazer milling around on the opposite side of the chasm while Mr. Johnson wrapped his arms around Carolina.

"Come on," Henrietta said, grabbing his arm and tugging him into the hole in the stone. "The faster we retrieve this piece, the faster we return to them."

They ducked into the low corridor and bent forward at the hips to fit. After several steps, they were forced to their hands and knees to fit in the small space.

"If this gets any smaller, we may have to go back for Carolina's help," Henrietta groaned.

"How do you think I feel? You may be larger than Carolina but far smaller than me."

"I see an opening ahead. At least, I think so." She shoved

her torch forward, smiling at the larger space that spilled open.

"Thank heavens," Clif said as he continued forward in a belly crawl.

Henrietta reached the opening and rose, dusting off her pants as she lifted the torch.

"There!" She poked a finger at a chest placed across the room. An opening in the rock's ceiling allowed a small amount of light to shine through, illuminating the shiny gold exterior of the box.

"Good," Clif said. "I wonder if we can escape through that hole rather than go back through the cave."

"I doubt it." Henrietta shifted her torch away to study the light. "It's a pinpoint. We cannot fit through there."

Clif muttered a curse under his breath as she handed him the torch and eyed the treasure chest. With shaking hands, she lifted the lid. Her breath caught in her throat when she caught sight of the inside.

She lifted the gemstones out along with the map piece. "Clif, look. How beautiful!"

"Indeed. And there will be plenty more if we can manage to find these islands."

Henrietta nodded as she slipped them into her pocket along with the map piece. "Come on, let's–"

She swung around toward the small passage leading back to their party but stopped short, her back arching backward and her eyes wide.

"Clif," she breathed.

"What is–"

Clif froze, too, as a pair of pit vipers snaked their way down from the ceiling, their mouths open in a hiss and venom dripping from their pointed fangs.

CHAPTER 17

"No sudden movements," Clif said as he slowly slid the torch toward the snakes, hoping the flames would drive them back.

Henrietta swallowed hard as she nodded. "Do you think we can get past them?"

"I aim to try. I'm hoping the flame deters them from getting too close."

Henrietta pressed a hand against her brother's back, staying close to him as he swung the torch between the snakes.

They hissed as the flames came closer to them but remained too close for comfort.

"Clif," Henrietta whispered, squeezing his shoulder, "there is another at your feet."

Clif let his gaze fall to his boots before he slid his eyes closed. The viper slithered on the ground, probing the toe of his shoe as it searched for flesh to bite.

Delicately, Clif lifted his foot and tried to step over the creature. The snake reared back and snapped at his shoe as soon as it moved.

"Careful, Clif," Henrietta said. "Stargazer said they are extremely poisonous."

"Yes, I know." He breathed shallowly as he tried to navigate around the snake while keeping the other two at bay. "We must get away from them, but they've surrounded us."

"Perhaps if we backtrack and loop around the one on our left. We may be able to squeeze past."

Clif bobbed his head ever so slightly. Henrietta glanced over her shoulder, her voice catching in her throat. "Abort. There are two now behind me."

"They've surrounded us."

"Smart buggers." Clif slowly moved a hand toward his sword. "Are you able to reach a weapon without startling them?"

"Maybe," Henrietta said, "though drawing my sword when I am nearly standing on top of you will be tricky."

"Don't kill me accidentally, Ri. I will never forgive you for it."

She inched her hand toward her sword's hilt. She'd worry about removing it when she had a hold of it. "Would you rather die by my sword or snake bite?"

"Neither. I would rather live," he murmured.

"I have hold of the hilt. I'm drawing the sword ever-so-slowly now."

Henrietta held her breath as she inched the long blade from its sheath.

"Stop!" Clif hissed. "They are growing restless."

One snake writhed closer before it snapped at them and hissed. The snake at their feet slithered closer to Clif's boot as he placed it on the floor.

Henrietta stiffened as scaly skin slithered against her neck. She sucked in a sharp breath. "Clif."

"What is it?" he asked, strafing the fire back and forth to drive the snakes as far back as he could.

"One of the vipers is sliding down my shoulder."

"Don't move."

"Yes, and while that is sound advice, I would very much like to remove it from my person."

"I dare not turn my back on them."

"Perhaps it is time for us to make a move. You will need to dive forward and escape the circle they've created."

Clif tugged his eyebrows together. "What will you do?"

"On your movement, I will fling the snake away from me and follow."

"I'm not certain we will be quick enough."

Henrietta lifted her chin, flinching as the viper turned its head toward her face and wriggled closer.

"I'm not certain we have a choice."

"Fine. On my count. Three, two, one."

Henrietta grabbed hold of the scaly reptile and tossed it to the side as Clif flung himself forward, somersaulting across the floor and leaping to stand with his sword drawn.

She ducked as one of the snakes struck out at her. It knocked her hat from her head as she shot forward through a tiny opening and rolled across the ground.

Clif stuck his hand out to pull her up as the nest of vipers dove forward to attack the feathered cap.

She scrambled to her feet with wide eyes. "Let's go."

Clif bobbed his head up and down, shoving his sword into its sheath and grabbing her hand as he headed for the entrance.

"You see?" she said, still breathless from her maneuvering. "My hat saved my life this time."

"There probably would have been no snakes had you not worn the blasted thing," he countered, stepping onto the small path leading back to the others.

"Did you find it?" Carolina called, her voice echoing across the chasm.

"We did." Henrietta carefully leaned around Clif to grin at her sister. "And beautiful gems indicative of what we may find at our destination."

"I cannot wait to see them."

Stargazer crossed her arms, her eyes narrowing. "And did you run into any trouble?"

"A few snakes, nothing we couldn't handle," Clif answered as he reached the midway point on the bridge.

"Are you certain about that?" Stargazer asked.

Henrietta tugged her eyebrows together before she shot a glance over her shoulder. Her eyes went wide. "Clif, go faster. The snakes have discovered that my hat is not me. They are slithering from the cave and moving toward us quickly."

Clif flicked his gaze behind him before he tried to move faster, wobbling toward the opposite side.

Henrietta followed behind him, more surefooted on the path with her smaller stature. The snakes slithered across the almost invisible bridge with ease.

"Go! Go into the next chamber!" Clif shouted with a wave, nearly toppling over had Henrietta not grabbed his arm.

Mr. Johnson shoved Carolina through the opening ahead of him before he disappeared through it.

Stargazer motioned with her hand. "Throw the torch behind you."

Clif passed it to Henrietta, who lobbed it a few feet from her onto the path. Clig grabbed her arm and tugged her back to the outcropping before he shoved her through the passage to the other chamber. She followed behind Stargazer, aiming for the light she carried.

"They are still coming despite the torch we tossed," Clif announced as Carolina and Johnson crept around the perimeter. "Move as quickly as possible and go straight into the water."

"They can follow us, but if we make it past the dive, we should be safe," Stargazer said as she pressed against the wall and hurried toward the water cavern.

Henrietta followed her with Clif bringing up the rear. The snakes slithered into the cavern, careful to avoid the quicksand.

"Move!" Stargazer boomed. "They are leery but can cross the quicksand more easily than we can and may try for it."

Carolina and Johnson disappeared through the passage. The sound of splashing water reached their ears moments later. Henrietta quickened her pace as the snakes raced toward her brother.

They pushed into the water cavern a moment later, finding the other three swimming toward the rock wall.

"Do not bother with the rope, we have no time. Leave the torch, let's go," Stargazer shouted as she swam toward Carolina and Johnson.

Clif tossed the torch to the ground as he dove into the water behind Henrietta. They swam toward the wall as the snakes slithered into the chamber, approaching the water without fear.

"Deep breath, dive, and swim," Stargazer said before disappearing under the water.

Johnson wrapped his hand tightly around Carolina's. "Do not let go of my hand."

She nodded before taking a gulp of air and following him below the surface.

"Ri," Clif began as she clutched his arm and sucked in a breath. He followed her lead, breathing deeply before descending below the surface.

With a hard kick, he swam forward, opening his eyes to

find the underwater tunnel. Henrietta matched his pace, swimming alongside him through the passage.

They surfaced on the other side with gasps for air. Carolina, Johnson, and Stargazer had already climbed from the water on the other side of the cavern.

They swam toward them as Stargazer retrieved a lit torch they'd left behind and breathed the fire back to life.

"We should leave this place now. The island wants to take something from you for stealing from her."

"Too bad for her," Clif said, snatching the torch from the woman's hands and leading the group back through the tunnels. "Let's move. And this time, we take the most direct route back to the beach."

"Commodore—" Stargazer began.

"No!" he said sharply. "We go the fastest way possible."

"Clif, I want to leave this place as much as you, but we should not be hasty. If Stargazer feels we should take another route, we should follow her direction. She has been correct at every step so far."

Clif sighed as they approached the main cavern. "I do not wish to spend more time than we must."

"But if it is too dangerous of a route, we may lose more than we intend."

They rejoined the others, and Clif shooed them from the cave. "Everyone out. There are snakes inside; they may have followed us."

The crew hastily moved out into the sweltering hot jungle.

"Commodore," Johnson said, "perhaps we should make camp. The heat is oppressive."

Clif shook his head. "We should leave this place. I have a bad feeling."

Henrietta nodded in agreement. "He's right. We should leave and plan to retrieve the next component."

Johnson pressed his lips together, clearly disagreeing but unwilling to speak against either of them.

Clif clapped him on the shoulder. "I know your concerns, Johnson; I share them. However, the other dangers heavily outweigh the heat."

"We can do it. The crew is used to rough conditions. They are well-rested," Henrietta said.

Johnson's eyes lingered on Carolina for a moment.

"She will be fine, Johnson," Henrietta promised.

He offered her a slight smile and a nod.

"Stargazer, take us through the fastest way to the ships that is safe." Clif flicked his gaze to Henrietta.

"Follow me and stay close. I will take us through the fastest way; however, there are some dangers." Stargazer sipped her water before she set off through the jungle.

The group fell in line behind her. Sweat beaded on their brow mere steps into their journey. A dark cloud covered the sun, allowing them some time to recover from the brutal heat.

Henrietta's shirt stuck to her skin, slick with sweat. She puffed with exertion as she pushed herself to move forward.

She glanced back at her fair-skinned sister. Her cheeks were red from the heat's toll on her body. Her other crew members had a similar look as they wiped at their brows or fanned themselves with their hats.

"Clif, perhaps a break," Henrietta said.

Clif scanned the group before he nodded and held up his hand. "Yes, good. Let's stop for a few minutes."

The group readily settled on the ground, leaning against the trees. Only Stargazer remained on her feet, shifting her weight from side to side as she kept her gaze constantly moving, searching the jungle for threats.

Groans went up through the group as the cloud sailed away, and the sun's rays heated the air again.

"All right, let's continue," Clif said after a moment.

More moans resounded as they climbed to their feet. They followed behind Stargazer as she trekked closer to the beach.

"How much farther?" Henrietta asked her.

"We should reach the beach before nightfall. I hope."

Henrietta wrinkled her nose at the statement. She didn't care for uncertainty. Despite the heat, her skin puckered into goosebumps. They'd had an easy time making their way back toward the skiffs so far. How long would their luck last?

Without warning, Stargazer stopped. "There is a cat in the tree ahead and on the left."

"We should circle out of its territory," Clif said.

She nodded without answering verbally before side-stepping her way, without letting her gaze leave the cat. Clif guarded the way forward, pushing the group to the side to follow Stargazer.

"Things are going too easily," Henrietta said, her hand on the hilt of her sword.

"I know. It makes me uneasy." Clif eyed the cat over his shoulder. "I don't like this at all."

"Me either. Let's hope this detour does not cost us much more time. I have a bad feeling."

A shout sounded from their right. Clif and Henrietta exchanged a glance, their blood running cold. Had their luck just run out?

CHAPTER 18

*H*enrietta raced toward the shout with Clif hurrying behind her. They pushed their way through the group gathered around something of interest.

When they reached the front, Henrietta stopped short, her jaw dropping open. "Oh no."

"What is it?" Clif asked as he reached her. "Oh no."

Henrietta carefully inched around one of Clif's crew members, already sinking in quicksand. "We need to pull him out. Does anyone have a rope?"

The stuck man thrashed as he tried to escape the sinking sands.

Carolina rushed to the edge, squatting and reaching a hand to him.

"No, no," she called, "you must stay still. The movement will only make you sink faster."

"We left our length of rope in the cave," Clif said with a shake of his head. "Mr. Johnson, do you have another?"

"I do not, Commodore."

"A vine," Henrietta said as she scanned the trees, wrapped her fingers around a long, leafy rope, and tugged it.

"I will cut it from above," Johnson said as he scrambled up the tree.

The man whimpered as the quicksand rose to his chest. "I'm going to die."

"No, you will not. They almost have the rope prepared. Stay still," Carolina counseled.

Seconds later, the tension on the vine gave way, and it dropped to the ground. "Here," Henrietta said, thrusting it toward her brother after she tied a loop in it.

Clif tossed it toward the quickly sinking crew member. He missed catching it the first time and sank further into the earth.

"Calm down, man." Clif tugged the rope back as quickly as he could before he threw it again.

The hole swallowed the man further, leaving his head and shoulders poking out, but he managed to grab hold of the vine.

"Wrap it around your wrist and snug it tight," Clif ordered.

The man followed the instructions, sinking even further into the hole. A whimper escaped him as the sand reached his lips.

Clif leaned back, tugging against the sand. Henrietta grabbed hold of the vine and helped. Several other crew members grabbed the length of the vine and threw their weight into the work.

The man rose out of the hole slightly.

"Remain as still as you can," Clif instructed as he pulled again.

They continued their work until only the bottom half of the man remained stuck. He scrambled, trying to climb free, but sank further.

Clif struggled to hold the vine as it yanked back against him. "It's slipping."

"Keep a firm hold," Henrietta shouted over her shoulder to the crew.

They heaved back again, pulling the man out of the hole again. The tension on the vine stretched it taut.

"Pull!" Clif shouted again.

The crew shifted their weight, but no tension pulled back against them this time. They toppled over backward in a heap as the vine snapped. The man on the other end thrashed as he desperately tried to scramble from the hole, only to sink further.

Clif climbed to his feet, expecting to see an empty pit of quicksand. Instead, Carolina stretched over it, her hand clutching tight to the man's arm. "I still have him."

Clif grabbed hold of his sister's legs before she was dragged into the pit, too. Henrietta rushed to help. Mr. Johnson hurried forward and grabbed hold of her, too, and together, they tugged her back while she, red-faced with effort, struggled to keep hold of the man's wrist.

She groaned with effort as they wrenched her body backward. Henrietta let go of her grasp on her sister's hips and leaned forward to grab the man's arm as it came closer. "I've got hold of him, Carolina, let go."

"I can't, you'll fall in."

Several of her crew members grabbed hold of her legs. "They've got hold of me. Let go of him."

Carolina glanced back to check before she released her grip on the man's wrist. Henrietta's shoulders immediately pulled from the tension, but she kept a firm hold while they dragged her back.

Within a quarter of an hour, they had freed the man. Everyone sat exhausted on the ground for several minutes, nursing their sore muscles and wiping sweat from their foreheads and necks.

"Please tell me there will be no more of that," Henrietta said to Stargazer.

"I told you she's angry and wants payment."

Henrietta climbed to her feet with a shake of her head. "Too bad. She's going to remain angry. Now, get us off this island."

After another moment of rest, they moved forward, exercising extreme caution and testing open areas with a stick before crossing them.

The sun had already set when they reached the beach and slogged into the boats to row back to the waiting ships.

"We should sail tomorrow morning," Clif said as he paced in Henrietta's cabin.

"Agreed," Henrietta answered as she studied the map piece. "The crew will need a long rest after that island."

"Thank goodness we made it off with everyone alive," Carolina said. "I hope fetching the next piece will not be as taxing."

"It will be more so," Clif answered, staring out the window at the night sky.

Carolina's features blanched.

"It is with a pirate enemy," Henrietta explained. "Not another island like this."

Carolina nodded at her in understanding. "Perhaps a trade. Don't pirates trade?"

"This one would only accept my head on a platter for the item, nothing less."

"Oh, dear," Carolina murmured with a frown.

"Yes. It will be quite a treacherous retrieval if he has any inkling that I am the one behind this."

"Perhaps it is best if you stay away and allow us women to handle the matter. We may have much better luck."

"While I have no desire to set foot in his domain, I know him better than anyone. I will be able to detect where he keeps the item. And I am quite skilled at...entering locked places."

Carolina's brow wrinkled at his statement, but she chose not to press the matter.

"Fine, then we shall both go. Carolina, you will remain aboard. There is nothing you should see on that island."

She puckered her lips but nodded. "All right."

"Then we have our plan. We'll take another group, perhaps Abby and Johnson, with us and retrieve the last piece of the map. How long will it take to reach his stronghold?"

"We should arrive tomorrow evening, which will be perfect for sneaking ashore and doing a little thievery."

Henrietta studied her brother, noting the gleam in his eye. "Admit it. You are thrilled to be doing this."

"I will be thrilled when we are finished."

She shook her head. "No, you enjoy the challenge. You are quite looking forward to robbing another pirate who hates you."

"I am quite looking forward to being alive at the end of it, too."

"Perhaps if Henrietta asked for the trade?" Carolina suggested.

Clif shook his head. "I'm quite certain he will not trade. And more than a little worried about what he may try to do instead."

Henrietta shrugged as she kicked her boots up on her desk. "I'm certain I can handle whatever he throws my way."

"That's not what I meant," Clif said. "If he should learn who you are...that we are related...well, I worry we'll have another Tortuga on our hands."

"Tortuga?" Carolina questioned.

Henrietta studied the map piece in her lap. "It's a pirate town."

"I don't believe she was asking what it was, but rather what happened there."

"None of your concern. Suffice it to say that we normally find ourselves in hot water whilst there," Henrietta answered, never lifting her gaze.

Carolina's eyebrows pinched further together. "I think it is my concern. I am sailing aboard this vessel. I have the right to know what we are sailing toward."

"You will know what I tell you," Henrietta answered.

"That's unfair!" Carolina said as she balled her fists and leapt to her feet.

Henrietta shot her a surprised glance. "Are you joking? I am not Mother who will bend to your whim because you throw a tantrum."

Carolina poked a finger at her older sister. "You threw most of the tantrums, not me."

"Well, now the shoe is on the other foot."

"She deserves to know," Clif interjected. "It is the reason we went to Hideaway Bay."

Henrietta sighed as she tossed the map piece onto her desk and swung her feet to the floor. "Fine. There was an incident with another pirate. It did not go well. We left and came to warn you since he threatened your life. There. Done."

"That's no explanation."

Henrietta rolled her eyes as Clif stepped in to explain. "I ended the life of an enemy pirate, and his son took exception. He has been on a mission to ruin me since. It is the reason Henrietta and I disappeared."

Carolina eyed her brother. "And he has threatened you again?"

"He nearly killed Ri."

Carolina's features crumpled, and she flicked her gaze to her sister. "What?"

"He exaggerates. We had the situation well in hand."

"You nearly swung, Ri," Clif answered, heat entering his voice as well as concern.

"I trusted your aim," she shot back.

"While my aim is enviable, it is hardly the matter at hand. These men should not be taken lightly."

"I am not taking them lightly, but this is part of the lifestyle. I am not fooling myself into believing what we do is not dangerous."

"Then you should face the fact that this could be extremely dangerous on the island."

Henrietta bobbed her head. "Then we should take care. We'll spend the evening planning, sail in the morning, and raid the island tomorrow night under the cover of darkness. Where do you suppose he keeps it?"

Clif sucked in a deep breath, flicking his gaze out the window again. "Unfortunately, close to him. I am fairly certain he keeps it on his person at all times."

Henrietta screwed up her face. "Are you certain? He carries the map around with him?"

"I believe so. We must find his chambers, wait until he is asleep, and attempt to steal it from him whilst he slumbers."

"That is the worst plan I've ever heard," Carolina said.

"And what do you propose?" Henrietta asked, her eyebrows raised high.

"Something that will allow us access to him without him slitting our throats."

"First," Clif said with a wave of his hand in the air, "you are not part of this. You will have no access to him whatsoever. Second, what plan would that be?"

"Perhaps someone should ensure he drinks quite a bit. Or give him some sort of sleeping draught."

Henrietta knitted her brows. "How do you propose we get close enough to do that?"

Color rose into Carolina's cheeks as she outlined her plan. "I assume this…pirate…enjoys the company of many women?"

"Certainly," Clif said. "He is well known for enjoying the company of many women."

"We are on a ship filled with women. Perhaps one of them could slip into his midst and drug his drink. Would he even know she is unfamiliar?"

Henrietta tugged back one corner of her lips. "Interesting. Yes, I think that could be a very good approach."

"Are you insane? We should not push one of the female crew members to expose themselves, possibly quite literally, to this man."

"No one is exposing anything. I will do it myself." Henrietta lifted her chin.

"You're mad. You are incapable of putting up with what he may do to you. You will kill him or end up killed yourself."

Henrietta wrinkled her forehead. "I will not."

Clif arched an eyebrow. "Ri, when a drunken man slurs a compliment in your direction, you draw your sword. You cannot stand to be treated as a harlot."

"If the situation calls for me to play a role…" She lifted one shoulder in the air.

"Oh?" Clif strode across the room and kicked open a trunk. He drew his sword, used the tip to catch a dress from the container, and waved it in the air. "And you are fine donning this? Which you hate?"

"Surely, he would not object to a woman in pants."

"You may be surprised. This man may object to a woman in clothes."

"I will do it," Carolina said.

Both siblings swung their gaze to her before Henrietta chuckled as Clif groused, "You will do no such thing."

"I can do it. I am used to abusive men. I would not bat an eyelash."

"I will not have that man help himself to any bit of you that he feels is appropriate."

Carolina shook her head. "I know how to handle myself. I am not an idiot. I have lived for many years with an abusive man. I know how to be small. I know how to not call attention to myself. I can do it."

Clif shot a glance to Henrietta. "Would you like to talk her out of this?"

Henrietta eyed her younger sister, who firmly stood her ground. "No. While I understand the urge to stop any harm from coming to Carolina, she is making an informed choice. She knows the dangers, and she wishes to continue. I support her decision."

"Support her…" Clif heaved a sigh, sliding his eyes closed to gather himself before he opened them to speak again. "This is not a women's issue. There is no sisterly support needed here. What is needed is a firm hand to stop her from doing something dangerous."

"Stop her from doing something dangerous? I thought you were open-minded about women's rights."

"I was… I am. This is not about her rights, it's about her safety."

Carolina approached her brother and laid a hand on his shoulder. "Clif, I am perfectly safe. But Henrietta is correct. You cannot and should not protect me from the world. I am a grown woman. Besides, you didn't stop Henrietta from becoming a pirate."

"There isn't any stopping Ri from doing whatever she wants."

Henrietta smirked as she crossed her arms. "It's true."

"I want to be like her. I want to make my way. Do my things."

"Now is the worst time to strike out, Carolina."

"Now is the best time. I can do this. I can prove useful."

"If this is about earning your keep on the ship, I'm certain Ri can give you a job."

Carolina shook her head. "It's not. It's about doing what I can to help and be a part of this."

Clif let his gaze sink to the ground as he sighed. "Fine. I suppose I cannot stop you. And with both of you against me, you'll sneak off and do it alone."

"I'm starting to worry. I've run out of ways to surprise you," Henrietta said.

"I'm certain you'll think of something," Clif answered dryly. "Now, I suppose we should all get some sleep before we sail tomorrow."

"Clif," Carolina said before he stepped away, "please don't be angry."

Clif offered her a warm smile. "I'm not. Merely disappointed that neither sister seems to need my protection anymore."

She grinned at him before she kissed his cheek.

"I'll walk you out," Henrietta said, slipping her arm through his and tugging him toward the door.

Once outside, she said, "You shouldn't be disappointed. You should be proud. We no longer need you because of what you've done for us. And now we merely want to be around you because we like you."

"I suppose that's a good thing," he said. "But we must ensure nothing happens to her. She is striking out because she is away from James for the first time. She may have bitten off more than she can chew."

"And she may be the perfect person for the job."

"I will trust your judgment on that. Until tomorrow, sleep well."

They said their goodnights, and Ri returned to the cabin,

finding Carolina already soundly asleep. She tossed and turned most of the night as she planned the assault on the enemy pirate's island. The sun crested the horizon, and she rose, bleary-eyed, to begin the long day of sailing.

Trailing *The Henton* on the port side, they sailed toward the rising sun. They enjoyed an easy journey toward the pirate's stronghold with calm waters and a good wind, arriving as the sun set behind them.

Henrietta eyed the island refuge from her spyglass as purples and reds painted the sky.

"What do you think, Captain?" Abby asked.

Henrietta slammed the spyglass closed and handed it to her second-in-command. "I think our smooth sailing was the calm before the storm.

"Your sister's plan is a good one, Captain. It will work."

"I hope so."

"Are we ready?" Carolina asked from behind them.

Henrietta and Abby twisted to face her. "I believe Clif would prefer to wait until the cover of darkness is a bit stronger."

"We risk being unable to enter or get close to him before his meal if we wait that long," Carolina argued.

Henrietta mulled it over before she bobbed her head. "All right. I'll speak with him."

She stalked to the railing and called over to the crew of *The Henton*. Clif strode toward her moments later. "It is too early."

"Tell that to your sister," Henrietta said. "She wishes to reach him during his meal if we cannot gain close access to him after."

"This is extremely dangerous. We could be spotted rowing ashore."

"I suppose we should be careful then," Henrietta said.

Clif shook his head as he sighed, but fifteen minutes later, the small party rowed toward the island, using the jungle cover to hide their approach.

They tugged their skiff ashore on the small beach before carrying it into the cover of the trees and fighting their way through the thick foliage until they spotted the smattering of buildings built high on a cliff.

They climbed up to the large palace in the center.

"This is his place," Clif answered before sucking in a breath after the difficult climb.

Henrietta arched an eyebrow as she stared at the large stone dwelling. "He must have done quite well for himself."

"He did," Clif said. "Stormrider was quite adept at pirating."

"I shall sneak inside and administer the draught, then come to find you."

Clif grabbed her arm. "Wait, we will go with you."

"That would look suspicious. I will find the dining hall and slip this in his drink." Carolina held up a vial of clear liquid before she tugged her arm free.

"Carolina, wait," Johnson said, stepping forward between Clif and her.

"Mr. Johnson?" she asked, her brow crinkling.

His lip bobbed up and down, his features pinching.

Carolina slid her head forward as she awaited the words, but none came. Instead, Johnson lunged forward, grabbing Carolina in his arms, bending her backward, and kissing her full on the lips.

"Oh, you must be joking," Clif said with a sigh.

Henrietta tapped him on the chest. "Let them have their moment."

After what seemed an eternity, Johnson returned her to her feet, both of them gasping for breath. "Be safe, Carolina. Come back to me."

A red-faced Carolina swallowed hard before she nodded. "I plan on it."

She leaned forward and gave him another kiss before she trotted off toward the house.

Clif glared at his first mate.

"I'm sorry, Commodore, I don't know what came over me."

"I can guess," Henrietta said with a wry glance.

Clif flung a hand in the air. "Get hold of yourself, man. We need to focus."

Henrietta crouched behind a bush as she watched her sister disappear into a doorway. "Yes, we do. We must be ready…in case Carolina cannot pull this off."

CHAPTER 19

"**I**'m worried," Johnson answered.

Clif shook his head as he crouched next to Henrietta. "We should not have let her go in there alone. She cannot do this."

"I fear the opposite, Commodore. She is so lovely that he will want her immediately upon seeing her. I worry his attention will be so focused on her that he will forget everything else."

Clif wrinkled his nose as he glanced sideways at the man. "I worry she will be caught and strung up."

"He will never see her put the draught in his drink. He will be fixated on her sparkling eyes, her beautifully formed, supple lips, her rosy cheeks, her ample–"

"That's enough," Clif said with a slice of his hand through the air. "I do not need to hear more. Please focus, Johnson."

"I am focused, Commodore. Focused on keeping Carolina safe."

"Are you…asking for her hand?"

Johnson flicked his gaze sideways to Clif. "I was waiting for a suitable mourning period, but yes, I intend to propose."

Clif sucked in a breath.

"You do not approve," Johnson answered, lowering his eyes. "May I ask why?"

"I...do not object," Clif said with a roll of his eyes. "I only..."

He puckered his lips and shook his head before he wagged a finger at his first mate. "If you should ever harm her..."

"I wouldn't think of it, Commodore. I have more respect for her and you to do anything. The fact that you would think–"

"I don't think it, Johnson," Clif said, waving his hand, "I just...she's my baby sister, man. I have to say those things. It's my role as her brother. I want nothing but happiness for her. And if you can provide that, I can't think of a better man for my sister to spend her life with."

Johnson offered him a warm smile and extended his hand for a shake. "I suppose we will be brothers."

Clif accepted it, pulling the man into an embrace. "We already are. Now, we will also be brothers-in-law."

He leaned back and gave the man another finger wag. "Just don't get yourself killed. I do not wish my sister to be a young widow."

"I am always the more cautious of us." Johnson cracked a smile.

"Well, with that squared away, I suppose we should discuss our next moves, shouldn't we, Ri?" Clif twisted to face his older sister, his smile dissolving into a confused frown. "Ri?"

He pushed a limb aside as though he'd find his sister hiding behind it before he snapped a shocked glance at Johnson. "Where the devil is Ri?"

* * *

Henrietta rolled her eyes at the bickering men. They acted as though Carolina had no mind of her own in the matter.

Yet, she supposed Clif needed to come to terms with the idea that his first mate would soon become his brother-in-law.

Mr. Johnson brought up a good point, though. Carolina was entering the viper's den. What if he took too much notice of her? What if the draught did not work, or she could not get close enough to slip it into his drink?

The two men continued to babble next to each other. She considered interjecting but decided against it. Let them have out whatever they needed to; she would handle the matter herself.

With a huff, she rose, skirted the bush, and strode toward the stronghold. She'd provide her sister the backup she would need in there was any trouble.

She reached the door Carolina had disappeared through moments ago and slipped inside. After waiting a few moments for her eyes to adjust to the dim light, she followed the scent of food down the long hall.

A kitchen spread out in front of her as she peered through the doorway. Women bustled around inside preparing food. She searched among them for her sister but did not find her.

She must have already gone up to the dining room. Henrietta lowered the brim of her hat and scurried across the kitchen.

When she had nearly reached the exit, a voice shouted, "Hey, you!"

Henrietta froze for a millisecond before she took another step forward. Perhaps the voice wasn't meant for her.

"Yes, you in the feathered hat."

Her heart dropped. She'd been spotted. She hoped that wouldn't spell trouble for her sister.

* * *

Clif rose to stand, scouring the area. "She was just here. Where could she have gone?"

"Captain?" Johnson hissed into the trees surrounding them. "Captain, where are you?"

Clif pushed aside a few bits of foliage before his eyes settled on the sprawling house before him. "Oh, tell me she didn't."

"Didn't what, Commodore?"

"She went inside. Probably to give backup to Carolina after our discussion. I was so distracted by your...liaisons with Carolina I wasn't paying attention."

"Do you think she'd be that foolish?"

Clif pushed forward past the bush. "I don't think it, I know it. Whilst we argued, she went inside in case something happened. Now, they are both in danger."

Johnson hurried to catch up with Clif as he thundered toward the house. "Commodore, this may make things worse."

"And it may save their lives. I will not leave them inside alone. We go in, too."

"Wait," Johnson said, stepping into Clif's path and holding a hand up to stop him. "We should not do this. I do not wish the women to be angered with us if we ruin their plan. Perhaps we should wait at least an hour until night has fallen. Then we enter."

Clif swallowed hard, staring at the house again. "They may be in trouble now."

"I doubt he would kill them immediately. However, we should allow the plan to work. We don't know it has failed."

Clif wrinkled his nose as his mind pushed through the scenarios. It landed on one where they did not retrieve the map piece, and Ri berated him for ruining her perfect idea.

With a sigh, he retreated to the jungle to wait. He gazed at the house, trying to see inside through the walls. He hated that his sisters roamed the halls that close from his mortal enemy.

He desperately hoped hiding behind the bushes was not a mistake that cost either of his siblings their lives.

* * *

Heat prickled Henrietta's skin, and the hairs stood up on the back of her neck. She spun slowly to face the accusing voice behind her.

Before she could question anything, a stout woman shoved a tray into her hands. "Don't go up empty-handed. Take this before Stormrider has my arse again about being late with his first course." The woman glanced up and down Henrietta's form before she clicked her tongue. "Strange taste in women, that one."

Henrietta stared down at the silver tray before she accepted it and plastered a smile onto her face. With an obedient nod, she spun and hurried from the kitchen, searching for a set of stairs.

When she found them, she followed behind another woman hurrying up with a goblet of something in her hands.

"Hurry up," she barked at Henrietta before she froze on the stairs.

Henrietta nearly plowed into her before she bounced back a step, struggling to hold the tray straight. "What are you doing? Keep going. I must get this food to Stormrider before it's cold!"

"Dressed like that?" the girl retorted.

Henrietta narrowed her eyes at the blonde. "And what is that supposed to mean?"

"It's your first night, isn't it?"

Henrietta lifted her chin. No sense in lying. "Yes."

The girl's features softened, and she bobbed her head up and down. "I figured as much." She dumped the goblet on the edge of Henrietta's tray before she tugged her shirt open further and lowered it. "There, that ought to do, though you should wear something more revealing next time. He doesn't like playing with boys, you know? And you look too close to one of them."

Henrietta stared down at her exposed cleavage for a moment before she mustered a wrinkled-nose half-smile. "Thanks."

"Oh, you're welcome," the girl answered as she retrieved the goblet. "Now, come along."

They climbed a few more stairs while the blonde girl chattered on. "Don't worry, love, you'll get the hang of it. And don't feel too bad if he doesn't pick you the first night you're here. Sometimes, he likes to see how the girls behave before he takes them to his special place."

"I'll bet," Henrietta said, swallowing the bile creeping up her throat.

"Oh, but with a face like yours, I'm certain you'll get a turn."

It took all in her not to roll her eyes. "How thrilling."

The girl giggled, her curls bouncing up and down as she shot an amused glance over her shoulder at Henrietta and nodded.

What an insipid fool.

They strode into the dining hall. Henrietta's eyes widened as she scanned the long table, overflowing with food, men, scantily clad women, and a tiger chained to the wall that pulled apart a cooked chicken.

"Amazing, isn't it? Now, hurry; he doesn't like his special food coming late."

Henrietta followed the woman as she swept past the long table. A few men reached out to slap her behind or pinch it.

"Oh, what have we got here? Playing pirate?" a man said as she passed.

Another took a gander at her before he winked. "I don't mind, but I'd prefer a short skirt to the trousers. You've gone too far, sweetheart."

Henrietta bristled at the statement, ready to drop the tray and draw her sword, but held back.

"I prefer them with no skirt at all," another man jested before laughter burst out at the table.

She searched the crowd for her sister. Had Carolina been accosted by one of the other drunken sailors around Stormrider's table?

They reached the midpoint, and she focused on the dark-haired man at the head of the table. He slumped in his chair with one leg dangling over the arm. A woman poured wine directly into his open mouth before he waved a hand in the air, and she stopped.

Henrietta wondered if the wine had already been drugged, but she hadn't yet spotted Carolina. Where was her sister?

He clapped his hands, and another woman scurried closer. She flicked a lock of blonde hair over her shoulder before she fed him a peeled grape.

Henrietta breathed a sigh of relief as she recognized her sister. Had she been able to use the sleeping draught, or was she stuck on grape duty? She'd soon find out.

With her attention focused on Carolina, she failed to see Stormrider set his sights on her. He shoved her sister aside, swung his leg forward, and leaned toward her.

"It's about bloody time. What have I told that hag about being late with my food?"

Henrietta tried to catch Carolina's eyes to determine how

far along their plan was, but Stormrider grabbed her wrist and tugged her forward before she could.

She stumbled closer to him, nearly dropping the tray.

"Are you simple, girl? Do you not know your focus should be on attending to my needs?"

Henrietta forced her expression to remain as neutral as possible before she said, "Sorry. It's my first night."

"Ohhhh, is it?" he answered his grasp on her wrist tight enough to hurt. "Well, I suppose you must be broken in properly."

Another girl relieved her of the tray and set it on the table before him. He ignored it, tugging Henrietta closer until she lay over his knee.

"What do you say, men? Does she need to be schooled in our ways?"

A cheer resounded through the group. Henrietta reached for her pistol. She would not be treated like a plaything by anyone.

Before she could tug it loose, wine drenched her. In the next second, she found herself dumped on the floor.

"You fool!" Stormrider shouted, leaping to his feet. He brushed droplets of liquid from his red-stained shirt.

"I am sorry, sir. I-I tripped," Carolina stammered, offering him an apologetic glance.

Stormrider's features turned stony, indicating his nonacceptance of her attempt at atonement. He lunged forward and grabbed her by her hair, tugging her closer to him. "You soaked me with this swill. It is not even our best wine, and I stink of it."

Carolina groaned as her head tugged backward from his iron grip. "I am so very sorry. I shall clean the shirt and fetch another drink for you."

"You will do more than that to appease me." He offered

her a vicious grin as he dragged her away from the table amid shouts from his fellow pirates.

Carolina stumbled next to him as Henrietta scrambled to her feet and freed her pistol. "Don't move, or I will shoot you."

The man whipped around and glared at Henrietta before he burst into laughter. He shoved Carolina to the side, and she stumbled and fell to her knees.

"Which one of you buggers put her up to this?" He scanned the crowd of men. "Was it you, Ironwood?"

He eyed a man halfway down the table before he pointed a finger at another. "Or you, Marlow?"

The man held up his hands in front of him as he chuckled.

"Well, someone must have. This fine young lady didn't dress up as a pirate out of her mind."

"I'm not dressed up, you fool. I am a pirate," Henrietta growled.

The statement brought Stormrider an even louder laugh. He doubled over and slapped his thighs before he leaned back and grabbed his belly as he shook with laughter.

"Did you hear that, men? She's a pirate."

Another round of chuckles escaped them. Stormrider approached her, and Henrietta cocked her pistol, her nose wrinkling as she stood her ground.

"That's a solemn expression. I prefer my women pleasant-looking."

"Sorry to disappoint, but as I've already explained, I am not your woman. Neither is she." She jutted her chin toward her sister.

"No!" Carolina shouted.

Stormrider puckered his lips, offering Henrietta an amused glance. "I see; you like to play games." He yanked the gun from her hands and tossed it across the room before he tugged Henrietta closer to him and planted a rough kiss on her lips. "So do I."

She groaned as she struggled to pull away from him. "Don't you touch me?"

He lifted her off her feet and carried her to the door. "I plan to do more than that."

Cheers and hoots rose from the crowd as Henrietta kicked her feet, trying to free herself from the man's grasp. "Let go of me, you brute."

"I plan to once we reach the confines of my chambers."

She kicked and flailed until he set her on her feet. Before she could speak again, he grabbed her and tossed her over his shoulder.

With a pat on her rear, he continued down the hall. "You're a feisty one. I do so enjoy that."

She pounded against his back with her fists, but he remained unfazed. He kicked open a set of double doors before he stalked across the room and tossed her onto his messy bed.

She kicked her feet to scramble backward away from his as he tugged off his vest and tossed it aside. "You stay away from me."

He climbed onto the bed next to her.

Henrietta rolled over the edge and stood, tugging her sword from its sheath. She held it at his chin, raising her own. "I said stay away from me."

The man narrowed his eyes at her. "And I said I prefer my women pleasant. Now, this act has gone too far. I insist you cease this show at once and join me in my bed."

"I think not. I already told you I am not here to warm your bed but for something else entirely. I am no tramp, I am a pirate."

Stormrider's forehead wrinkled as he stared at the blade. "A pirate? You're being serious."

"Yes, I am. And I demand what I came for before I leave, or I will kill you to find it."

He ducked away from the blade and climbed from the bed. "And what is it that you came to find?"

"Your piece of the map to the Gemstone Islands."

Surprise shown on his face as he studied Henrietta. He stalked across the room to a dresser and tugged it open. When he twisted to face her again, he shoved a cocked pistol toward her and uttered one word, "No."

CHAPTER 20

*H*enrietta swallowed hard as she stared down the barrel of the gun pointed at her. Her sword would do her little good against that weapon, and she'd lost her pistol after drawing it in the dining hall.

She raised her chin. If it was her time, it was her time. She would not submit to him no matter what. Her eyes slowly scanned the room in search of a way out of the situation.

"You will not find an escape. But before I kill you, I'd like to know more. What led you to me?"

Henrietta pressed her lips together, refusing to answer the question.

"Nothing to say?"

"No. Nothing. I have my sources. I will not reveal them."

"That would be foolish. You could buy yourself some time if you did. You may even walk away with your life."

"Suddenly, you don't wish to kill me?"

He flicked his eyebrows up. "I could be persuaded."

"Why? What has changed?"

He tugged one corner of his lips back. "You intrigue me. A

female pirate. I imagine you are quite popular among the rest of the crew."

Henrietta flexed her jaw, her irritation building. "I have an all-female crew."

"You have? Are you a captain?"

"Yes. Captain of the *Grandmistress.*" She lifted her chin again.

He puckered his lips, letting the pistol fall back to rest against his shoulder. "Hmm, interesting. And this female crew serves you well?"

"They serve me better than the drunkards in your dining hall who couldn't raise a sheet to get your ship out of port at the moment."

Stormrider chuckled at the comment. "Those men have earned their time off."

"Have they? Well, my girls haven't. But they soon will if I can get what I came for. I aim to be the pirate who finds these islands."

"Do you? An ambitious goal, though a foolish one."

"Is it? Then give me the map and let me go along my way. If what you say is true, this will be the last you see of me."

He paced in front of her as he shook his head. "My apologies, dear lady, but I cannot do that."

"Why not?" Henrietta eyed his motions, wondering if she could strike with him when he was not on his guard.

"It is my most prized possession. I cannot simply let you walk out of here with it."

"Why is it so valuable to you? If this is impossible to reach, it's worthless, isn't it?"

"Difficult is not impossible. And it would be quite a haul. I may choose to go for it myself one day."

Henrietta arched an eyebrow, growing weary of the conversation. He was taunting her, and she disliked being toyed with. "Really? Well, you'll find that impossible."

He slid his gaze sideways to her. "Why?"

"Because I have the other half of the map. And I will not give it to you."

Stormrider pressed his lips together as he rubbed the stubble on his cheek. "Well, I suppose then, we are at an impasse."

"Seems so," Henrietta answered.

"Seems I'll need to kill you, then." He leveled his weapon at her again.

Henrietta's heart skipped a beat as she hoped she could talk or fight her way out of this situation. Before she could react, the doors burst open.

Carolina's blonde hair streaked behind her as she dashed into the room. With shaking hands, she thrust the pistol forward toward Stormrider. "Do not do anything, or I will shoot."

Stormrider swung his gun toward her before he raised his eyebrows. "I suppose this is another of your crew."

"Yes," Henrietta started when Carolina gave her head a vehement shake.

"No, I am her sister. And I will shoot if you threaten her again."

"Sister?" Stormrider asked, his face showing his surprise. "I never would have guessed. You are quite different, aren't you?"

"In some ways, yes," Henrietta answered. "But make no mistake, we are both deadly. And now you are outnumbered."

Stormrider flicked his gaze back and forth between the two women. "I doubt that."

Henrietta scoffed. "Can't you count?"

"I can count just fine. I see two women. Both frightened, one whose fear will ensure she misses her shot."

"That's not true," Henrietta said. "And even if she misses, which is unlikely, I will not."

"But you have no pistol. And if she fires at me, I will kill her faster than you can kill me. So, again, I say, it looks as though I still hold the advantage."

"You are a fool," Henrietta growled as she raised her sword.

He seemed unfazed by the action, giving her a casual shrug in response. "I disagree. Now, perhaps we could discuss some...alternate ways for you and your sister to bargain for your lives."

Henrietta narrowed her eyes. "Never."

"I suppose, then, I will simply have to kill you outright. It's a shame. We could have had so much fun together."

"You want to talk compromises?" Henrietta asked, seizing an opportunity to free herself and her sister. "Perhaps you can give me the map piece in exchange for a cut of the find."

Stormrider resumed pacing, rubbing his temple with the barrel of his weapon. "Hmmm, tempting, but no."

"Why not?"

"I'd rather keep my map piece than send a simpleton in search of such a prize."

Henrietta stamped a foot against the floorboards, heat rising into her cheeks. "I am no fool! I have many conquests under my belt."

"Do you? Tell me, darling, have you successfully learned to sail out of a port?"

Henrietta let out a shriek. "I have done much more than that. Ask Blackheart. Are you familiar with him?"

"I am." He stuck his leg against a chest in the room and leaned his elbow against it. "Have you warmed his bed?"

"Keep talking that way, and I will be certain to make your death painful."

Stormrider tugged his lips back into a devilish grin. "So, you have."

"I have not. But I have disabled his ship. His main mast crumpled like a delicate lady on a summer day."

Stormrider threw his head back with a loud laugh. "And this was at your hands?"

"Yes, it was."

"You're trying to tell me that Blackheart engaged you at sea, and you bested him?"

Henrietta swallowed hard as she considered her answer.

Before she could answer, Carolina spoke. "No, we snuck behind him as he engaged my brother's ship and attacked to end the battle decisively."

"Is that so? And your brother, is he a pirate, too?"

"No," Henrietta said quickly. "He is a merchant. Blackheart attacked his vessel, and I defended it."

"Oh? Your brother is a merchant, and you are a pirate? I find that hard to believe."

"Why?"

"You seem to be on opposite ends of the law. Does your brother approve of this way of life?"

Henrietta frowned as she worked out an answer in her head. How could she talk her way out of this? Stormrider clearly had his suspicions about the bogus story, and she needed every advantage she could get.

"Yes, he does. She's lying. He's a pirate, too. And one of the best." Carolina lifted her chin, her hands steadying as she pushed the gun forward again.

"Let me guess, your brother is Blackheart, and you broke his main mast in a bit of family fun." Stormrider offered Henrietta an amused smile.

"My brother is far better a pirate than Blackheart," Carolina spat.

"And who is your brother?" Stormrider asked. "If he is such a wonderful pirate, I should know his name."

"I'm sure you do, it's—"

"Nothing," Henrietta interrupted. "He's no one. She is lying. Merely trying to buy time."

Carolina screwed up her face as she flicked her gaze to her sister. "Henrietta! That's not true."

"Yes, it is," Henrietta said without taking her eyes from Stormrider. "He is a merchant. He disapproves of my line, but he is my brother. Do you have a sibling?"

"I had one brother."

"Then you should understand," Henrietta said.

"I do not," Stormrider said simply. "I killed my brother."

Henrietta's stomach dropped. The man clearly had no scruples. And his weapon was pointed at her.

"Why? What did he do to deserve that?" Carolina asked.

"He protested to my being a pirate. So, I killed him. It no longer seems to bother him." Stormrider chuckled before he thrust his gun forward toward Henrietta. "Now, wench, tell me who your brother is."

Henrietta rallied, steeling her nerves. "I told you. He is a merchant. My sister is lying. Merely trying to talk her way out of the situation."

"I don't believe that!" he shouted before swinging his gun toward Carolina. "And if you do not give me his name, I will begin with a bullet to her leg, then her other, then her arm. You get the idea. How many bullets will she take before you break or she dies? Do you wish to find that out?"

Henrietta's pulse raced, but she forced herself to be calm. The man appeared to be volatile. In one instant, he was intrigued, and in the next, riled. Perhaps she could shift his mood again.

"I prefer to go back to discussing ways in which we can come to a compromise. Only moments ago, you offered one.

"The time for that is over. Your lies have changed my mind. I prefer now to be rid of you."

Henrietta sheathed her sword and started across the room. "Well, then, we shall be out of your hair. Sorry for the interruption."

A bullet whizzed past her, lodging itself in the wall across the room. She snapped her gaze to the smoking pistol still pointed in her direction.

"Move again, and the next one will not miss its mark."

She swallowed hard. "So, you mean to kill us then?"

"I do. I need to determine which of you I prefer to kill first." He narrowed his eyes as he slid his gaze between them. He waved the gun at Carolina first. "You are very pretty. Perhaps I should off your sister and keep you for my pleasure before I end your life."

A tear rolled down her cheek, and her lower lip trembled.

"No," Henrietta shouted. "Let her go. She is not a member of my crew. Merely my sister who has sailed with me for a short time."

"If she sails with you, she is a part of your crew."

"No," she said with a shake of her head, "she...was alone. Her husband passed, and she could not stay alone. She should not be punished for my actions."

"Yet, here she is in my house helping you. You sent her here."

"No," Henrietta lied. "She followed me. I had no idea she came. Let her go. Keep me."

Stormrider eyed her from head to toe with a flick of his eyebrows. "Truthfully, you were my choice. She is pretty. But you...you are beautiful. And most intriguing. I shall look forward to breaking that spirit."

Henrietta raised her chin. She would endure whatever she had to at his hands to save her sister.

"But I cannot allow her to simply leave. So, I will have to kill her first." Stormrider aimed his weapon.

Henrietta cried out and shoved her sister aside as the weapon fired. Carolina fell sideways, her blonde hair flying in the wind. Henrietta stumbled into her sister's former position as the bullet barreled across the space.

A second later, it struck its mark. Henrietta stood straight as she searched the wall for the hole. Something trickled down the skin of her abdomen.

She twisted to stare down at her side, pressing a hand against it. When she pulled it away, blood-tinged her fingertips. He'd shot her. And the world began to blacken at the edges of her vision.

lif watched as darkness descended over the island. His lower lip ached from chewing it incessantly since he'd learned Henrietta had disappeared, following his younger sister into his enemy's camp.

He rose to stand with a shake of his head. "I can take no more. We must go inside."

"I am growing concerned, too, Commodore. Perhaps the passage of time has seemed slower to us than it is, but it seems that Carolina should have delivered the draught by now."

Clif eyed the glowing windows. "We should not enter where they did."

"No, two men bursting through that door may set off trouble. I brought a rope. We can climb to the balcony and enter." Johnson pointed at a stone structure on the second story of the sprawling house.

"Wonderful idea, Johnson. Let's not dally." Clif strode toward the house as he spoke, with Johnson hurrying behind him.

They reached it quickly and tossed a rope attached to a

small grappling hook onto the stone railing. Clif shimmied up the rope first.

He swung his leg over as Johnson climbed behind him. Lights glowed from the French doors across the ample outdoor space. Clif eyed them, wondering if they could enter or if someone lurked inside the room.

He crept forward as Johnson swung onto the balcony and hurried to follow. "Is it clear, Commodore?"

"I do not know yet." Shadows shifted inside the room, indicating a presence inside. Clif clicked his tongue. "Looks like we are out of luck."

"Wonder who it is? Perhaps a woman who can be easily overpowered."

Clif stepped out of the light glowing onto the balcony and into the shadows before he crept toward the room. "Let us hope so. We need a way into this place. I am more than uncomfortable with my sisters being in there."

He pressed himself against the wall and tugged his pistol from its holster.

"And then we need to find them quickly."

Clif nodded at his first mate. "Yes. To hell with the map piece."

"You'll need more than luck to convince the Captain to give up on this."

"Do not remind me," Clif said as he leaned over to peer through the glass in the door. "Ri will not be easy to—"

"Convince is the word you're looking for, though others could be used," Johnson said with a chuckle.

Clif held up a hand to silence him. His heart skipped a beat, and for the first time as a pirate, his knees went weak. "We have a large problem, Mr. Johnson."

Johnson craned his neck around Clif's shoulder to peer into the room.

Henrietta and Carolina stood in the room with Stormrider. Carolina pointed a pistol at him while he aimed one back at her. The trio exchanged words they couldn't hear.

Clif reached for the door, intending to burst inside and fire at his enemy, but before he could, one of the pistols went off.

Clif's stomach dropped, and his mind whirled as his trembling hand slipped from the knob. He shouldered through the door into the chaos. Another shot was fired.

Johnson raced in behind Clif, weapon drawn. Stormrider gasped out a breath as he clutched his stomach. When he pulled his hands away, blood covered them.

He snapped his surprised gaze toward the balcony, his shocked features twisting angrily. "Jack…"

Clif studied his wound briefly before flicking his gaze across the room. Carolina sat on the floor with a smoking pistol still clutched in her trembling hands. Henrietta lay next to her, blood soaking her shirt.

Johnson pushed past Clif and hurried to the women as the heat rose in Clif's face. He lunged at the wounded pirate and wrapped his hands around his neck.

"You bastard. You shot my sister."

"Sister," the man slurred, blood trickling from his lips.

"Yes, they are both my sisters. And now I'll see you take your last breaths for harming them."

Stormrider grasped for his sword, but Clif increased his pressure on the man's windpipe, crushing it. His eyes rolled back in his head as his body went limp.

Clif let the body slump to the floor before he lifted his gaze to the scene across the room.

Henrietta cried out in pain, reviving when Johnson pressed a hand to her wound. Clif raced to her side. "Ri…"

She gritted her teeth as she smacked Johnson's arm. "Stop pressing it, it hurts."

"I must stop the bleeding, Captain."

Carolina rummaged through the drawers, found a shirt, and hurried to her sister to stop the bleeding. "Here, use this."

She dropped to her knees and shoved Johnson's hands aside before she pressed the white blouse against her sister's bloody shirt. "We must move her back to the ship immediately."

"No," Henrietta growled before she let her head thud against the floor. "We must find the map piece."

"Forget the map piece, Ri. You're wounded. It doesn't look good. You are what matters." Clif stroked her forehead.

She slapped his hand away. "Don't tell me you've gone soft, brother. Find that map piece. I shall live."

"Let's be sure of that," Clif answered.

"We can be sure of it after we find the map piece." She struggled to push herself up to sit, groaning as she moved. "It appears I will have to take matters into my own hands."

Clif pushed her down by her shoulders. "Now, Ri..."

"Don't know, Ri, me, go find that map piece. This is a flesh wound."

Clif eyed his first mate, who shrugged.

Carolina flicked her gaze back and forth between them before she clicked her tongue. "Honestly."

She grabbed Johnson's hands and pressed them against Ri's wound, earning another screech of pain before she hurried across the room to the deceased pirate. "It is somewhere on his person, isn't it?"

"Carolina, we should–" Clif started.

"She is not going to leave without this map piece."

"What happened, Carolina? Why did you not administer the draught?"

Carolina checked his pockets before she struggled to roll him over. "I tried, but before I could, Henrietta appeared. He noticed her, which was not a good thing."

"Let me guess, she charged in, guns blazing," Clif said.

Henrietta clenched her teeth, her nostrils flaring as she breathed through her pain. "I did not."

"No. I think he noticed her beauty." The body flopped over, and Carolina breathed out a sigh as she sat back on her haunches before she studied the pool of blood from his wound.

Sweat beaded on Henrietta's brow as she wiggled under the pressure Johnson placed on her abdomen. "He acted most inappropriately, and Carolina spilled the draught-infused wine on him to temper the situation."

"And then?" Clif asked, his brow crinkled.

"He brought me to his bedroom," Henrietta answered, "intending to...break me in. Carolina appeared, and after several rounds of arguing, he decided to kill one of us."

"Me," Carolina said as she searched under the man's bloody shirt.

"I could not let that happen."

Carolina stopped her search and shifted her gaze to her sister. "You took a bullet for me. You continue to save me, Henrietta."

"I will consider us even if you find that map piece."

Carolina huffed out a laugh as she tugged the shirt from his pants. A piece of bloody fabric flopped to the floor. Carolina picked it up and unfolded it. "I found it."

Henrietta tried to push up to sit again, raising her eyebrows as she reached for the discovery. "Give it here."

Clif stepped between them and snatched it from his sister's fingers. "No. We will look at it once we've assessed your wound on the ship."

Henrietta huffed but allowed Johnson to lift her into his arms. "I can walk."

Clif stuffed the map piece into his pocket and motioned for Johnson to hand Henrietta to him. "Give her here. I can withstand the ear-beating I shall receive for carrying her."

"I do not find this amusing." Henrietta winced as Johnson handed her off to Clif.

"Neither do I. My sister is shot. Not even I have managed to be shot in all my pirating days."

"I am pleased to have one up on you. Perhaps I should be the Commodore."

"Very funny," Clif answered.

"Which way shall we go, Commodore?" Johnson asked his arm firmly around Carolina's shoulders. "It may not be wise to take the ladies over the railing."

Henrietta kicked her feet with another groan of pain escaping. "I am no lady. I am a pirate. Take me over the railing."

"But Carolina–" Johnson began when the youngest Nichols cut him off.

"Is capable of escaping that way, too." She raised her eyes to Johnson's face. "With your help, of course."

He smiled down at her as he cupped her face in his hand. "Of course."

Clif heaved a sigh, following behind them onto the balcony with Henrietta still in his arms.

"There is nothing–"

"I know, I know. Johnson and I have already had a lengthy discussion about it."

"And?" Henrietta asked, watching as Johnson helped Carolina climb over the railing and loop the rope around her midriff to lower her down.

Clif eyed the couple across the way, noting his sister's loving stare into Johnson's eyes before he lowered her to the ground. "And it appears we shall have a new brother-in-law soon enough."

"Perhaps you could marry them as a ship's captain," Henrietta teased.

"Do not make the situation worse than it already is. I have

accepted Johnson into the family just barely. Let's not take it further."

She chuckled, wincing as the pain in her belly increased. "Put me down. I can climb down myself."

"I don't think so."

"You cannot lower me down. The rope around my abdomen will be far worse than me climbing."

"Honestly, Ri, what sort of pirate do you think I am? I will hold you in one arm and swing down with the other."

Henrietta wrinkled her nose at her brother. "Just let me climb down."

"I think not." Johnson, already on the ground, tossed the rope up to Clif. With it wrapped around one hand, he climbed onto the stone railing and leapt into the air. The rope pulled taught as he swung away before his feet touched the ground. "There we are."

Henrietta offered him an unimpressed stare. "I could have climbed down myself."

She grumbled as they he kept hold of her, and they hurried away from the house. After thirty minutes of grousing while they crossed to the beach, they arrived at their skivvy and rowed back to their waiting vessels.

A flurry of activity descended on Henrietta as they hauled her aboard. Clif hurried after her. "She is shot. Wounded badly and needs immediate attention."

Abby ripped open her shirt as they laid her on the bed and studied the wound. "Water!"

Clif hurried to retrieve it from the washstand across the cabin, handing it to Abby as Carolina and Johnson entered.

Carolina hovered over Abby's shoulder. "Please tell me how I can help. I am alive because of Henrietta."

"Stand aside for a moment whilst I assess this." Abby splashed the cold water onto Henrietta's abdomen to wash away the blood and study the bullet wound.

Henrietta cried out as the icy water hit her skin. Clif unscrewed the cap of his flask and poured some of the alcohol into her mouth. "Drink this, and it will ease the pain."

"Says the man who was never shot," she said through gritted teeth. "I was fine until Abby splashed that water on me."

Abby stared at the wound's ragged edges before wrapping her fingers around Henrietta's hip and rocking her to the side. "No exit wound."

"What does that mean?" Carolina asked.

"It means the bullet is still inside her," Abby said with a frown.

"Perhaps we should leave it there."

"No. We must remove it and close the wound. But she may bleed inside. And removing the bullet may cause her to lose enough blood to die."

"I have been shot and haven't died yet," Henrietta growled.

"Because the bullet is stopping you from bleeding to death," Abby informed her as she raced to the desk to search the drawers for a knife.

"Then leave the damned bullet where it is," Henrietta said with labored breaths.

"We can't. That's dangerous, too. It could also kill you."

"So, I am doomed either way?"

Abby held up a knife and swiped a lit candle from the desk. She held the blade against the flame, , and slid her eyes sideways to Henrietta. "No, I am going to operate."

CHAPTER 22

"*N*ow, wait just a moment, Abby," Henrietta started, trying to raise herself to her elbows.

"I have done it before," her first mate said.

"Let her help you, Ri," Clif said, stroking his sister's hair.

"Stop that. I am fine. I…" Her voice quivered.

"You must stop moving, Captain. You could do more damage. If the bullet shifts the wrong way…"

Henrietta collapsed backward to lay on the bed.

"Here, take another sip of the rum," Clif said, bringing the flask to her lips.

"That won't matter much, Commodore," Abby said. "She will likely lose consciousness from the pain. But we should give her something to bite on so she does not chew her tongue in half."

"I insist you stop this instant," Henrietta cried.

"I am sorry, Captain, but the bullet must come out."

Johnson hurried across the room, tugging his leather belt from his pants before he thrust it forward. "Bite this."

"What?" Henrietta questioned. "No!"

Clif stuffed it into her mouth and held it firmly. "Go ahead."

Abby glanced at her fellow sailors. "Hold her down firmly. This will not be pleasant."

Carolina swapped positions with her brother as he took hold of Henrietta's shoulders. Johnson threw himself across her legs. Henrietta tried to protest, but with the belt stuffed between her teeth, only muffled noises came out.

Abby blew out a deep breath. "Here we go."

The knife pierced Henrietta's supple skin, and more blood poured from the wound. She shrieked in pain, the noise again dampened by the belt she bit into it. A moment later, her body went limp as she fell unconscious from the pain.

"She's out cold," Clif reported.

Abby bobbed her head up and down as the group let the pressure off their patient. "Keep close. She may come to when I begin to remove the bullet. One mistake on my part..."

Clif lay a hand on her shoulder and squeezed. "Take your time, Abby."

Carolina rubbed her sister's sweaty head as a tear rolled down her cheek. "You must save her."

"I will. I promise. I would never let anything happen to the Captain." Abby stared down at the bloody mess in front of her before she dabbed away the liquid with a cloth and searched for the bullet.

Clif kept a hand on both of his sisters. "Abby is very good at what she does, Carolina."

Carolina bobbed her head up and down as she continued her quiet sobbing. "She saved my life."

"Of course, she did. She loves you despite the animosity she sometimes shows."

"I know," Carolina choked out. "And I love her. It is my

fault she was there. She wanted to protect me. She would not leave me alone. She fought for him to release me and offered to sacrifice herself."

"Well, then she cannot die," Clif said.

Carolina snapped her glassy eyes to him with a questioning glance.

"Ri would not let her last act on Earth be so selfless. She will return to us, demanding we take her to the Gemstone Islands." He grinned down at his sister as he brushed a lock of hair away from her cheek.

She stared at him for a moment, unable to determine if he meant to lighten the mood or was being serious.

"Bullet is out," Abby said with a sigh of relief. "That's half the battle won."

"How does it look? Is she losing too much blood?"

Abby dabbed at the wound again and studied it. "She is bleeding quite a bit. I will need to cauterize the inside before I sew her shut. Hold her steady, this may revive her."

Abby wiped the blood off the blade before she retrieved the candle from the desk and held the knife to its flame. The others braced Henrietta's body in anticipation of the painful fix.

With the blade hot, Abby nodded to them. "First, the inside."

Johnson dabbed the blood away inside, and with a quick motion, Abby pressed the knife against the bleeding vessel inside. Henrietta remained unconscious as the smell of burning flesh filled the air.

"Done," Abby reported as she withdrew the knife's edge, cleaned it, and set it aside. "Now, I will stitch her closed."

Abby retrieved the materials needed to close the wound, threaded her needle, and carefully slid it through the edges of Henrietta's wound.

Sweat beaded on her and her patient's brow as she delicately tugged the skin closed. Carolina dabbed at her sister's forehead while Clif wiped at Abby's.

She finished the work and collapsed backward with a sigh. "Finished. She should be fine now, but we must take care that she does not tear the wound open, particularly inside. She could bleed to death without us even realizing."

"How can we ensure that?" Carolina asked.

"We must keep her quiet and resting."

Clif barked out a laugh. "We have our work cut out for us, then, don't we? Henrietta does not care for rest. She will be running about the ship demanding we set sail for the Gemstone Islands immediately."

"Perhaps we should set sail, Commodore," Johnson said. "It is only a matter of time until Stormrider's people realize what's happened. I do not wish us to be anywhere near his island."

"Very true. Ready the ships; we will sail to–" Clif stopped as he considered it.

"We do not know where," Carolina answered.

Clif pulled the map piece from his pocket and slapped it onto the desk, finding the second piece and matching it up.

"What is the bearing, Commodore?" Johnson asked.

"I remain uncertain. This map is inconclusive."

Johnson stared down at the crudely drawn symbols. "It is coded."

"Yes, and we will need to solve it. Carolina, perhaps you can work on this. We will sail west away from this island, in the hopes that we have a bearing soon."

Carolina nodded as she took a seat at the desk. "I will try, Clif. I was quite good at this when we traveled in the jungle."

"I will ready the *Grandmistress* to sail," Abby said, "and send a crew member in to tend to the Captain."

"I will stay," Clif answered. "Mr. Johnson, I leave *The Henton* in your charge."

"Aye, Captain." Johnson nodded before he and Abby disappeared from the cabin.

Silence filled the space for several moments as Carolina eyed the map. Clif paced the floor, his eyes darting between his older sister and his younger.

She offered him a glance through her eyelashes before settling her focus on her work again. "Are you going to scold me?"

"For?" he asked.

"Henrietta and I had a long discussion about my...interest in Mr. Johnson. She seems to encourage it, yet I know you do not care for it."

"That's not..." Clif heaved a sigh. "I only want you to be happy, Carolina."

"He makes me happy."

"Perhaps you should take your time. You've just suffered–"

"Greatly at my husband's hands," Carolina finished for him. "His death is a relief."

She slid her eyes sideways to her brother. "I will not rush into anything."

"Good. That's all I can ask for."

She studied the map pieces for another moment before she flicked her gaze to him again. "Though we had an immediate connection."

Clif heaved a sigh, letting his head fall back between his shoulder blades. "Carolina–"

A groan from Henrietta drew their attention away from the conversation and to their injured sister. Clif rushed across the floorboards to kneel at his sister's side as she thrashed her head back and forth.

"Ri? Easy, Ri."

Her eyelids fluttered open, and her features pinched.

After retrieving a washbowl and cloth, Carolina joined

her brother at Henrietta's side. She pressed the damp rag against her sister's forehead. "Easy, Henrietta. You've been shot and are still recovering."

"Yes, I know," she snapped. "I fell unconscious when Abby cut me, I did not lose my mind."

Clif offered his sister a sheepish glance and shook his head, trying to tell her silently to allow Henrietta her outburst.

"I thought perhaps you'd blocked out the surgery."

"No, I haven't."

"Well, what you do not know is that you cannot move."

"What?" She huffed as she stared down at her legs. "Has Abby crippled me?"

Carolina wet the rag again and pressed it against her sister's skin as she chuckled. "No, no, nothing like that. But she had to dig the bullet out and cauterize the wound inside, then sew you shut. She does not wish her lovely work to be fouled up with your jumping about.

Carolina wrung out the cloth again and dabbed it across Henrietta's forehead. Henrietta shoved it away. "Stop that."

"I'm trying to soothe your pain."

"You're making it worse," Henrietta answered. "I'm less soothed by all this fussing."

Carolina dumped the cloth in the bowl and set it on the desk while Henrietta struggled to sit up.

"No, no," Clif said, holding her shoulders down. "You mustn't. Not until you've rested more."

"I do not need rest. I am perfectly fine."

"Ri, do not put on a brave face, as it may cost your life."

Henrietta glared at him. "Let go."

"I will not. And I will have you know there is no reason to get out of this bed. We have everything under control."

"Then we are sailing for the gemstone islands?"

"Y-y-yes," Clif stammered. "In a way."

"In a way? What does that mean?"

"The map is coded. We have not broken the code yet," Carolina said, "though we are trying. For now, we sail west away from the island."

Henrietta heaved a sigh. "Give me the map pieces."

"Ri…"

"I can use my eyes, Clif," she answered. "Though I would prefer to sit up."

"I think we should ask Abby about that first," Clif answered.

Carolina retrieved the map pieces from the desk and stuffed them into the pocket of her dress. "She should be able to sit, and it may even help. But no standing and no walking for at least the night."

"Who made you captain of this ship?" Henrietta groused.

"You did when you got shot. Abby is busy tending to the sailing, leaving me in charge of you not dying. Now, Clif, ease her to sitting. Tell me how the pain is once you are up whilst I adjust your pillows."

Henrietta frowned at her sister. "You are worse than Clif."

"Oh good, I'm so pleased not to be the target of your ire as on most other occasions." Clif eased her upward.

Henrietta groaned and grimaced, panting as she moved.

Carolina arched an eyebrow at her. "The pain?"

"Fine," Henrietta forced out between clenched teeth.

Clif wrinkled his nose at her. "It hardly seems fine, sister. You can barely breathe."

"I am fine." Sweat beaded on her brow as she ground out the words.

Clif flicked his gaze to his younger sister.

"Ease her back against the pillows."

He nodded and gently shifted his sister back against the cushion.

"How is the pain now?" Carolina questioned.

Henrietta's breathing eased, and she slid her eyes closed for a moment. "Much better."

Carolina dug in her pocket and thrust the two pieces of paper forward. "Good. Then, you may sit up and review the map. If the pain becomes too much–"

"I will drink rum. That ought to soothe it."

"Or you can rest and sleep," Carolina countered.

"I'd still wish to know why you are suddenly giving orders. When did you become a doctor?"

"I haven't. Though I have tended to a few wounds in my day. I know what to expect."

Clif snapped his gaze to her. Had she tended gunshots? Had that been one of the wounds her now-deceased husband had inflicted on her? "Have you been–"

"No, I have not been shot. One of the men in our camp was, though. And I tended him. Not moving is as dangerous as moving."

"There, you see?" Henrietta said as she peered at the two pieces of map. "I must move."

"Not much," Carolina corrected. "But you mustn't lie about if you are able to be up. The danger of pneumonia is too great."

"At least someone has an ounce of sense in this cabin."

"I have many ounces of sense. And I must confess, I am not fond of having my sisters sailing with me. You gang up on me."

"Poor Clif," Henrietta teased. "Once a feared pirate, and now at the whim of two women."

"Someone ought to feel sorry for me. I used to sail these seas and be feared. Now I slink about, hoping to remain alive."

Henrietta began to chuckle, but her face soured immediately. "Oh, do not make me laugh. That hurts."

"At least your spirits are good," Carolina said. "That is an excellent sign."

"My spirits will be far better when I have solved this puzzle."

Clif perched on the edge of the bed and peered at the map spread on her lap. "You mean you haven't already."

Henrietta offered him a narrow-eyed glare. "Give me a few extra minutes. I have lost some blood."

"And it seems to be slowing you down quite a bit. I expected you to have this all worked out at first glance."

"I need paper, ink, and my quill, please."

Clif grinned as he bounced from his seat to retrieve the material from the desk. "Well, I am pleased to know you are going to live. Your Ri attitude is back in full force with you barking orders."

"And as soon as I am able, I shall be up and about and barking them to my crew." Henrietta grabbed the writing materials from her brother as he offered them and set about making notes on the symbols.

"Solved it?" he asked.

"Just a moment. I believe I may be on to something."

"Are you being serious or joking?"

Henrietta offered him a coy grin as she continued to scribble on her paper. "What do you think?"

Carolina hurried to peer over her sister's shoulder. "Joking, I think. I cannot make heads or tails out of this."

Henrietta poked at her with the quill. "Just because you cannot see it does not mean I do not almost have this solved, and I'm quite certain I do."

She leaned forward with a wince before she settled back and jotted a few more notes. "There. Solved."

"Solved? Really?" Clif furrowed his brow. "That quickly?"

"You thought I should have solved it quicker," Henrietta retorted.

"All right, then, smarty pants, where are they?"

Henrietta crossed her arms and lifted her chin. "On Orion's belt."

"What?" Carolina said, her delicate features crinkling.

"Look at these markings," Henrietta said.

Clif leaned over her. "What about the symbols?"

"Allow me a moment to explain, and you will know what they mean."

After pausing to let the statement sink in, Henrietta continued, "These markings looked oddly familiar to me. Then I noticed their pattern."

"Constellations," Clif said. "They are constellations."

"Yes. Just like Mother taught us as children." Henrietta nodded. "And once I figured that out, I realized the formations on the island line up with this constellation."

"Orion," Carolina said.

"Yes, specifically, Orion's belt."

"Then we have our bearing." Clif strode to the door. "I shall inform the crews. We shall be at the islands in no time."

Before he could finish his statement, a loud blast shook the ship. He tumbled to the floor as a shout resounded into the cabin. "We are taking fire!"

CHAPTER 23

"aking fire?" Clif asked with a crinkled brow.

Henrietta tried to rise from her bed, but Carolina held her in place. "No, you could tear that open and bleed to death."

"I will not lie here whilst my ship is blown to bits."

Clif scrambled to his feet and yanked the door open. "Never fear, sister. I shall not allow that to happen."

"Go find Abby and bring word to me about what is happening."

Carolina nodded and hurried across the room to the door to find answers. Left alone, Henrietta winced as she swung her legs over the edge of the bed. Moving sent pain through every fiber of her body, but she couldn't sit back whilst a battle raged outside her cabin. She was the captain of this ship, and she should have been giving orders.

Grinding her teeth, she inched to the edge of the bed and let her feet slide to the floor as she slowly put weight on them. Her vision darkened at the edges before she plopped back onto the bed. She'd have to give orders while remaining abed. She could not risk passing out in the middle of the battle.

She'd saved Clif once already in this venture, he could return the favor. The idea didn't sit well with her, but there was little she could do.

Before she could give it any further thought, Carolina darted through the door. "What are you doing out of bed?"

"I am not out of bed," Henrietta retorted. "Merely stretching. Though now I have become stuck. I cannot lift my legs back onto the blasted platform."

"Here, let me help." Carolina hurried to her and lifted her feet, swinging them onto the bed.

Henrietta groaned with pain as she adjusted herself back into her seat. "Who is firing on us? Why? What is being done to counteract?"

"Just a moment, I'll get to all of that. I want to check the wound and make sure you did no damage with your shenanigans."

"Shenanigans?" Henrietta asked as Carolina peeled back the bandage to eye it. "There were no such things."

"It looks fine. Stop moving about before you ruin Abby's work."

"Stop lecturing me and tell me what is happening to my ship. Who is attacking it?"

"It appears to be Stormrider's group. They must have found him dead and followed us. Clif has the matter well in hand. *The Henton* is being charged with fending off the attack."

"*The Henton*? Why? The *Grandmistress* is perfectly capable of defending herself."

"Yes, of course, but Clif felt it best that this ship does not receive any strikes that could injure you further."

Henrietta clicked her tongue and huffed. "How ridiculous." She held out her hand. "Help me up. I shall go handle this myself."

"I will do no such thing. The matter is in hand. Mr. Johnson is most capable. And while we wait, you should focus on this."

"What?"

Carolina grabbed the map pieces from where they had fallen at Henrietta's side and flipped them over. "What does this say?"

Henrietta knitted her brows as she stared down at the symbols scribbled on the back of the map. "I don't know."

"We ought to find out before we charge ahead to these islands unwittingly."

"And I suppose that will be my job since I am useless at anything else."

"You are not useless, Henrietta, merely wounded. Also, the smartest among us, so it falls to you."

"You cannot make me stay here by flattery alone," Henrietta retorted as she eyed the cryptic symbols.

"No? Are you certain? It would be easier than if I tied you down." Carolina crossed her arms and arched an eyebrow.

"You wouldn't dare," Henrietta answered, side-eying her sister as an explosion sounded further than it had before.

"Wouldn't I?"

"No, you wouldn't." Henrietta shrugged as she used a matter-of-fact tone. "You spent years cowering to a man–"

"I did not cower. Had I cowered, I would never have survived. I merely…took the path of least resistance."

"Yet you think tying me to the bed will be met with none?" Henrietta clicked her tongue.

"I didn't say none, but it will be the easiest if you continue to flout the instructions everyone has given you."

"I don't care for this tone."

"Too bad. You should not have emboldened me. You have only yourself to blame."

Henrietta wrinkled her nose at her sister. "This ship is not big enough for both of us. With this newfound attitude, we may have to get you your own vessel to command."

Carolina slumped into the chair with a pout. "No. But I must do all I can to prevent you from harming yourself. You cannot die after you saved my life. I need the chance to repay you."

"Fine," Henrietta said, wiggling around as the wound bothered her. "I will not move so you can repay the favor later."

"Favors," Carolina reminded her. "Oh, Henrietta, you have given me a new life. And I mean to see that it does not cost you yours."

Henrietta snapped her gaze to her sister's delicate face. "My, you have taken this quite to heart, haven't you?"

"Of course, I have. We have had a difficult relationship. Though when it mattered the most, you helped me. You saved me."

Henrietta offered her sister a slight smile. "You are my sister. You will always be my sister. Difficult or not, I love you."

Tears formed in Carolina's eyes, and she thrust a hand out toward Henrietta. Henrietta wrinkled her nose and turned back to the map pieces. "Let's not take it too far, shall we?"

"Oh, Ri." Carolina bounded from the chair and flung her arms around her sister's shoulders.

"No," Henrietta said with a shake of her head. "This is too much. We are sisters. We do not need to shower each other with affection."

"Too bad. You are a captive audience, and I mean to shower you with affection." Carolina plastered her sister's hair, still damp with sweat, with kisses.

"Oh, stop. It's becoming embarrassing."

Carolina giggled at her sister. "You are as easy to tease as Clif."

"Stop this nonsense and pull over that chair. You can help me decipher this."

The cannon blasts resounded, now further in the distance than before. "Sounds like the battle continues," Henrietta said. "And here we sit deciphering gibberish."

"I hardly think it's gibberish. Often, these bits contain clues about important information for navigating."

"Hmm, yes, and I suppose it will pass the time while we sail. After your Mr. Johnson defeats those pesky pirates, that is."

Carolina blushed as she smiled at Henrietta before the grin faded. "You do believe he will win, don't you?"

Henrietta patted her sister's hand. "Mr. Johnson is an excellent pirate. He will have no problem defeating a few drunken sailors."

Carolina bobbed her head, satisfied with the answer, as Henrietta focused on the symbols.

"It appears as though this symbol occurs most frequently," Henrietta said. She cast a gaze into space, narrowing her eyes. "If I am not mistaken, the letter E appears most frequently in the English language."

"E? Could these be E's?"

Henrietta searched for a fresh sheet of paper and dipped her quill in the inkwell. "Let us assume they are."

She filled the page with blank lines and inserted the letter E in each slot where the frequently used symbol sat. "Now, we must search for something else that is familiar to us."

"Oh, it is a puzzle," Carolina said. "Each symbol is a letter. We must determine what they correspond to."

"Right." Henrietta tapped the feathered end of the quill against her lips as she stared at the configuration of letters.

"How can we guess at the others?" Carolina asked. "Do you know of more letter frequencies?"

"T is fairly common, along with S."

Carolina scanned the page. "Here is the next most used symbol. Could it be a T or an S?"

Henrietta jotted a T and S above the blank lines corresponding to those symbols and stared at the results. "This cannot be a T. See here where there is a TTET. I know of no words with that pattern at the end."

"But SSES could work for the end of the word. Yes. Let's try that." She filled in the blanks with the letter S, then pointed to a three-letter word. "Perhaps this is the word THE."

"Try it, and I will search for other T and H symbols." Henrietta filled it in before Carolina pointed to other locations to fill in the appropriate letters.

Henrietta pointed to another word, her voice speeding with excitement. "This word must be THOSE."

"Which means we can fill in many more letters." They worked together to fill in the Os in the phrases and were able to identify several more words.

Henrietta pointed to the first solitary letter. "This must be an I or an A."

"Hmm, if it is an I, this word would take on a strange form."

"Yes, you are correct. It must be an A." Henrietta filled it in along with all other instances.

"This word may be ALL." Carolina excitedly pointed to a word on the first line.

"Yes, I believe so."

Henrietta stared down at what they had deciphered so far with their deductions.

. . .

A _A_ _ _ _ _ TO ALL THOSE _HO E_TE_
   ASS _ E _ EASTS _ _ A_ _ THE _SLA_ _ S, A_ _ _ OA
_ H _ _ O_ THE _ O_TH
   _O_ _ ASSES _ _LL _OT _ O _ _, _EE_ THE _O_ _ TA_
_ O_ _O_ _ LE_T AL_A_S

Carolina furrowed her brow. "It still looks like gibberish to me."

"We have made good progress," Henrietta said as she scanned the letters. "There must be something else we can guess at."

"Such as?"

"Here," Henrietta poked her quill at the top line. "To all those *who*."

"Oh, yes, that could work. Which means there are Ws here and here, too." Carolina pointed toward two spots in the bottom line.

Henrietta filled them in and studied the result. "This last word must be always, though it does not help much. There is only one other Y in the puzzle here."

"Could this word be not?" Carolina pointed to the third word in the last line.

Henrietta considered it. "Perhaps. It will not make sense. And gives us several N's."

A WA_ N _ _ _ TO ALL THOSE WHO ENTE_
   ASS _ E _ EASTS _ _ A_ _ THE _SLAN _ S, A_ _ _ OA
_ H _ _ O_ THE NO_TH
   _O_ _ ASSES W_ LL NOT WO _ _, _EE_ THE _O_
NTA_ N ON YO_ _ LE_T ALWAYS

. . .

"I'd wager the word before not is will." Henrietta filled in the Is.

A WA_ N _ _ _ TO ALL THOSE WHO ENTE_
    _ASSI_E _ EASTS _ _ A_ _ THE ISLAN _ S, A_ _ _ OA _
H _ _ O_ THE NO_TH
    _O_ _ ASSES WILL NOT _ O _ _, _EE_ THE _O_
NTAIN ON YO_ _ LE_T ALWAYS

Carolina pointed to a word in the middle of the second line, her voice rushed with excitement. "And this word is islands."

"A fair bet, though it provides us with no further information; however, this could." Henrietta filled in an R to make the last word of the first line ENTER.

"This word must be warning," Carolina said, "which finishes our first line."

Henrietta filled in the G.

A WARNING TO ALL THOSE WHO ENTER
    _ASSI_E _ EASTS G_ARD THE ISLANDS, A_ _ ROA _
H _ RO_ THE NORTH
    _O_ _ ASSES WILL NOT WOR _, _EE_ THE _O_
NTAIN ON YO_ R LE_T ALWAYS

Henrietta read the phrases allowed so far, trying to reason through the other letters. "A warning to all those who enter, blank blank blank the islands, blank blank blank the north. Blank will not blank; blank the blank on blank blank always."

"That sounds…unhelpful."

"Indeed. A warning." Henrietta rubbed the quill against her lips. "Of what? Something about the islands."

"This second word blank easts. Is it some direction?"

"No, there is only one east, not multiple. It must be another word that sounds like east." Henrietta started through the alphabet with letters. "Beasts."

She stopped, a grin spreading across her lips. "Beasts!"

A WARNING TO ALL THOSE WHO ENTER
_ASSI_E BEASTS G_ARD THE ISLANDS, A_ _ ROA _ H _ RO_ THE NORTH
_O_ _ ASSES WILL NOT WOR _, _EE_ THE _O_ NTAIN ON YO_ R LE_T ALWAYS

"The warning is that some sort of beasts—"

"Guard!" Carolina exclaimed. "They guard the islands."

"Yes, excellent, Carolina. Which gives us one more word."

A WARNING TO ALL THOSE WHO ENTER
_ASSI_E BEASTS GUARD THE ISLANDS, A_ _ ROA _ H _ RO_ THE NORTH
_O_ _ ASSES WILL NOT WOR _, _EE_ THE _OUN- TAIN ON YOUR LE_T ALWAYS

They stared down at the unfinished pieces. "Some sort of beasts guard the islands. Something something the north. Something will not something, something the something on your something always," Henrietta murmured.

"Let's pick another word to work on," Carolina said. "This

one. Wor blank. What letters could go there? Not a b, not a c."

"D is used, E is used, F does not work."

"K!" Carolina shouted. "Work. Work fits. Something will not work."

"All right," Henrietta said, filling it in and finding the same letter next to it.

A WARNING TO ALL THOSE WHO ENTER
    _ASSI_E BEASTS GUARD THE ISLANDS, A_ _ ROA _ H _ RO_ THE NORTH
    _O_ _ ASSES WILL NOT WORK, KEE_ THE _OUN-TAIN ON YOUR LE_T ALWAYS

"Keep! Something will not work, keep the" Carolina said.
    Henrietta filled in the Ps.

A WARNING TO ALL THOSE WHO ENTER
    _ASSI_E BEASTS GUARD THE ISLANDS, APPROA _ H _ RO_ THE NORTH
    _O_ PASSES WILL NOT WORK, KEEP THE _O_ NTAIN ON YOUR LE_T ALWAYS

"Aha," Henrietta said with a grin. "Approach. Approach from the north. Oh, Carolina, I think we almost have it."

A WARNING TO ALL THOSE WHO ENTER
    MASSI_E   BEASTS   GUARD   THE   ISLANDS,
APPROACH FROM THE NORTH

COMPASSES WILL NOT WORK. KEEP THE MOUN-
TAIN ON YOUR LE_T ALWAYS

"Massive," Carolina said as she pointed at the second to last unfinished word.

"And left. We have it." Henrietta filled in the remaining blanks, and they read the message together before giving each other a stunned glance.

A WARNING TO ALL THOSE WHO ENTER
  MASSIVE   BEASTS   GUARD   THE   ISLANDS,
APPROACH FROM THE NORTH
  COMPASSES WILL NOT WORK. KEEP THE MOUN-
TAIN ON YOUR LEFT ALWAYS

CHAPTER 24

*C*lif popped in through the door as the two women stared at each other. "We have successfully removed ourselves from the conflict."

No one answered him.

"Is no one going to applaud my efforts as Commodore of this fleet?"

"Wonderful, Clif. What an excellent pirate you are," Henrietta said as she focused on the phrases before her.

"That was less than enthusiastic."

Henrietta flicked her gaze to her brother. "While you were sending Mr. Johnson to do the hard work, we were deciphering the back of this map."

Clif wrinkled his nose at the insinuation. "I hardly sent him to do the hard work. He merely had to fire off a few cannons and slink away."

"Whatever. Here is what we have learned. Some large beasts guard those islands; the safest way in is from the north."

Clif crossed to them to stare down at the decoded

message. "This is what I've heard, yes. Knowing to approach from the north is helpful."

Henrietta tapped a finger against the last line. "And our compasses will not work to help us navigate. We must keep the mountain on our left at all times."

"Well, at least we have solutions to the problems presented by the Gemstone Islands. Hopefully, they will be sufficient for us to navigate them. It would be a terrible shame to have come this far and go home empty-handed."

Henrietta glanced up at her brother. "I think you're quite excited for this haul."

"I am," he answered as he crossed to the hammock and sank into it. "I always have been. Now that we have the approach figured and know how to navigate the islands, this should be simple."

Henrietta slid her eyes sideways to her brother's reclining form. "Simple? That's quite a statement. I hope it proves true."

"So do I. Though you will not find out until we return."

"Return? Return from the islands? I will be there, too."

Clif shook his head as he pulled his hat over his eyes. "No, you will not be. With that wound, you will remain aboard."

"Clif!" Henrietta cried. She searched for something to throw at him but found nothing that would make the distance. She pointed to her leather book on the desk, looking at Carolina. "Give me that journal."

Carolina collected it and handed it to her sister, who promptly flung it across the cabin to smack her brother in the gut.

"Ooof," he said, expelling air as he pulled up his hat. "What did you do that for?"

"I did it because you are a nitwit. I will certainly go to the islands. I will go if you have to carry me on your shoulders."

"Ri, you are wounded. You will stay aboard the ship, . I am speaking as your commanding officer, not your brother. You would do well to listen."

Henrietta crossed her arms and frowned as he settled back into the hammock with his hat tugged over his eyes.

"You probably should listen," Carolina whispered.

"You may have kowtowed to men, I will not."

"He only means to help you. You are seriously wounded. Shot, in fact. And you nearly died."

"That is a gross exaggeration." Henrietta rolled her eyes.

"Henrietta, you were unconscious."

"Because Abby sliced me open."

"To remove a bullet because you were shot." Carolina fussed with the covers over Henrietta.

"I know what happened to me. I was there, remember?"

"Then you should know how serious it is and heed the advice of those who saved your life."

Henrietta flung her arms at her sides. "I did not solve this conundrum and get us to the Gemstone Islands to sit in my cabin whilst everyone else enjoys this."

"We will reassess when we awake. For now, sleep." Carolina blew out the candle as she climbed into the bed next to Henrietta.

She snuggled closer to her sister as the ship rocked from side to side. Henrietta sat in the darkness as her sister's rhythmic breathing filled the air, followed by her brother's snoring.

With a click of her tongue, she let her head fall back against the pillow. She shifted a bit, testing her wound. With a wince, she conceded that it still hurt like the dickens.

Clif's words rang through her mind. He was right. She shouldn't push too hard. She may end up hurt more than she already was. But she hated to miss the opportunity.

Even now, she could not sleep as the sheer excitement coursed through her. She closed her eyes, imagining herself pushing through a jungle. She wiped at her sweaty brow before pushing a leaf aside.

The corner of her lips turned up as she stared at the ground, littered with gemstones of every size, shape, and color.

Before she could scoop them up, though, something pinched in her side. She glanced down at her shirt, finding it soaked in blood.

"Oh, no," she murmured. She pressed a hand against her wound. Blood oozed between her fingers. Her head swam, and her vision blackened on the edges.

"Ri?" Clif asked.

Her brows knitted as she offered him a sad glance. "Clif... I'm bleeding again."

"Yes, I know. This is why I told you to stay back."

"I should have listened. But now you must help me."

Clif glanced down at her wound. "I don't think I can."

"Call Abby." She groaned as the pain coursed through her entire body.

Shouts resounded through the group, though they sounded miles away from her. As her first mate rushed forward, she collapsed to her knees.

The world further darkened. Her heart slowed, as did her breathing. Her eyelids turned heavy, threatening to close.

She flopped forward onto her face. Someone rolled her over. She stared up at the bright blue sky as activity buzzed around her. But it would all be too late. She wouldn't live.

She would bleed out among the glittering jewels of the Gemstone Islands.

* * *

Henrietta gasped awake, pain blooming in her side as she shifted. Next to her, Carolina still slept soundly, as did her brother. The ship rocked lazily under them as they sailed toward the islands.

Henrietta let her head fall back against the pillows.

In another moment, she realized the reason for her waking. The ship shook underneath them. Something was wrong.

"Clif!" she hissed across the darkness. "Clif!"

Her brother's arm fell over the side of the hammock as he snorted a deep breath and wiggled around.

"Clif!" she tried again, raising her voice a little.

He didn't budge. She glanced down at her sister, still nestled in the covers, and considered waking her. Someone needed to check on whatever was happening.

She'd have to do it. With a wince, she wriggled her way around Carolina and dangled her legs over the edge of the bed.

After a few deep breaths, she rose. In the blackness of the cabin, she couldn't tell if her vision was normal or darker on the edges.

She took a tentative step forward, finding that her legs held her. Emboldened, she tried to take a few normal steps but found her side still ached. She adjusted her gait and ambled across the cabin to tug the door open.

Shouts shot across the deck, turning her stomach. Something was wrong, and no one had bothered to tell them, likely afraid to disturb her rest.

Heads would roll if something happened because they refused to follow the chain of command.

Henrietta stepped onto the deck, grabbing the arm of a woman as she rushed past. Her features pinched as her side pulled. "What's going on here?"

"There is something in the water, Captain. And it seems drawn to the ship."

She let go of the girl's arm, allowing her to sprint to her destination as she searched the chaos for her first mate.

She found her hurrying down from the helm. "Captain!"

"Abby, what is going on?"

"What are you doing up? You shouldn't be on your feet."

"Never mind that, Abby. What is going on here?"

Abby swallowed hard. "We aren't quite certain yet. There is something in the water. We are doing our best to navigate away from it, but it seems intent on following us. We have slowed until we can assess it once dawn breaks."

"Slowed? Perhaps that was a mistake. You should have woken me."

"Absolutely not. You should not even be up now. And I'd like to see how that wound is progressing."

"It's perfectly fine. I am fine. Show me this creature that is following us. Is it a whale? A dolphin? What?"

"I don't know," Abby said with a shake of her head. "It isn't very large."

Henrietta's mind ran through the warning she'd deciphered. If it wasn't large, what was it? The warning said massive beasts, not small ones.

"Dolphin, perhaps," Henrietta said. "They are known to be attracted to large vessels."

Abby wrinkled her nose but bobbed her head up and down.

Henrietta cocked her head. "Is there something you wish to say, Abby?"

"Only that...well, it does not look like a dolphin. It's...not gray."

"How can you tell? You said you cannot see it clearly."

"In the moonlight, it...had a reddish appearance."

Henrietta arched an eyebrow at the detail. "Red?"

"When light breaks, perhaps we can get a better look at it. Until then, we should look at that wound. You should not be running about this soon after a bullet wound."

Her dream flashed in her mind, and she nodded. "Fine, perhaps it is best to have it checked."

Abby stepped toward the cabin, but Henrietta grabbed her arm and led her below deck. "No, both Carolina and Clif are asleep."

She lifted her shirt, finding the bandage Abby had used earlier soaked with blood. The woman stooped to peel it back with a shake of her head. "You really should not be up, Captain. You've bled through this bandage."

"How can I be a ship's captain whilst I am confined to my bed?"

Abby retrieved a fresh bandage to redress the wound. "If anyone can manage it, I'm certain it is you."

"Don't patronize me. I would very much like to determine what is going on *and* travel to the islands to see these gems."

"I fear there will be no talking you out of it, so I will be certain to keep a close eye on you."

Henrietta's nose wrinkled as her dream flashed through her mind again. "Yes, please do. I refuse to be sidelined but want to be as safe as possible."

"That would be to—"

"Don't say it," Henrietta warned with a wag of her finger.

Abby pressed her lips together as she finished with the bandage and rose. Henrietta winced as she climbed the stairs, though the pain seemed to lessen now that she'd been moving around. At least, that's what she told herself.

"Any further sightings?" she asked as she stepped into the pale morning light.

"Nothing yet, Captain, perhaps it has given up," her helmswoman said.

Clif poked his head from the cabin below, craning his neck to peer up to the helm. He pressed his lips together and shook his head as he crossed to the stairs and climbed. "I see you cannot be trusted."

"I can be trusted perfectly, but there are matters that need tending to, and as this ship's captain, I–"

"Should be resting."

"Well, I called to you…twice. You slept through it. I had to take matters into my own hands."

Clif twisted to face the first mate. "Abby, should she be up?"

"No, and she has already bled through a bandage, though there is nothing to be done other than to keep a careful eye on her."

Henrietta rolled her eyes. "Stop fussing over me and start fussing over whatever has been attacking the ship."

Clif stalked to the railing and peered into the still-dark waters. "Something is attacking the ship?"

"We spotted a small, reddish creature," Abby answered.

"Reddish?" Clif screwed up his face. "Have you consulted with Mr. Johnson?"

"Not as yet."

Clif arched an eyebrow before he returned to the wheel. "Hail them. I'm certain Johnson will know the cause of this."

"Aye, Commodore," Abby said with a nod.

"Show off," Henrietta said with puckered lips.

"Well, no reddish creatures are lurking about in the sea. The girls must be making up tales."

"My crew do no such things. You'll see once your precious Mr. Johnson tells you." Henrietta crossed her arms as her crow's nest signaled to *The Henton*.

The ship ahead slackened its sails, slowing and allowing them to pull alongside.

"Good morning, Mr. Johnson," Clif said with a grin. "It

appears the adventure of the Gemstone Islands is nearly upon us."

"Aye, Commodore. And good morning, Captain. I am surprised to see you on your feet so soon."

"Never mind that," Henrietta said with a shake of her head. "My crew says something has been following the ships. Have you spotted it?"

"Aye. Whatever it is has been banging into our hull."

"Dolphin or whale?" Clif asked.

Johnson tugged his lips into a wince. "Neither, Captain. It has none of the qualities of either. Small, like a dolphin, but reddish in color.'

Henrietta offered Clif a haughty glance.

"How did you come to see this red color?"

"It beached itself on rocks in the distance. I caught sight of it in the moonlight. By the time I extended the spyglass, it had returned to the water."

"Small, reddish in color?" Clif rubbed his finger along his lips. "What could it be?"

"I am not certain, but it—"

A massive boom shook the ship. Clif and Henrietta struggled to stay on their feet, with Henrietta wincing as her side ached from the effort to stay upright.

"What in the world was that?" she cried.

"I'm not certain, Captain," Abby said, rushing to the railing. "But that felt larger than when the other thing bumped into us."

Another tremble shot through the large vessel, and it leaned starboard.

Abby scanned the water for the culprit.

"What do you see?"

"Nothing," she cried. "But another hit like that and we'll—"

Another loud bang slammed into the ship's side. It rocked

precariously as several crew members lost their footing and slid toward the railing.

Abby clung to it to stay upright, desperately searching the waters. Her features were betrayed when she found what she sought. She shot a panicked glance at Clif and Ri.

"This is a different creature. A whale. And she's large enough to capsize us."

CHAPTER 25

"What?" Clif cried. "You must be joking. The *Grandmistress* should be able to withstand a whale."

"This is no normal whale, Commodore," Abby said with a grim shake of her head.

"Let me see." Clif stalked forward and peered over the ship's edge as it righted itself.

Abby lifted a finger toward a section where the waves parted as it barreled toward them. "There."

Clif's eyes went wide. "That is no normal whale. Brace!"

The thing slammed into the ship's hull again, shaking it as it sent it keeling sideways.

"We need to get out of these waters!" Henrietta shouted. "Full sails."

Clif rose from his crouch and peered over the side again. "What are those creatures swimming with it?"

"I told you," Abby said. "Reddish. Unknown. But they seem to be guiding it to attack the ship."

Moments later, a shudder shook *The Henton*.

"We are also being attacked!" Johnson shouted.

"Same whale?" Clif asked before they sustained another hit.

"No. There is more than one. We must make for the open sea."

Henrietta shoved her helmswoman aside and adjusted, sending the ship sliding off course for waters away from the islands they approached.

"We're never going to make it," Clif shouted. "We must fight back."

"With what?" Henrietta asked. "We'd never be able to spear that thing. It'll break the spear."

Clif clung to the railing as they took another hit at the back. "Cannons."

"What do you propose, brother? That we sink them underwater."

"No, we'll need to aim them." He shouted across to his first mate, still boarding *The Henton*. "Johnson! Prop the cannons up on blocks and aim them into the water. Fire at it. Maybe it will drive the creatures off, at least."

"Aye, Captain, we will try it."

"Shall I have ours do the same?" Abby asked Henrietta.

She nodded. "Yes. It's worth a shot. We won't escape otherwise."

Orders passed to belowdecks, and the sideboards opened, but no cannons poked from within until they were raised at the back.

They took two more hits as they awaited the appropriate configuration.

"We're ready, Captain," Abby said with a nod.

"Commodore! Cannons are readied!" Johnson called.

Both siblings gave the order at the same time. "Fire."

As the creatures snaked through the water toward them, the orders were passed to those manning the cannons. The waters parted as the massive whale-like creature lined up for another hit.

Cannons thundered to life under them, firing cannon-balls into the water. It did not stop the blow they took, though, rocking the ship hard and threatening to overturn it.

"Fire again," Henrietta said as she clung to the ship's wheel.

Next to them, *The Henton* fired off its first round before being rocked by a hard hit to its underbelly.

Grandmistress's crew reloaded the cannons and prepared to fire. A second volley pounded into the waves but did little to save them from the attack.

"This is not working," Henrietta growled.

"No," Clif answered, rubbing his chin. "And I am not certain how much more these ships can withstand."

"They are firing too late."

"Late?" Clif questioned. "I'd wager it's too early. We must hit it in the center."

"No," Henrietta said. "The thing is massive with skin likely thick enough that a simple bombardment of cannons is only wounding it slightly. We must strike its head. We should fire before it closes the gap."

"Interesting. We will try it." Clif shouted a new set of orders across to this first mate.

"Fire early, Commodore?" Johnson crinkled his brow.

"Yes, fire before you think you should."

Johnson offered him a wary glance but bobbed his head. "Aye, Commodore."

"Here it comes again," Henrietta reported. "Fire now."

"Captain—" Abby began.

"FIRE!" Henrietta shouted.

Cannons boomed below their feet, and cannonballs roared into the water. *The Henton* fired her cannons, too.

This time, nothing hit the ship. Abby flung herself over the railing and studied the waters. "I don't see anything."

"Perhaps they are gone," Henrietta said. They waited another moment, each holding their breath to determine if they'd won the battle.

"It seems–" Clif started before another massive shake knocked him from his feet.

"There is another!" Henrietta called. "Load cannons and prepare to fire!"

The remaining creature slammed into the side of *The Henton* before it circled back for the *Grandmistress*.

With its cannons readied, she fired into the water before it could close the distance.

Outside of the lapping waves, silence pierced the air. They waited for several moments before Henrietta spoke. "Are we clear?"

"It seems so," Clif answered.

"Dare we proceed back to our course toward the island?"

"We shall never know if we do not try it."

With a nod of her head, Henrietta gave the order, relinquishing the wheel to her normal helmswoman. She scratched her head as the ship swung toward its original course. "Why did that not work? We entered from the north."

"Perhaps you translated something incorrectly," Clif suggested.

Henrietta glared at him, and he shrugged. "Or the writer was merely incorrect."

"That is more likely the case. But that makes me nervous about following the rest of the instructions."

"We shall need to keep our wits about us. How is your wound?"

Henrietta pulled up her shirt and studied the bandage. "Not bleeding. I am healed. Good thing, now I can go with you."

"I prefer you to rest, but only slightly. I'd much rather have your wits at my side for this trek."

"I'm glad we agree."

Henrietta offered him a playful smile as Carolina emerged from the cabin, stretching and yawning. "Are we nearly there?"

"Are you just waking?" Henrietta asked.

"Yes, I had the most luxurious rest."

"Did you not feel the shuddering of the ship?" Clif asked.

"No," she answered with a shrug. "Was there something wrong?"

"Never mind. We are nearly at the island." Henrietta pointed a finger toward the land rising from the sea.

"Remember, we must keep the mountain–"

"On the left, yes, but we have reason to suspect that the writer of that may have been mistaken about a few things."

"Oh." Carolina wrinkled her nose. "Well, then we must take care when we traverse it."

"I cannot believe you did not feel those massive hits we took from the creature. You are the heaviest sleeper I've ever met."

"I never woke up as a child when you and Clif caused all those problems."

"Problems," Henrietta cried, "what problems?"

"You know, the sneaking out and so on. I only heard about them after when Mother spoke to the ladies."

Henrietta sucked in a breath as she frowned at her sister. "Well, I suppose we will not worry about waking you with any issues on the ship."

"How long until we can go ashore?"

"We don't know. I am hoping the approach to the islands this time is riddled with fewer problems," Clif answered, "though we should proceed with caution."

They continued forward slowly, careful to keep an eye on

the seas for any more incredibly large sea creatures. Also noticeably missing were the reddish-colored creatures. Unaccosted, they approached the island and weighed anchor.

After observing the water for a period, they deemed it safe to send the skiffs to shore. With fresh bandages packed, Abby allowed Henrietta to climb aboard one of the skiffs with Clif and Carolina.

Among the crew members joining them were Abby, Johnson, Stargazer, and several others. Henrietta eyed the jungle-covered island as her stomach twisted in a knot. She couldn't wait for the discovery, if she made it that far.

The ache in her side worried her. She desperately wanted to see the gemstones but worried she'd collapse before then. Perhaps she should have listened to her first mate.

When they reached the shore, she shoved any concern aside. The adrenaline coursing through her body masked any pain she'd felt as she sat stiff, waiting for their boats to run aground.

Clif helped her out and carried her to dry land before he returned, splashing through the water to deliver Carolina to the first island.

"It appears as if land bridges connect these islands," Stargazer said, pointing to an elevated spit of land stretching toward the second island.

"Keep the mountain on your left," Henrietta murmured. "Which means we would go straight toward that bridge. This shouldn't take long."

After securing the skiffs, they trudged forward. The sticky heat made their clothing cling to them despite the early morning hour.

Henrietta kept her eyes trained on the land bridge, counting the seconds until they reached it as each step sent a sharp pain through her side.

"How is it?" Abby asked as they walked.

"Perfectly fine," Henrietta assured her.

Abby offered her a glance with raised eyebrows.

"Hurts like the dickens," Henrietta said. "Don't tell Clif."

Abby tugged the corner of her lips back into a half-smile. "I will not. Just assessing you. Perhaps we should break."

"We'll break once we reach that land bridge."

They continued forward until Henrietta knitted her brows. "Is that land bridge getting no closer?"

"It may be an illusion," Abby said. "I feel the same way."

Henrietta continued forward before she stopped. "Something is wrong here. No matter how many steps we take, it is no closer."

"Perhaps…this is what the note meant about islands being disorienting," Abby said.

"Something amiss, Ri?" Clif asked as he noticed her stop.

"Yes. That land bridge is getting no closer to us."

Clif twisted to view it and spun back to her. "I thought we were making good progress."

"We've made no progress! I've assessed it multiple times, and it is always the same distance."

Clif studied it again.

"Go forward several steps, and you'll see. Run ahead. I'll wait here." Henrietta flicked her fingers at him.

Clif puckered his lips before he trotted a few steps forward. He stopped, narrowing his eyes at it before he shimmied up a tree. After sliding back down, he hurried forward again and climbed another.

He landed on the ground in a crouch and stalked back toward them.

Henrietta drummed her fingers against her forearm. "Well?"

He wrinkled his nose. "You are an astute observer, Ri. I climbed the tree and estimated the distance using a rough guess of the number of trees separating us. When I moved forward ten trees and tried again, the distance remained the same."

"We are disoriented, that's why."

"But we've kept the mountain on our left," Carolina said. "That's what the note said."

"The note also said to go in from the north, which we did, which did not work."

"Perhaps we should do the opposite of the note," Abby suggested.

"Yes, let's try that. Going away from the land bridge would be counterintuitive, but it just might work."

They changed their direction with the group trekking away from the land bridge.

Henrietta wiped at her brow. "Now, I have nothing to keep my sights on."

"We should have rested," Abby said.

"I did rest whilst Clif assessed the distance, but it is hot and uncomfortable. The bandage is sticking to me. And I am in quite a foul mood."

"No different to always, then," Clif said with a grin.

"I still have a sword and a pistol, Clif," she retorted. "And I can still use either."

"You wouldn't dare shoot your brother, would you?"

"Wouldn't I?" she asked.

He trotted a few steps forward and grinned. "No, because I present to you...the land bridge."

Henrietta pushed herself to hurry forward, cursing the stitch in her side. "How did we make it here? How odd. I thought we'd have to traverse the entirety of the island."

"Apparently, Abby's idea was a good one."

"I am not surprised by that," Henrietta answered. "My crew surpasses most."

"Except mine."

"Oh?" Henrietta asked as a few crew members climbed

the steep natural staircase leading to the top to test the bridge. "I did not hear Johnson suggest it."

"No wonder." Clif offered an unimpressed stare over Henrietta's shoulder.

She twisted to discover the man grinning at Carolina as they spoke about a flower they'd found. "He has other things on his mind."

"Obviously." Clif frowned as the crew members who had climbed up to the land bridge began to venture across it.

Henrietta watched them make the slow trek, each footstep prodding. When Abby reached halfway, the land crumbled, sending rocks and earth skittering down into a whirling whirlpool underneath.

"Careful, Abby!" Henrietta called.

The woman bobbed her head up and down as she inched forward, trying to venture safely across, but her next step proved too much. The land gave way, and she plunged toward the angry whirlpool below.

CHAPTER 26

*D*espite being unable to help from her position, Henrietta lurched forward, pain splitting her side. Her eyes went wide as she saw her first mate falling.

Clif raced toward the stone stairs, but he'd never reach her in time. Stargazer dove forward and grabbed her wrist. Locked together, they slid toward the sea.

Stargazer dug her feet into the earth behind her as she struggled to bring herself to a complete stop. She managed it, and then one of Clif's crew grabbed hold of her legs to steady her.

Abby dangled from one wrist, kicking her feet desperately to find her way back up to the land bridge.

More earth broke away from the bridge, sending Abby into another fall. "Abby, stay still. Let them pull you up."

The woman's taut features betrayed her fear, but she heeded the advice and ceased her frantic movements. Carolina, her concerned eyes trained on Abby, slid her arm around Henrietta as Johnson scrambled up the land bridge to help with the rescue efforts.

Together, the crew pulled her onto the remaining bits of crumbling earth. She lay staring at the sky, panting but safe. Henrietta let out a sigh of relief as the danger passed, wincing as her side pinched.

The land bridge, though broken, held, for the moment, a reminder of the dangerous nature of the islands. The islands seemed to throw obstacle after obstacle. Though they had been warned, the near loss of her first mate made the danger hit home.

With Abby safe, Henrietta turned her attention to her brother. He shot her a concerned glance before he returned to assessing the gap they'd now need to cross to continue their journey.

"What do you think?" Henrietta called up to him.

Clif squatted at the edge of the break in the bridge. "It's wide, but not too wide. You may not be able to jump it."

"Says who?" Henrietta called. "I can jump that."

"With your wound?" he shouted back.

"If we are able to move forward, we shall. We did not come all this way to turn back empty-handed."

The crew rose to their feet. Abby pulled herself up and dusted her clothes off before she hurried over to the stairs to help Henrietta, who worked to climb up.

"Come on, start hopping across. Let's see if it holds," Henrietta said.

"Who do you propose goes first and risks the plunge into the whirlpool below?" Clif asked. Henrietta groaned as she struggled to scramble upward.

She made it to the top and adjusted her shirt. "I will."

"Ri!" You can't go across first with your wound. You're the worst to try."

"I will try again, Captain," Abby said with a determined nod.

"No, you've already done your part."

Abby hurried away from her. "You cannot stop me. It is my duty as your first mate."

"Clif, stop her," Henrietta said with her eyes wide.

Before her brother could reach the woman, she inched to the edge, swung her arms, and propelled herself forward.

She landed on the opposite side with no trouble and whipped around with a grin. "I did it. It was quite easy."

"Well, I suppose then I shall go next," Henrietta said.

"No, wait. First, Abby should go to the end of the bridge. We don't want too much weight on it. And second," Clif answered, "I should go first. I will wait for you if your side causes any issues with the leap."

"Fine. Though, wouldn't it be better to have Abby wait for me since she is lighter?"

"But not as strong. If you fall, I can catch you and pull you up. She cannot."

"All right," Henrietta agreed with a wave of her hand. "Proceed."

Abby scrambled to the end of the land bridge and climbed down until only her eyes peered over the top. Clif threw himself in the air and landed neatly on the other side. He spun to await Henrietta. "After she jumps, Carolina, you come next. Then we will vacate the bridge to allow the others to come across one by one."

Henrietta stared down at the water swirling below her. Her heart thudded hard against her ribs as the memory of her nightmare crept across her mind again. She swallowed hard, preparing for the jump.

"Hold your side, Captain," Abby called. "Try not to jar it."

Henrietta pressed her opposite hand against her wound before she pushed away from the ground. She sailed across the air and plowed into Clif on the other side, who caught her and eased her to the ground.

She sucked in a deep breath as she nodded to her brother before she hurried toward Abby.

"Have you pulled your stitches?"

Henrietta sucked in a sharp breath as she tugged up her shirt. No blood stained the bandage. "No, it seems fine."

"Good. I'd hate to have to restitch you here."

Carolina sailed across next, and she and Clif joined Abby and Henrietta as the others came across one by one.

"Now," Henrietta said when they all stood on the second island. "What is the trick with this island?"

"We have no information on that," Carolina answered. "Perhaps this is where we keep the mountain on the left. Is it the more northerly?"

"No," Johnson said, pointing back at the island they'd come from. "That one is."

Carolina frowned. "Then we have no information about this island."

"Which makes me nervous," Johnson replied.

Henrietta took a few steps toward the lush jungle before them. "Everything makes you nervous, Mr. Johnson. The only way we will learn is to test."

Clif eyed the thick foliage. "Perhaps we should leave a contingent here if we need to find our way back. We may be able to use the sound of their voices to guide us."

Henrietta bobbed her head. "Yes, perhaps two people should stay behind. Carolina and Mr. Johnson, you would be–"

"The worst two to stay behind," Clif finished for her.

"That was not my take," Henrietta said.

"Yet, it is true. We should take them along with Abby, Stargazer, and Williamson. The others stay behind."

"Aye, Commodore," Clif's crewman answered. "We shall wait and listen for any calls from you."

"Good," Clif answered as the others gathered behind him, ready to move forward.

The dense jungle swallowed them as they stepped past the large leaves gatekeeping it. An eerie silence pervaded it.

"There are no sounds of life here," Carolina said as she wrapped her arms around her midriff.

"No," Henrietta agreed. "Not even the call of a bird. How odd."

"I hope there are no large cats about," Johnson answered. "The last time we traipsed through a soundless jungle–"

"Clif found his new best friend," Henrietta said with a grin.

"Don't remind me. I do not see any wildlife at all here."

Henrietta continued behind her brother. "We shouldn't encounter too much trouble. I am wearing my lucky cap."

Clif narrowed his eyes at her. "Any cap of yours with a feather poking from it is hardly lucky. I would be shocked if we returned to our fellow crew members unscathed."

"My hats are not unlucky."

"They are so. Every time we've been faced with danger, your hat has been involved."

"Suppose it's your hat, brother. You *always* wear that battered old tricorn. It, too, has been on every adventure with us. Perhaps it is unlucky."

"No. This hat has survived since my days as Black Jack, and I was quite lucky then."

"Until O'Rourke, Junior," Johnson said, his arm now snaked around Carolina.

With a grumble, Clif continued to push through the thick jungle, hacking at leaves and vines to clear a path. Before he could return a comment about his misfortune with Redbeard's son, he abruptly stopped, staring ahead with wide eyes.

He snapped his gaze to Henrietta. "Do you still believe your hat to be lucky?"

She eyed their newest predicament. A wide chasm yawned in front of them, deep enough for the bottom not to be visible and wide enough to make crossing impossible. "This is...not very lucky."

"No. Perhaps if we throw the feathered cap in as a sacrifice, it will close."

Henrietta drew her sword and held the tip toward her brother. "Touch my hat at your own risk."

"Merely a joke, Ri." He strode a few steps away before he shimmied up a tree and studied the expanse.

"Well?" Henrietta called to him.

"It is as long as it is wide. I'm not certain we can find our way around it." He slid down the bark and landed on the ground.

"There must be a way," Henrietta said as she sheathed her sword.

"Here," Carolina answered.

Henrietta whipped her head in her sister's direction.

She studied a thick tangle of vines. "There is a stone structure here."

Clif hurried toward her and hacked away some of the foliage. "Yes, there is. Though I fail to see how it will help us."

"There are markings. Perhaps they provide some direction," Carolina answered as she studied the pieces of the now visible plinth.

Henrietta tugged away several more pieces and studied the symbols. "These *are* instructions. They show someone on the top of the plinth along with a series of symbols."

"What are they doing?" Johnson asked.

"Perhaps activating a mechanism with the symbols," Henrietta answered before she craned her neck to search for the top. "It is quite a climb."

"I can do it, Captain." Abby shed her belt and leapt high to grab a handhold. She shimmied up the vine-laden structure to the top before she slipped a knife from her boot and hacked away at the foliage.

"There are buttons. Tell me the order of the symbols."

Henrietta pressed a finger to the first. "An eye."

"Eye," Abby called out, grunting as she depressed the tile. A large clang resounded through the jungle.

"Next is a jungle cat."

"Jungle cat," Abby repeated, followed by another loud bang.

"Then, a moon."

"Moon." Abby pressed the button, but this time, no clang sounded. The earth shook underneath them. Abby struggled to remain on top of the structure.

"What happened?" Henrietta called when the turmoil stopped.

"I pressed the moon. The circle."

"No, no," Henrietta said with a shake of her head, "the crescent."

"Oh, that may make a difference," Abby answered. "Just a moment, I'll try again. Eye, Cat, Crescent Moon."

This time, only three clanks echoed through the air without the rumbling. "What is the final one? Circle, Tree, or Man?"

"Tree," Henrietta called.

With a press of the button, the plinth rumbled again, though this time, it did not threaten to knock them from their feet. Instead, a whirring noise accompanied it as a vine wound its way into a hole in the front.

Henrietta gasped as a rickety rope bridge emerged from the darkness of the chasm. Stretched taut, it provided a way to the other side for those who dared to cross.

The crew stared at it as Abby descended to the ground.

"Well, I suppose we should try it," Henrietta said. "Who wants to go first?"

"Perhaps you and your lucky cap," Clif suggested.

Henrietta blew out a sigh. "Fine, if only to prove that my cap is lucky."

"No, Captain, I will go. I can test the bridge."

"No, no. I shall do it." She placed her hands on the two ropes at her waist level and set a foot on the single string for her feet.

"Ri, I was joking. I wouldn't–"

"I would." Without further hesitation, she shifted her weight onto the rope. It protested with a creak but held. With her teeth sinking into her lower lip, she continued on the treacherous path, one step at a time.

"Halfway!" Clif called as she reached the middle of the chasm.

She glanced downward before she swallowed hard. She could do it. She took another step, and the bridge swayed as a gust of wind swept across the chasm. It knocked her hat from her head. She watched helplessly as the prized feather cap fell into oblivion. "Damn."

"Unlucky," Clif called to her.

Henrietta shook it off and continued forward until she reached the opposite side. "There, I have made it. Now, the rest of you come across."

One by one, they made their way over to her. As Stargazer, the last of them crossed, they continued through the thick foliage.

Henrietta slashed at a massive leaf blocking their path. As it fell away, a rainbow sparkled in front of them. She stopped, her jaw falling open in awe.

"We've done it," Clif breathed.

They stared down at the bowl in the earth. Gemstones

were scattered, contrasted against the brown earth. Vibrant greens, yellows, reds, and blues glittered in the beating sun.

Henrietta rushed forward, scooping a sizeable pink gem up and wincing as her side pinched from the motion. A smile spread across her features, and she whipped around to face her brother. "We've done it!"

The crew with them hurried forward, collecting gems as excited chatter filled the air. Clif wrapped his arms around his sister in a tight embrace. "We are legends, aren't we?"

"Yes, we are," she said. "And with this haul, we shall also be rich."

"Again."

She chuckled at him. "Yes, again. Though my diamonds were lonely without some colorful friends."

"We shall have plenty to give them." Clif scooped a large blue gem from the ground and held it to the sun.

"You know," Henrietta said, "getting to the island was more difficult than navigating the island itself."

Clif bobbed his head. "Yes, and with our knowledge about the clues and their opposite nature, we should have no trouble returning. It will be much easier getting off the island with our bounty."

"Yes. And wait until we move to the next adventure."

Clif snapped his gaze to her. "What next adventure?"

Henrietta offered him a mischievous grin. "I have been reading your journal avidly. I have an entire list."

"Oh, please, let us enjoy this one for a moment."

"Alright, I'll give you your moment. Because we also need to discuss the dispatching of one Ronan O'Rourke, Junior."

"I have some ideas for that."

"Oh, good," Henrietta said. "It sounds like we will have much to discuss when we return to the ship."

Clif sighed. Even after taking a bullet, his sister's energy seemed to know no bounds, and it appeared their lives would continue at a fever pitch. At least for now.

The End
To be continued…

<u>Want to Read More About Clif & Ri?</u>
Look for more adventures coming soon!
Until then, try the Maggie Edwards Adventures.

An unexpected package with a mysterious note and an ancient artifact catapults Maggie Edwards into an unbelievable adventure.

When her archeologist uncle sends her a strange item, Maggie is unknowingly plunged into a world of danger. A terrifying phone call alerts her to the danger both she and her uncle face.

After a break-in at her apartment, Maggie has nowhere to turn. She is forced to trust her uncle's self-proclaimed associate. Is he leading her one step closer to finding Ollie alive or deeper into the dangerous web of the tomb raiders? The tiny scarab could lead Maggie to the biggest archeological discovery of the modern world… if she lives long enough to find it.

Indiana Jones meets Lara Croft in this globe-trotting adventure series by Nellie H. Steele. Find out why Indies Today calls Cleopatra's Tomb "the perfect page-turning getaway."

Find out what happens in *Cleopatra's Tomb* available on Amazon Now! **https://geni.us/CleopatrasTomb**

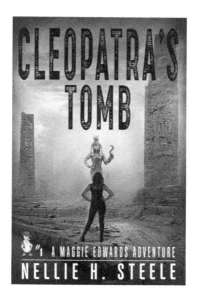

<u>Click HERE to get your copy of Cleopatra's Tomb</u>

Let's keep in touch! Join my newsletter and receive five free books!

ABOUT THE AUTHOR

Award-winning author Nellie H. Steele writes in as many genres as she reads, ranging from mystery to fantasy and allowing readers to escape reality and enter enchanting worlds filled with unique, lovable characters.

Addicted to books since she could read, Nellie escaped to fictional worlds like the ones created by Carolyn Keene or Victoria Holt long before she decided to put pen to paper and create her own realities.

When she's not spinning a cozy mystery tale, building a new realm in a contemporary fantasy, or writing another action-adventure car chase, you can find her shuffling through her Noah's Ark of rescue animals or enjoying a hot cuppa (that's tea for most Americans.)

Join her Facebook Readers' Group here!

OTHER SERIES BY NELLIE H. STEELE

<u>Cozy Mystery Series</u>

Cate Kensie Mysteries
Lily & Cassie by the Sea Mysteries
Pearl Party Mysteries
Middle Age is Murder Cozy Mysteries

<u>Supernatural Suspense/Urban Fantasy</u>

Shadow Slayers Stories
Duchess of Blackmoore Mysteries
Shelving Magic

<u>Adventure</u>

Maggie Edwards Adventures
Clif & Ri on the Sea

Made in the USA
Las Vegas, NV
17 October 2024

97003619R10154